Sign up for our newsletter to hear about new releases,
read interviews with authors, enter giveaways, and more.

www.ylva-publishing.com

Turning
for
Home
Caren J. Werlinger

Acknowledgments

EMILY DICKINSON WROTE A letter to the world that never wrote to her. This book is my apology—not to the world, but to one woman in Rocky Mount, North Carolina, who wrote to me. It was sometime in the early 2000s, and it would have been March, because it was spring break, and we were driving north from Florida. We stopped at a tiny place, one of those stops that was a combined gas station/convenience store/diner. Much like Jules's experience in *Turning for Home*, someone slipped a note to me under the restroom door, asking for help getting out of her small town and giving me an e-mail address.

I never responded.

All I can say now is that I had very little experience with the Internet, and the world was a much scarier place for lesbians and gays. We had no legal protections of any sort. My partner worked in public education. I simply wasn't brave enough to risk contact with an unknown dyke from a small Southern town, who may or may not have had the sense to be discreet.

I never responded, but I have always remembered. And regretted. I hope she found the courage to get out if that's what she really wanted to do. I'm not sure how I could have helped, but I'm sorry I wasn't braver and willing to at least reach out.

From that one little incident, this entire story grew. It has nothing to do with the woman in Rocky Mount, but it has everything to do with all of us who have ever felt alone and lost in being different. I hope this story helps at least one person who feels isolated to know that she's not really alone.

I owe many people a debt of gratitude for helping to bring this book to life: my readers Marty, Marge, and Lisa T (I owe you big time!). Thank you for catching what my eyes could not.

To my partner, Beth, none of this would be possible without your support.

To Astrid Ohletz of Ylva Publishing, your openness and support helped me feel it was the right time to work with a publisher again. Thank you to Paulette Callen for your insightful comments and edits. To Sandra Gerth, you are an extraordinary editor, and you gently pushed me to make this book better than it could have been without your input. Together, we have created a book I am very proud of.

I always create a playlist of music that I listen to as I write a book. Mary Chapin Carpenter's song "Jubilee" became the theme song for this book. In my mind, it became Jules's song. Kenny Loggins's version of "The Last Unicorn" also resonated strongly, as did "Meet Me in the Dark" by Melissa Etheridge. Just in case any of you want to check out the songs that helped inspire this story.

As always, thank you for reading.

Dedication

To Beth, always

CHAPTER 1

THE FIRST RAYS OF the sun crept through the dormer window and hit the mica panels of the night-light on the bedside table. Becoming translucent as the beam of light hit the lamp, the paper-thin sheets of mineral glowed in amber shades of gold, with dark copper silhouettes of figures visible where a moment ago all had been dark. Smiling, Jules squinted at the familiar cowboy, slouched near his campfire while his horse grazed nearby. She reached out and twirled the lampshade on its base to the next panel with ducks and geese flying over a grassy marsh and then again to a fish leaping from a stream. One more turn of the lamp showed a panorama of foxes trotting through a meadow, hopping a fence.

Jules allowed her eyes to slide out of focus into a half-awake haze and put herself in the field with the foxes, feeling wet grass tickle her belly and long, fluffy tail as she hopped after mice and tumbled and played with the other foxes....

"Can't you smell the earth, Jules? Look up and see the trees and bushes and the whole, wide sky over you..." She could hear Pappy's voice, see his strong hands as he twirled the lamp. "If you use your imagination, you can go anywhere, do anything. You'll never be lonely again—"

CLANG!

Her eyes snapped open at the bang of a heavy cast-iron skillet being dropped on a burner. *More effective than any alarm clock.* She heard the familiar scuff of slippers and the sounds of the refrigerator door opening and closing. She reached for the cell phone next to the lamp and pushed a button.

"Hi," came a sleepy voice over the phone.

"Hi," said Jules, speaking low to avoid being heard downstairs. "Sorry to call so early."

"I thought maybe she'd sleep in a little today."

Jules snorted. "What, Mae Calhoon let a little thing like a funeral disrupt her routine?"

"What time's the service?"

"Funeral home at ten, cemetery at eleven, and then everyone will come back here."

"You okay?"

"I guess," said Jules softly. "It's not like I'd seen him much in the past umpteen years."

"If that gets you through this, fine. But I know you don't mean that."

Jules swallowed hard. "I love you, Kelli."

"I love you, too."

"I'll call you later."

Jules rolled onto her back and looked up at the slanted ceiling above her, the wide white boards covered in faded posters. Smiling down at her were the eternally young faces of the Beatles, the Brady Bunch, and the Partridge Family.

On the other side were movie posters from *Dr. Zhivago* and *Love Story.*

"These were your mother's, weren't they?" Kelli had asked the one time she'd come to Aldie with Jules. "How old were you when you came to live here?"

"Three, I think," Jules had said. "I don't really remember living with my mother. I only have one vague memory of her; I think we were at a pool. All my other memories are of being here with Pappy and Mae."

As if on cue, "Are you coming down, or do you expect breakfast in bed?" called Mae's voice from the kitchen.

"Coming," Jules called back. Sitting up, she quickly brushed her hair back into a tight ponytail and pulled on jeans and a T-shirt.

When she got downstairs, her grandmother was standing at the stove, wearing her blue-flowered housedress, her white hair up in curlers. She flipped the bacon as grease spit from the skillet and glanced disapprovingly at Jules. "That's not what you're wearing, is it?"

"Of course not," Jules said. "But it's only six and the funeral isn't until ten."

Cool air was coming in through the screen door opening onto the backyard, where birds were singing a morning chorus.

She got two glasses out of the cupboard and poured orange juice as Mae laid the bacon on a paper towel and cracked four eggs into the skillet, the grease sputtering and crackling madly.

"Coffee?" Mae asked.

As much as Jules needed a cup of coffee, she wasn't sure she could stomach the boiled sludge coming from Mae's old

Corning percolator. "No, thanks," she said. "I'm trying to cut back."

A few minutes later, they were seated at the 1950s diner table—"probably the only new thing Mae ever agreed to buy," Jules often joked—the aluminum banding around the edge still gleaming and spotless even if the gray-speckled Formica on the tabletop was a little faded. The red vinyl on the chairs was cracked at the corners with little tufts of stuffing peeking through the cracks. They ate in silence, eyes focused on their plates.

No need for conversation.

Jules ate quickly and carried her dishes to the sink, where she washed them and placed them in the dish drainer.

"I'm going for a walk," she said, heading for the screen door.

"Just don't be late," Mae called after her as the screen door slapped shut.

Jules stepped out into the yard. Funny how little it looked now. Except for the birds, all was quiet at this hour, but soon, garbage trucks would be rumbling along the dirt road that ran behind all these houses to the town dump.

Walking around to the garage and driveway, she looked through the overgrown hedge to the brick house next door. The shrubs and trees surrounding the little house had grown so that the house itself was almost engulfed. She walked down the driveway to the sidewalk and quickly passed the neighboring house, relieved to see all the curtains drawn and no sign of anyone peering through the windows.

The sun was just high enough to cast dappled shadows along the sidewalk as she made her way downtown. Sniffing, she could already detect the stink of the paper mill in

Chillicothe. She knew the smell would get stronger as the mid-summer day warmed.

"That will make the cemetery service lovely," she muttered, but then, Pappy had worked at the mill for forty-five years, so maybe it was appropriate.

Ten minutes' brisk walking brought Jules to Aldie's tiny downtown, consisting of not much more than a couple of stores, a bank, "and the diner," she muttered aloud. Craving coffee by now, she headed toward Sandy's Diner. The counter seats, as always, were mostly full with locals visiting with one another. A few of the old men nodded as she entered, and she wondered if they recognized her as Carl's granddaughter. She slid into a booth and flipped the upside-down coffee cup in front of her.

A waitress appeared almost magically with a pot of coffee. "What can I get you, hon?" she asked, one hand on her hip as she poured.

"Uh," Jules said, remembering she had just had breakfast. "Got any chocolate pie?"

"Sure do. Be right back," the waitress said, already halfway back to the counter, refilling coffee cups as she went.

Cradling her cup in her hands, Jules sipped the hot liquid. She savored the flavor, wondering again what they did to their coffee to make it taste so good. Outside, a few cars rolled by, people on their way to work, she supposed.

Diagonally across the intersection was the Aldie Five & Dime, where she had spent hours and hours—"and all my allowance," she remembered with a wry smile—buying comic books and bubble gum and warm cans of grape pop because the cold cans cost five cents more. That store was where she had first seen her night-light, not long after she had come to live with her grandparents. She remembered having to pull herself up on tiptoe because she wasn't big enough to see over the edge of the shelf. She could barely reach the light, twirling the shade to look at all four panels, around and around and around.

"You like this, Jules?" Pappy had asked, squatting down beside her, where she could smell his Old Spice. He lifted the light down so she could see it more closely as she nodded mutely, mesmerized by the copper cut-outs fixed to the illuminated panels. A few minutes later, she had walked out of the store, proudly carrying the boxed-up light in a shopping bag nearly as big as she was, but her happiness was short-lived.

"You paid what?" Mae had demanded angrily when they got home.

Upstairs, crouching in the door of her room, the bag next to her, Jules heard Pappy say, "But Mae, she's scared up there all alone in the dark. It'll help this house feel like home for her."

"You're going to spoil her, Carl, just like you did—" Mae said, still angry. "She's going to end up like her mother."

"Mae—" But there was only the sound of a door slamming.

Picking her bag up high to avoid thumping it on the stairs, Jules carried it back down to the kitchen.

Pappy looked at her. "What's this?"

"We should take it back," Jules said.

Pappy smiled, his eyes suddenly shiny, and said, "No. Let's plug it in and see how it looks."

Together, they went up to her room and set the night-light on the bedside table. Jules turned it on. They sat on the bed, Pappy's arm around her, turning the light from scene to scene.

"Can't you smell the earth, Jules..."

Jules blinked, and hot tears leaked down her cheeks. Keeping her head turned toward the window of the diner, she covertly swiped her hand across the wetness. She was startled by the clatter of her pie being set down in front of her.

"Thanks," she mumbled.

"Excuse me," said the waitress, "but aren't you Jules Calhoon?"

Jules glanced up. "Yes."

"You probably don't remember me," the waitress said with a shy smile. "I was a year behind you in school. I'm Trish Gregory. Well, Bayliss now. I married Gilbert Bayliss. You two were friends, weren't you?"

Jules felt her face get hot. "Kind of, I guess."

"We were all sorry to hear about Carl," Trish said. "He was a nice man." Her face brightened. "You should come by while you're in town. We live in Gilbert's home place. Bought it from his parents. Where are you now?"

"Virginia," Jules said. "Near Charlottesville."

"Couldn't wait to get out of Ohio, huh?" Trish joked and, suddenly, her smile faded. "Oh... um..." She backed away. "Well, enjoy your pie."

———— ❖ ————

"Mae, you sit down," said an older woman, her beehive hair dyed an impossible shade of black—"country-singer black," Kelli would have said with a giggle—as she ushered Mae to the sofa and waved to another woman to bring a glass of lemonade. Fans were whirring from every available electrical outlet to move the air in the un-air-conditioned house.

The kitchen table and counters were filled to capacity with platters of ham and cold cuts and deviled eggs, casserole dishes filled with lasagna and potatoes au gratin and green bean casserole. There were bowls of pasta salad and chicken salad and egg salad.

"I don't know what in the world she's going to do with all the food," Jules said to Kelli, stepping out onto the back stoop to call her as dozens of people, most of whom she didn't know, snaked around the kitchen, filling plates.

"How was the service?" Kelli asked.

"It was okay," Jules said, shrugging. "Typical Methodist funeral. Everyone in black. Everyone sings 'Amazing Grace' and recites the 23rd Psalm and then pats Mae on the hand..."

...and goes to the cemetery, the place I haven't been since... That was the hardest part; only it wasn't Pappy I was thinking of.

Kelli chuckled. "And what would Pappy have wanted?"

Jules went around the far side of the garage and sat in the plastic lawn chair Pappy always kept there to hide out of view of the house and smoke his pipe, pretending Mae didn't know. "He loved to dance, just jigs around the kitchen. I never saw Mae dance with him, but I did sometimes. And he loved musicals. He probably would have preferred 'Climb Every Mountain' to 'Amazing Grace.'"

"I wish I could have known him before he got sick," Kelli said.

"Me, too."

"How much longer will you stay?"

"Only until tomorrow," Jules said. "I want to get home."

"Call me tonight?"

"I will. Kell?"

"Yes?"

"I love you," Jules said.

"I love you, too."

Jules clicked her phone off and slid it into the pocket of her black slacks.

"You're wearing pants?" Mae had asked, glowering in her direction when Jules came down dressed for the funeral.

"Mae," said Jules—"I knew this was coming," she almost said wearily—"you haven't seen me in a dress since the first day of kindergarten..."

"Here, here," Pappy said when he found Jules upstairs, facedown on her bed, crying as if her heart would break. "What happened to my girl?" he asked as he rubbed her back.

Sniffing, Jules rolled over and looked up at him and said, "The other kids made fun of this stupid dress Mae made me wear. They said it's about a hundred years old." She got off the bed and yanked the dress over her head, standing there in her underwear and undershirt. "It was my mother's, wasn't it?"

"Well," said Pappy slowly, scratching the cleft in his chin, the way he usually did when he was thinking. "Your grandmother thinks it still has plenty of wear left in it... and your mother did look awful pretty when she wore it."

His eyes misted as they always did when they talked about Jules's mother.

"I don't care," Jules said, crossing her arms, her socks scrunched around her ankles. Her legs were so skinny, her socks never stayed up. Pappy stared at the large scab on one knee as she stomped her foot and declared, "I'm not pretty, and I don't want to be pretty. I won't wear it again or any of her other clothes. I'm wearing my own clothes, or I won't go to school."

Pappy's mouth twitched as he looked at her. "All right. I'll talk to your grandmother."

"But what will people say?" Mae asked a short time later. "They'll think we can't afford to dress her properly. She can't run around like a little hobo."

Jules lay on the floor at the top of the stairs, listening to their voices carry through the kitchen and up the stairs from the living room.

"Mae," Pappy said. "She's not Joan. We have to let her be herself."

"But they're still going to make fun of her," Mae said. "She's such an odd creature."

"She says if she's in her own clothes and they laugh at her, she can at least punch them in the nose," Pappy said and Jules could hear him laughing....

———◆◇◆———

Jules blinked to clear her vision at the sound of more car doors slamming from the direction of the street. More food, more well-meaning friends or neighbors or church members. People would be coming and going all afternoon. She leaned forward in Pappy's lawn chair.

"I don't think I can take much more of this," she muttered, wishing she could leave for home this very minute.

"Pssst."

She swiveled her head.

"Pssst."

Craning her neck around, Jules realized the hiss was coming from next door. There, standing almost in the hedge, was the neighbor. She waved Jules closer.

Hesitantly, Jules approached. She nearly didn't recognize her. The woman was thin and worn-out-looking, with bags under her eyes. Her scant, graying hair was greasy and lank as if it hadn't been washed in a very long time, and her pale blue eyes were watery and red-rimmed. Silently, she held out a towel-wrapped object through the branches of the hedge.

Jules accepted it and could feel it was still warm. She peeled back a corner of the towel to reveal a fresh loaf of bread.

"Thank you, Mrs. Fahnestock," Jules said, but the woman had already disappeared back to her side of the hedge.

CHAPTER 2

THE AFTERNOON WORE ON, and a handful of Mae's
friends were still at the house, showing no inclination to
leave anytime soon. Half of them were already widows,
and, in a small town, drama provided the only relief from
the sameness of the days. Carl's death and Mae's new
widowhood would sustain them for weeks to come.

After changing back into jeans and a T-shirt, Jules called
from the kitchen, "I'm going for a walk." When she got no
response, she let herself out through the screen door.

"Do you think she loved him?" Kelli had asked once.
"You know, romantically?"

Jules had stared off into space, trying to imagine an
affectionate, loving Mae. "I don't know," she said. "Maybe
early on, when they were young."

"Don't judge your grandmother too harshly," Pappy had
said to her more than once. "Life hasn't been easy for her. I
never amounted to much," and Jules remembered the sadness
in his eyes as he said that, "and when your mother left..."

"You mean when she ran off," Mae would have
said bitterly—her anger, her sense of betrayal over that
disappointment never far from the surface.

"...well, it took some of the joy from her," Pappy said. "She used to sing and laugh," but Jules always frowned at him, having a hard time imagining her grandmother laughing.

Outside, Jules took a deep breath at her escape from the house. Retracing the path she had taken earlier that morning—*it feels like days ago*—Jules glanced at the Fahnestock house as she passed. She thought she saw one of the closed curtains twitch, but she couldn't be sure.

Coming into town, she took a detour one block east of Main and came to Johnny Clem Elementary. She walked around the three-story brick building, still not air-conditioned by the looks of it as some of the old sashes on the upper floors were raised to let in some air. She tilted her head, trying to remember which window it was she'd broken with a baseball. She wandered around behind the school, to the deserted playground and sat on a swing. Swaying as she pushed off, she held her feet up and closed her eyes, enjoying the swooping sensation in her stomach.

"Hey, kid, throw me the ball."

Joey Reynolds hollered to a chubby boy leaning against the school building where a foul ball had rolled to a stop. The boy, wearing a strange combination of too-long jeans rolled up several times at the cuffs paired with a too-small T-shirt that didn't quite cover his white belly, retrieved the ball and threw it awkwardly. It sailed high and landed twenty feet short amid howls of laughter.

"He throws like a girl!"

"The fat kid can't even throw a ball!"

Jules stomped up to Joey and shoved him in the chest with her baseball mitt. "I'm a girl, Joey Reynolds, and I throw as good as you. Good enough to throw you out from center field."

Scowling at the reminder, Joey picked up the ball and said, "C'mon. Let's get back to our game." The other boys followed, but he stopped after a few steps and called back to Jules, "You comin'?"

"You go on." Jules squatted down to tie up the laces of her sneakers.

As the sounds of the baseball game resumed, she stood and went to the fat boy, who was running a fingernail back and forth in a mortar line between two bricks. He looked as if he might cry.

"Hey," she said.

"Go away," he replied.

Stung, Jules waved toward the baseball game with her mitt. "I'm not like them."

"I said, leave me alone!" He turned his back on her.

"Fine."

Fuming, she stalked off and went back to the game. When they were called back inside after recess, red-faced and sweaty, she saw him lagging behind, making sure he stayed away from Joey and his gang.

Later that day, as she walked home from school, she noticed the fat kid walking ahead of her, tracing the same path she was. To her surprise, he turned into the driveway of the house next door. He paused, as if waiting for her to catch up.

"Hey," he said as she drew near.

She started to walk by him, pretending he hadn't spoken, but then stopped and said, "Now you'll talk to me?"

"Sorry," he mumbled. "But, at my old school, whenever someone seemed like they were being nice, they were usually just tricking me so they could play some kind of joke on me."

"That's awful," Jules said.

The boy just shrugged.

"My name's Jules Calhoon," she said. "I'm in Mrs. Davies's third-grade class."

"I'm Hobie Fahnestock. I'm in third grade, too. Mr. Black's class."

Now that he was looking at Jules, she realized he had the prettiest eyes she had ever seen, light blue with long, black lashes that made it look as if he had makeup on. He had dark hair and a pale face that made his eyes stand out even more. They lit up as he asked, "Jules? As in Jules Verne?"

She just looked at him blankly. "Who?"

"The writer," he said. "You know, *Twenty Thousand Leagues Under the Sea*? *Journey to the Center of the Earth*? *Around the World in 80 Days*?"

"No," said Jules, staring at him. She made a pained face. "Jules as in Juliet. Like *Romeo and Juliet*." Her fists balled up. "But don't you tell anyone."

Hobie backed up quickly as if he expected to be hit. "I won't. I swear."

Jules looked toward the house and noticed several cardboard boxes piled on the front porch. "Did you just move in?"

He nodded. "Two days ago. Me and my mom. And you live there, with your grandparents," he said, pointing. "My mom asked the mailman about some of the neighbors."

"Where's your dad?" Jules asked.

"Dead."

"Oh." Jules didn't know what to say. She'd never known a kid who had a dead parent. Her mom was still alive, somewhere, even if Jules didn't live with her. "Is that how come you don't know how to throw?"

Hobie shrugged again, scarlet patches rising in his pale cheeks.

"Want me to teach you?" she asked.

He nodded, his expression brightening.

"But we'll have to do it here, where no one will see," she said, knowing Joey and the others would make fun of Hobie while he learned.

"Okay," he said.

"Hobie?" called a woman's voice.

Jules looked over to see a pretty, brown-haired woman on the front porch.

"I better go," he said.

"Okay. See you, Hobie."

"See you, Jules."

Jules opened her eyes and dragged her feet to stop the swing. "Why are you doing this?" she asked herself harshly, getting up and leaving the schoolyard behind.

The schoolyard maybe.

It was almost five o'clock, and most of the downtown businesses were closing. Jules headed toward the diner. "With all the food in this house?" she could hear Mae bristling.

Glancing around as she slid into a booth, she was relieved to see that Trish wasn't working. Gilbert Bayliss. She rested her forehead on her hands. She hadn't thought of him for as long as she hadn't thought of Hobie.

"God, why did I come back here?" she mumbled.

"Excuse me?"

Jules looked up, embarrassed to realize a waitress was standing there, an older woman with a voice like a bullfrog and a face lined with fine wrinkles. "Um," she stammered, flipping open the menu. "I'll have a burger, medium-well, fries, and a chocolate milkshake."

She grinned as she imagined Kelli's reaction to that. "Your life insurance is all paid up, right?" or some such quip would be typical.

As the waitress left to place her order, Jules was hit by a strong wave of homesickness. Not for Aldie, not even for Pappy. For Kelli, for the million little things she did to make their house feel like home—baking Jules's favorite oatmeal cookies, arranging unexpected vases of flowers, leaving a card at Jules's place at the table to find after Kelli had gone to work—little reminders of how much she was loved.

Again with the stupid tears.

With a disgusted sigh, Jules went to the restroom, where she slipped into the only stall and dabbed at her eyes with a length of toilet paper. She heard the bathroom door open and close, and then open and close again almost immediately. She pulled off more toilet paper, blew her nose, and threw the used tissue into the toilet. She pushed the handle to flush and reached for the bolt on the door.

Her eye was caught by a piece of paper lying at her feet. She bent over to pick it up, certain it hadn't been there when she entered the stall. It was a blank diner check. Turning it over, she read:

Below was scrawled an e-mail address.

Her heart thumped as she re-read the note. She listened, but the restroom was empty. She folded the paper and tucked it into her pocket as she left the stall and washed her hands. Her face staring back at her from the cracked mirror was ashen. She returned to her booth, where her heart rate slowly returned to normal. *Relax. You don't live here anymore. It doesn't matter if somebody guessed.* Her meal arrived a moment later, and Jules looked at her waitress as she thanked her, but there was no sign of recognition there.

Glancing around casually as she munched a few fries, she saw no one who looked obvious. No one who seemed to be watching her covertly. No one who looked like a dyke. "And what does that look like?" she could hear Kelli say, laughing.

She ate the rest of her meal, watching people come and go, and still could not tell who had slipped the note under the door. She paid her check and stepped out onto the sidewalk. The sun was still high in the sky, and she wasn't ready to go back to the house, where she was sure Mae's friends would still be keeping her company. She began walking aimlessly and found herself several minutes later at the entrance to the cemetery.

The cemetery was built on the town's highest bluff, where the early residents had figured it would be safe from the occasional flooding of the Scioto River, flowing in a lazy arc below the cemetery's far side. It had been a favorite place to play twilight games of hide-and-seek, and the hill was a great place to go sledding in the winter, but this afternoon, in the back of the limo with Mae, was the first time Jules had been there since she was seventeen....

"There's a place, but you have to swear never to tell..."

"Down a hidden trail on the back side of cemetery hill..."

"It's only for us. No one else can know..."

But there had come a time when Jules had had to take other people there, police and firefighters and—"Stop," she said, screwing her eyes shut and turning away.

"Surely, they can't still go there, not after..." She pulled the scrawled note from her pocket and stared at it. *I'm like you...* Suddenly angry, she crumpled the paper and hurled it as she stalked away. "No one helped us!" she yelled, punching the sky. "No one told us it would be okay." She stopped after a few steps, her jaw working as she fought with herself. "Damn it." She shook her head and stomped back to pick up the little wad of paper. Carefully, she smoothed it on her thigh and refolded it before slipping it once again into her pocket.

CHAPTER 3

"You don't have to stay with me," Hobie said.

He and Jules were inside, drawing, while outside, they could hear the squeals and yells of a furious snowball fight beyond the school library windows. Despite months of coaching from Jules, Hobie could still manage only a mediocre throw—"you'll never throw someone out from the outfield," she'd said, shaking her head—and though she had managed to get him into some of the games when they were short a player or two, she always arranged for him to play right field, where he rarely had to worry about a ball coming his way. But a snowball fight... That would be asking for trouble.

"What do you mean?" she asked as she shaded in the horse she had copied from a library book. She wasn't as good a drawer as Hobie, but he was teaching her.

"I know you want to go outside with them," Hobie said. "It's okay. You don't have to play with me all the time."

She looked at him and thought again that one of the things she liked most about him was the way he could read her mind. That, and he was always honest. Hobie, for his part, had quickly learned to appreciate the protection his friendship with Jules gave him. The other kids—especially the girls—didn't always like her, but for some reason they didn't pick on her, either. She wasn't like other girls. "Other girls don't give you a black eye," Joey Reynolds could have told him.

There were places Jules couldn't protect him, though, and sometimes she could tell Hobie had been roughed up in the boys' bathroom or in the hall.

"They make fun of me, too," she had told Hobie. "Because I don't have any parents."

"Where are your parents?" Hobie asked. "Are they dead?"

Jules shook her head. "My mom ran away with a boy she wasn't married to," she said matter-of-factly, "and then she dropped me off with Pappy and Mae when I was three, and we haven't heard from her since."

"Why do you call her Mae?" Hobie asked. "Why not Grandma or something?"

Jules shrugged. "Dunno. It's what I've always called her. I don't think she wants to be a grandma."

Listening now to the noise of the snowball fight outside, Jules shook her head and said, "No. I'd rather be here with you."

Jules blinked as she came back to the present and, seeing a sign for Staunton, realized she had no recollection of the last fifty miles. "Pay attention to what you're doing." She couldn't help feeling the car was more crowded now than it had been going to Ohio.

Kelli was at work when Jules finally got home at the end of a very long seven-hour drive. In the backseat of her Subaru, carefully tucked into a box and cushioned with wadded-up newspapers, was her night-light.

"Well, I don't suppose you'll be back until my funeral," Mae had said when Jules finished loading the light and her suitcase into the car.

"Don't be silly," Jules had said. "I'll be back," but, as she drove, she tried to imagine what could possibly draw her back. There had been no tearful hugs good-bye, no promise to be back soon or call often—not as it used to be with Pappy.

"I know you have to go," he'd said in a choked voice the day Jules left for Ohio State on a hard-won scholarship. "You're better than this place." She had clung tightly to him, wishing she could tell him all the reasons she had to leave, why she could never come back. She knew he would go upstairs and sit in the empty bedroom both his girls had abandoned, nothing but an old night-light and faded posters left behind to remind him of them....

"Hello, girls," she said as she opened the door and was vocally greeted by two kittens, an all-gray named Mistletoe and a gray-and-white named Holly.

"They have to have Christmas names," Kelli had said when she brought them home last Christmas Eve. "Someone dropped them by the dumpster. I couldn't leave them." Jules had peered into the box at the two mewling kittens, their eyes barely open. Between Kelli's imploring eyes and the kittens' pitiful cries, "How could I say no?" Jules had asked in her most Scrooge-like voice, but her heart had melted as soon as the kittens, their little bellies full of kitten formula, had curled up on her chest and fallen fast asleep.

"Oh, you look so skinny and neglected," she said now as they wound around her ankles, complaining loudly that it was past their dinnertime. She went back out to the car to get her suitcase and the box containing the night-light and took them upstairs. She was back down in a moment, saying, "Come on, let's get some dinner while we wait for your mother to get home."

"Oh, my gosh, it smells so good," Kelli said an hour later when she came in the door.

Jules rushed to her and held her tightly. Kelli returned the embrace as Jules mumbled into her neck, "I missed you so much."

"I missed you, too." Kelli kissed Jules's cheek and then worked her way to her lips.

They stood, locked in a kiss for a long time, until Jules jerked away.

"Ouch!" she exclaimed as Holly stretched up on her hind legs, kneading her front claws into Jules's thigh. "Dinner's ready," she said, rubbing her leg. "Hope you don't mind tacos. We had all the stuff, and it's simple."

"Sounds great," Kelli said. "Let me wash up, and I'll be right down."

Though Kelli changed into and out of her ICU scrubs at the hospital—"you don't even want to know what they've been exposed to"—she always showered as soon as she got home.

She was back in ten minutes, smelling of soap and shampoo, her short, blonde hair dark now while it was damp.

"So," said Kelli as they sat with plates filled with a couple of tacos each, "tell me all about it."

Jules shrugged. "Not much to tell." She took a crunchy bite.

Kelli watched Jules's face closely. "I notice there's an addition to our décor upstairs."

"Oh, that," Jules said sheepishly. "I hope you don't mind. It was mine. Pappy bought it for me."

Kelli reached for her hand. "Of course I don't mind. I remember it from your room. How old were you?"

"About four, I think," Jules said. "Not too long after I came to live with them. Mae had a fit that he spent so much money on me."

"She does love you, you know. In her way," Kelli said.

<hr />

"Why does Mae hate me?" Jules asked Pappy one day. "All the other kids have mothers who bring cookies or cupcakes to school for their birthday." She sniffed and wiped her nose with the back of her hand. "I'm going to be nine this summer. The teacher said we could do a party for all the summer birthdays, and when I asked Mae if we could make cupcakes, she said it was the silliest thing she ever heard of."

"Oh, sweetie," said Pappy, handing her his handkerchief while he puffed on his pipe behind the garage. "She doesn't hate you. She loves you. A lot. She's just not real good at showing how she feels. She shows it in other ways. Like when she patched your overalls."

Mae, having long since accepted that Jules would wear what Jules would wear, no longer tried to get her into Joan's old dresses, but she couldn't help complaining about some of the things Jules did wear—like her old, faded overalls. They had been big on her when she was little, like seven, but they fit fine now—"except for the holes in the knees," Mae pointed out.

"I don't care," Jules said, crossing her arms. "They're all broken in. I like them this way."

But even Jules couldn't keep wearing them when she was climbing a tree and a branch caught in one of the back pockets, ripping the material away from her backside, letting everyone see her underwear. Joey and his gang of boys had roared with laughter as she climbed back down from the tree.

"I see London, I see France. I see Jules's underpants," they chanted over and over as she ran from the schoolyard.

"Oh, no," she wailed when she got the overalls off and inspected the damage. She sat up in her room for hours, tongue sticking out of the corner of her mouth in concentration as she tried to sew the ripped fragment back down. It looked awful, the stitches all puckered and uneven, "and it feels funny," she said when she tried to put them on and realized the ripped leg was now much shorter than the other.

She draped them carefully over the chair in her room when she went to bed that night, only to wake and find them missing. Scrambling out of bed and down the stairs to the kitchen, she was already hollering when she stopped short. There, on the kitchen table, were her overalls, tiny neat stitches replacing her jagged ones, with fresh patches on the knees.

"You fixed them!" Jules cried. She hugged Mae around the waist and ran back upstairs to try them on.

Jules looked at Pappy's smiling face as he puffed rings of smoke from his pipe. "I forgot about that."

The next Monday, Mae showed up at school with two large Tupperware containers of chocolate chip cookies.

"She does love you, you know. In her way."

Jules smiled and nodded as Kelli squeezed her hand. "You're right," she said. "Neither of us has ever been very good at showing how we feel about each other."

Kelli turned back to her taco, now falling apart where the grease had soaked into the tortilla. "She's going to be lonely now, even if she won't admit it. You'll need to call her more often."

"I guess."

"And maybe we could go visit in a month or so," Kelli said brightly.

"Oh, that'll be a joyful visit."

"And to think I used to wonder where you got your sarcasm from," Kelli said with a shake of her head.

"Hey."

Jules looked up from a student file she was going over. "Hi, Donna."

"You're back at work already?" Donna asked, pulling out a chair and sitting.

"Just looking over the list of students I'll be testing in August," Jules said.

Donna reached forward and laid her hands over top of the file, blocking Jules's view. "I'm not talking about work," she said. "For a psychologist—"

"School psychologist," Jules interrupted. "There's a difference."

"Whatever," Donna said with a wave of one hand. "I'm talking about family. You just lost your grandfather, the man who raised you."

Jules tugged the file out from under Donna's hands. "He was sick for a long time. It's not like this was sudden or unexpected."

"That doesn't make it any easier," Donna said.

"What are you doing here in July?" Jules asked. "I have to work twelve months, but you're supposed to have the summer off."

Donna gave her a sardonic look, and Jules knew that she'd recognized the abrupt change in topic.

Sitting back, Donna said, "We got our shipment of new textbooks. I was counting them to make sure the order's complete."

"Oooo, new history textbooks." Jules grinned. "Can't wait to get ahold of one of those."

"Smartass." Donna got to her feet. "You and Kelli still coming to Elaine's birthday party this weekend?"

"Yup. It's on the calendar."

"Good," Donna said. "Elaine went to a lot of work putting her party together. She'll be pissed if people don't show up."

"She's throwing her own party?" Jules asked.

Donna rolled her eyes. "You think she'd trust me to get it right?"

Jules chuckled. "Well, we'll be there, and we promise to be properly impressed."

"That will make my life much easier," Donna said with a smile before she disappeared through the door.

CHAPTER 4

"KELLI?"

"Back here," came Kelli's voice from a back room.

Jules found her hunched over her potter's wheel, turning a tiny pot, her pinky just fitting inside as the wet clay was shaped into a delicate curve, narrowing at the top. Shelves around the room—a converted sun porch—held pots of different sizes and shapes, some already glazed, but most still raw clay. An open kiln occupied one corner.

Jules sat down on an antique deacon's bench along one wall and watched Kelli work, admiring the play of sunlight on her blonde hair and the muscles of her forearms as her hands molded the clay.

"I love to watch you work," Jules said softly.

Kelli smiled but didn't take her eyes off her pot. Her pottery was her creative outlet for the stress of ICU nursing. Her schedule—three twelve-hour shifts a week—allowed her ample time to indulge her creative side.

She plucked a string from a bowl of water and, holding it taut between her fingers, slid it under her miniscule pot, breaking it free of the wheel. She set it aside and said, "Now, it's your turn," coming to Jules, who stood to hold her.

"Have you been in here all day?" Jules asked as Kelli gave her a quick kiss.

"Not all day," Kelli said, going to the sink to wash the clay from her hands. "I vacuumed the house and brushed the cats." She scrubbed her nails with a brush. "Oh, I did some laundry, too. Could you put it in the dryer for me while I go shower and get ready for the party?"

Jules went to the laundry room, where she could hear the water begin to run through the pipes from the bathroom upstairs. She pulled the wet clothes out of the washer and tossed them into the dryer. When she leaned over the washer to make sure she hadn't missed anything, a wad of damp paper in the bottom of the drum caught her attention. She plucked it out and carefully unfolded it.

I'm like you.

The writing was washed out, but still legible. "I completely forgot that was in my pocket," Jules murmured. She blotted it in a paper towel. The shower suddenly turned off. With a glance upwards, Jules folded the damp diner check and placed it in her wallet.

A couple of hours later, Jules and Kelli were walking through an impeccably landscaped yard to the front door of Donna and Elaine's home in Locust Grove. The buzz of multiple voices reached them as Donna opened the door and greeted them both with hugs. They entered an interior as beautifully decorated as the exterior.

"All Elaine, not me," Donna frequently joked. "I don't know a Chippendale from a Queen Victoria."

"It's Queen Anne," Elaine would point out with a roll of her eyes. *Does she even know Donna does it on purpose?* Jules often wondered.

Kelli spied Elaine in the midst of a knot of people—"holding court," Jules mumbled.

Kelli shushed her with an elbow to the ribs. "Come on," she said, taking Jules by the hand and leading her over.

"Oh, I'm so glad you could come!" Elaine exclaimed, her perfectly made-up face beaming as she hugged them and gave air kisses.

"You look wonderful," Kelli said.

Elaine spun around, showing off a new suit that did look fabulous on her, Jules had to grudgingly admit.

Kelli looked around, taking in all of the fresh flower arrangements and platters of artfully arranged hors d'oeuvres. "It all looks beautiful," she said. "Where did you get these flowers?"

She and Elaine started talking flower arranging, and Jules took the opportunity to slip away and get something to drink. She looked over to see Donna at the sideboard, holding a bottle of wine.

"Don't suppose there's any beer?" Jules asked.

Donna scoffed. "Are you kidding? Everything had to be just so, and beer doesn't fit that picture in Elaine's scheme of things. I just did what I was told to have the house the way she wanted it."

"What about the way you want it?" Jules almost asked but swallowed the words. *It's none of my business. If Donna's happy, that's all that matters.* "Who are all these people?" she asked instead, looking around.

"Most of them are clients." Donna poured two glasses of wine. "But some of our friends are here; I think they're all hiding in the kitchen." She leaned close and whispered, "Where you might find a smuggled beer."

"Thanks," Jules said with a wry grin, taking a glass for herself and one for Kelli.

"The grays and blues are selling really well," Elaine was saying as Jules handed Kelli her glass. "I'm almost sold out of those, so if you can do more in those colors, I know they'll go."

"Sure," Kelli said with a quick smile of thanks for Jules. "I'm just getting ready to glaze a new batch. They should be ready next week."

Jules wandered off, leaving them discussing Elaine's design studio. She stopped to chat with a few people as she grazed on various platters of food—*most definitely not like the food at Mae's house after the funeral,* she thought, peering at something she couldn't identify. She took a tentative nibble and then covertly wrapped the rest of whatever it was in a napkin and looked for the nearest trash can.

She slipped out the French doors to the patio, where the night was cooling, the sky an inky black dotted with brilliant stars. She heard the door open and close behind her and turned to find Donna standing at her shoulder.

"It's a nice party," Jules said, sitting on the side of a chaise.

Donna smiled. "It is, but I warned her, I only want a few people for mine—you and Kelli, maybe Barbara and Chris." She sat beside Jules on the chaise. "So, what happens to Mae now?"

"Nothing happens," Jules said. "She'll stay busy with church and volunteering, the same things she's been doing since before he went into a nursing home."

"But she had him keeping her there before. Will she stay there alone?"

Jules nodded. "She would never leave Aldie."

"Have you asked her?" Donna asked.

"No!" Jules said. "Why would I do that?"

Donna shrugged. "You're the only family she has left. At least the only family she knows of unless your mother resurfaces someday. What if something happens to her?"

"I'll deal with that if it happens," Jules said. "We would kill each other. You know that."

"She's going to be different without Pappy," Donna said. "She's going to need you more now." She gave Jules's shoulder a sympathetic squeeze before going in.

Jules, reeling a bit from even the suggestion that Mae should come to live with her, sat in the darkness, listening to the muted noise of voices coming from the party.

A few minutes later, the door opened again. This time, Kelli joined her, sitting beside her where, a moment ago, Donna had sat.

"You okay?" Kelli asked, slipping her arm through Jules's and giving her a squeeze.

"Mmm-hmm."

"I know being around all these people is probably the last thing you feel like right now," Kelli said softly. "Thank you."

Jules smiled and looked at her. Tenderly, she traced her fingertips over Kelli's cheek and kissed her. They sat in silence for a few minutes, listening to the laughter coming from inside.

"You know," Kelli said, leaning against Jules. "I think Elaine still has a hard time with you and Donna."

Jules turned to her. "What makes you say that?"

"The way she keeps looking any time you and Donna are off together, like when she was out here with you just now," Kelli said. "I don't think she's ever gotten used to the idea that you and Donna stayed friends."

Jules shook her head in bewilderment. "We were over years before Donna even met Elaine. It's not like it's a fresh breakup."

"I know," Kelli said. "But...it doesn't help that Donna is still in love with you."

Jules mouth dropped open as she stared at Kelli in the diffused light coming through the sheers on the French doors. "No, she isn't."

Kelli gave her a knowing smile. "The breakup wasn't her idea."

Jules didn't know what to say to that.

"On another topic," Kelli said. "Is everything all right with you?""

"Yes, why?" Jules asked, feeling a little defensive now.

"You've been really restless at night since you got home," Kelli said. "Last night you were kind of calling out in your sleep."

"What was I saying?" Jules asked.

"Nothing I could make out," Kelli said. "You just seemed really agitated. Anything you want to talk about?"

"Here? Now?" Jules joked. "Sure. Let me lie on the couch."

Kelli watched her face for a moment. "All right." She kissed Jules on the cheek and went back inside, the noise from the party spilling out into the night for a moment before the door closed with a snap, leaving Jules sitting alone in the dark.

———◆◇◆———

"Come on," Jules whispered to Hobie. "It's Saturday. The garbage trucks don't run on Saturday. Let's go explore."

"I should tell my mom," Hobie said.

"No, don't," Jules said quickly. She had learned early on that Hobie's mother was very protective. "She won't let you go if you tell her."

Hobie stood, looking back toward his house.

"Come on," Jules said. "I've been there tons of times." She had, in fact, been to the dump exactly once, but it was a treasure trove of good junk—old bicycle parts, fishing reels all tangled in impossible birds' nests, wheels and engine parts that could be used for a go-cart someday.

"I'm going," Jules said, turning toward the far end of the backyard.

"Wait!" Hobie called after her.

She grinned. It worked every time.

Together, they traipsed down the dirt road, kicking at rocks and empty cans until they came to an enormous pile of junk and garbage.

"It's like a mountain!" Hobie said, his mouth open.

"I know," Jules said. "Watch out for the real garbage. Some of it's pretty stinky."

Together, they kicked and poked through the pile, using a stick to prod some things out of their way. They were startled by a few rats.

"The rats are scared of us," Jules shouted to Hobie, who had bolted back to the dump road and was ready to leave at that point.

Reluctantly, Hobie came back, and they began to set aside a small collection of things to take home—a coil of copper wire, a sled with no runners, a broken radio Jules insisted Pappy could fix. They split up to cover more ground.

"Look at this!" Jules hollered from the far side of the mountain.

Hobie hurried to where she was holding up an army helmet and ammo belt. "Look at this stuff!" She dug out a backpack and canteen as well. "There's two! Two of everything," she said, pawing deeper into the junk pile as she handed Hobie another ammo belt and canteen and then a second helmet and backpack. "Genuine army stuff!" Jules crowed. Every piece was stamped with faded block letters spelling out "WALTERS" on one set of gear and "ANDERSON" on the other.

Ecstatic at their good luck, they donned the helmets and slid the straps of the backpacks over their shoulders with the ammo belts and canteens stuffed inside and proudly brought everything home, expecting to be congratulated on their find.

"What if there's infection in these things?" Mrs. Fahnestock shrieked as she made Hobie take everything off and drop it on the ground as if it were contaminated. "What if there were rats crawling around on them?"

Jules looked at her as if she were crazy. "Well, they're not here now," she said, throwing her hands in the air.

Mrs. Fahnestock shook her head. "There could be germs. Hobie is delicate. He gets sick so easily."

Mae, to Jules's surprise, came to their defense. "We can boil everything to disinfect it, and then they can play with no worries, Bertha."

And so the two women boiled large pots of water to sterilize the metal helmets and canteens while Jules and Hobie scrubbed the backpacks and ammo belts with rags and cleaner.

"Isn't this great stuff?" Jules asked as they cleaned.

"Yeah," said Hobie, his plump cheeks red with the effort of scrubbing. He beamed at Jules. "You're my best friend."

She looked at him with a grin. "You're my best friend, too."

Have I ever said that to anyone since? Jules wondered as she sat on the dark patio. She listened to the voices and noise of Elaine's party and thought about the things Kelli had just said. She knew Kelli was speaking from a place of love and honesty; she wasn't an angry or jealous person. Jules wished she could explain about her bad dreams—the dreams that had, in fact, started back up. She closed her eyes. "Please don't let this happen again," she whispered.

CHAPTER 5

JULES HUMMED ALONG WITH the radio as she drove to Clearbrook Elementary. She liked having a variety of schools assigned to her. The high school where Donna worked was her favorite, but she liked the mix of ages. This time of year, the pending start of a new school year, always brought a sense of excitement and anticipation—a feeling she remembered from when she was a child.

"I'll never get to sleep tonight," she remembered saying to Hobie the night before their first day of fifth grade as they sat out in the backyard on either side of an oil lamp, listening to the crickets.

"Me neither," Hobie said morosely, and Jules knew he was imagining all-new horrors awaiting him with the coming of a new year.

Summers were always Hobie's favorite times—"I wish it could stay summer all the time," he'd said to Jules several times over their two summers together. He loved it when he didn't have to be at school, when he could just read and draw all day. But this summer had been their best ever. She and Hobie had spent nearly every day playing—playing army with the gear they'd found in the dump, playing Indians in the woods, fishing in the smaller creeks nearby, even sneaking down to the river—a place they weren't supposed to be.

The Scioto River ran in a big, lazy loop around Aldie, its muddy waters moving in deceptively slow currents until they came to tangles of trees and brush ripped up and deposited by previous floods. "You stay away from there," Pappy had said in an unusually stern tone. "Every year, someone gets caught in those brush dams and drowns." So, they stayed on the bank, throwing rocks and sticks but never venturing into the water.

At night, they caught lightning bugs in jars and pretend-camped around an old oil lamp since they weren't allowed to have a real campfire. "You'll get burned," Mrs. Fahnestock had fretted.

"I wish it could just stay like this," Hobie had said that evening as he held a twig above the chimney of the oil lamp, watching the clinging green leaves curl and wither, "and we never had to go back to school."

"It won't be so bad," Jules said, trying to encourage him.

"For you, it won't." Hobie looked up at her, the dancing light from the oil lamp chasing shadows across his face....

Jules shook her head to clear it as she pulled into the school parking lot, gathering her briefcase and coffee cup.

"Hi, Sue," she called to the school secretary, who was already besieged by parents registering new students or wanting to know who their child's teacher would be this year. Sue gave a distracted wave as Jules went down the hall to the guidance office where they had a desk designated for her use when she was at this school. Even though the students wouldn't start until after Labor Day, the school personnel all reported on August 15. Jules had scheduled a meeting with the new assistant principal and the new special ed teacher to orient both of them on the forms they would be using for those kids who needed to be tested to see if they were eligible for special education services—"my chance to train them to get it right," she quipped to her colleagues. The other psychologists were similarly scattered throughout Albemarle County to their assigned schools, so that sometimes a week or two went by without their being in the central office at the same time.

Glancing at her watch, she saw that she was early for the meeting. She logged onto the computer and checked her personal e-mail. Aside from sales announcements from LL Bean, there was nothing worth keeping. She paused a moment and pulled her wallet from her pocket. There, dry now, was the note from the diner—the note that had been wadded up and thrown away, put through the wash, yet still refused to go away. *Maybe that's a sign*, she thought as she opened a new e-mail and typed the scribbled e-mail address.

She paused for a moment and then wrote.

> *You left me a note in Sandy's Diner. My name is Jules. Talk to me.*

She hesitated, her finger hovering over the send button before finally tapping it and shutting down the computer.

She went to find the classroom where they were scheduled to meet and knocked as she entered.

"The office is down the hall to the left," came a voice from the back of the room, where a stack of boxes sat near a set of bookshelves.

All Jules could see was a woman's rear end as she bent over to grab an armful of books and straightened to place them on the shelves. She caught herself appraising the woman's backside for a couple of seconds before clearing her throat.

"Can I help?" Jules asked.

The woman jumped and dropped a book that landed with a loud thud.

"Sorry," Jules said. "Didn't mean to startle you."

"No, it's okay," said the woman. "I can finish this later." She stepped over a box and approached, her hand held out. "I'm Carrie Sturdivant."

"Jules Calhoon," Jules said, shaking her hand. "I'm the school psychologist assigned to Clearbrook."

The handshake and the initial glances lingered just a few extra seconds.

"Yes, of course," said Carrie. "Bob should be here any minute. Sorry about..." She gestured toward the door. "I've had about a hundred parents bypass the secretary and come exploring on their own today."

"No problem," Jules said. "I'm sure it's hard, setting up a new classroom. Where did you come to us from?" she asked, trying to decide how old Carrie was. Her short, dark hair framed a face that could have been anywhere from twenty-five to thirty-five.

"Newport News," Carrie said. "I was there for seven years, the last four as a reading specialist." Her face flushed a little as she went to her desk, where she had a pad and pen waiting for this meeting.

Ah, Jules thought, *a breakup.* "Well," she said, "Newport News's loss is our gain."

"Hello, ladies." A male voice sounded from the doorway. "I see I'm a little late. Bob Manzella," said a rotund man, no taller than Jules and Carrie.

"Jules Calhoon." Jules shook his hand. "And you're right on time. Carrie and I were just getting acquainted."

He took the seat behind the desk, leaving the small elementary desks for Carrie and Jules.

Oh, no you don't. Pointing to the activity table at the back of the room, Jules said, "Why don't we all sit back here? That way I can distribute the handouts I've prepared for you and we can all see what the forms look like."

Carrie caught her eye, swallowing a smile as she and Jules headed back to the table, leaving Bob no choice but to follow.

An hour later, Jules was driving back to the central office, pleased with how the meeting had gone. Bob was a little pompous but had seemed amenable to taking direction from Jules when he realized the complexity of the paperwork he would be responsible for. This guy could make life easy or hard for her, and the trick, she had quickly realized during their meeting, would be to make it look like his idea.

Carrie had been very open to accepting Jules's input in the intervention and educational plans she would be writing.

"I'll be glad to help you with these," Jules had said when Carrie looked a little lost.

"Thanks." Carrie exhaled in relief.

Jules smiled as she drove. Carrie was definitely family. For a school system the size of Albemarle County, there weren't many gays and lesbians, or if there were, they were very good at remaining closeted.

"This could be an interesting year," she said to herself. She pulled into a parking space at the central office and felt her cell phone vibrate. She checked the screen. There was a text message from Kelli, asking her to call. Her expression darkened, and she tucked the phone back into her pocket as she walked into the building.

Kelli stretched into a reverse warrior with the instructor on the yoga DVD.

"Breathe into it," intoned the instructor, an impossibly lithe young woman. "Clear your mind of any distractions..."

Kelli snorted as she tried to make her spine bend that way. Her mind was nothing but distractions: her back was bothering her—a souvenir of a heavy patient lift several years earlier—the whole reason she forced herself to work out religiously and do yoga now; she was anxious to see how the latest set of pots would turn out with the new glazing technique she had experimented with; she and Jules had made love last night, the first time in ages, but....

Kelli dropped out of downward dog to lie flat on her yoga mat.

The night-light had been on, providing a romantic glow over their bodies. Kelli reached between Jules's legs, her fingers finding the wetness waiting for her touch as Jules opened to meet her. Just as Kelli could feel Jules riding her to a crescendo, Jules had looked over at the light and... nothing. The wave of excitement crashed without cresting into an orgasm.

"I can't," Jules had gasped, gently pulling Kelli's hand away.

Kelli lay with her head on Jules's shoulder. "Maybe our bedroom isn't the best place for that light," she murmured as Jules lay with her head turned toward it. Kelli could see the shadow of Jules's neck undulating with every beat of her heart. She reached up and gently placed her fingers over the pulsating artery.

Jules smiled. "Are you checking my heart rate?"

"Just feeling you," Kelli murmured, nuzzling into Jules's fragrant hair, which she only let down from its ponytail at night. "Your life, your rhythm."

They lay silently for long minutes, Jules's face still turned toward the light.

"What's wrong?" Kelli whispered.

She could see Jules bite her lip, could feel her weighing words. She waited, but Jules only said, "Nothing," reaching out to click the light off. "Maybe you're right. I'll move this tomorrow. It's like having my grandparents in here with us."

Kelli rolled onto her back as the woman on the DVD moved on to balance poses.

One of the things that had attracted her to Jules when they met was a sense of depth and mystery. It had intrigued her from the beginning. There was something—"not exactly wounded," Kelli had tried to explain to her younger sister, Mary Anne.

"No, no, no," Mary Anne had groaned. "Not someone else you're going to try and fix. Why can't you find someone healthy and whole?"

"She's not like that."

"No?" Mary Anne said, unconvinced. She reached out to grasp Kelli's hands. "How many relationships has she had before you?"

"Two," Kelli said.

"And how long did they last?"

Kelli frowned. "The first was eight years, the second was six."

Mary Anne's eyebrows rose. "And why did they end?"

Kelli's frown deepened. "She said they just grew apart. They're still friends. At least the first one is."

Mary Anne shook her sister by the shoulders. "'We grew apart' is code for 'I found someone else.' Don't you know that? Please don't set yourself up for this."

But Kelli was already in love and Jules—Jules was wonderful—laughing, kind, considerate, passionate.

"I couldn't have not loved her," Kelli tried to explain to a frustrated Mary Anne weeks later.

But if Kelli had thought that time alone would allow her access to the places Jules didn't let other people go, she was wrong. After five years together, Jules was still kind and loving, but from the beginning, there had been times when she seemed very far away—distant, brooding, uncommunicative. She always came back from that other place, *but will she always come back?* Kelli couldn't help wondering. Especially lately.

"It's just Pappy," she kept telling herself, but she wasn't so sure.

She had even thought about going to Donna, asking her about what Jules had never explained satisfactorily, about how and why they broke up, about whether what was happening now was part of a pattern... but she couldn't.

It felt too disloyal to go to Jules's ex to get answers, *and somehow it feels like I'm admitting our relationship is in trouble.*

"It's not," Kelli said aloud, staring at the ceiling as she lay on her yoga mat. "We're fine."

She rolled up her mat and went to the studio to check on her pots. The kiln had cooled from its last firing. She unlocked it and lifted the lid.

"Damn."

A pot had burst. It happened sometimes. Defects in the clay, air bubbles or moisture—unseen, hidden below the surface—could expand during the firing of the kiln, unable to take the heat. It was bad enough when it happened to one pot, after all the time and effort that had been put into making it, but sometimes the damage was more extensive.

"Oh, no."

Kelli reached in, picking up shards from all the surrounding pots that had been caught in the explosion. Nothing had escaped. Pieces of clay lay scattered everywhere.

"Everything is ruined," she moaned. She sighed and reached for a trash can. *Nothing you can do but clean up the mess and start over.*

CHAPTER 6

I can't believe you wrote to me! I hoped you would when I wrote you that note, but I didn't think you would. My name is Ronnie Yoder—well, really it's Veronica, but I like to be called Ronnie. I'm sixteen and a junior at Aldie High. I'm not sure there are any other girls like me in school. Sometimes, I think the girls on the sports teams might be like us, but I'm not cool enough for them, so even if they are, they wouldn't talk to me. But when I saw you, even with a ponytail, I knew you were.

We don't have Internet at home. I can only use e-mail at school or at the library. I know you're probably going to say I should talk to someone here, but we go to kind of a strict church, so I know better than to talk to our pastor. I heard there was a boy a couple of years ago when I was a freshman who told the school guidance counselor he was different—like us—but she went to his parents, and then he wasn't in school any more. I don't know what happened to him, but after that, I know I can't talk to a teacher or counselor, either. So there's no one here I can talk to. Not really talk.

I work at the diner, washing dishes. That's how I saw you. I heard Trish saying you were here for your grandfather's funeral and that you went to school a year ahead of her. So you know what it's like here. Why I have to get out as soon as I can. Write back when you can and tell me how you did it.

Ronnie

Jules re-read the rambling message several times, noticing how vague Ronnie was, describing herself in obscure language, never using the words "gay" or "lesbian." *Probably afraid of someone else reading it.* Or maybe... She thought back to how long it had taken her to feel comfortable calling herself by those adjectives, even when she had known for a long time that she was different.

She sat staring at the screen, feeling sick to her stomach, kicking herself for responding to that note—that plea for help. Alarm bells were sounding in her head; a large part of her wanted to pull back and protect herself. It seemed cowardly to feel that way, but she worked with teenagers every day. She knew how impulsive and indiscreet they could be. Another, stronger, part of her sympathized with Ronnie's sense of isolation, stuck in a small town where you felt utterly alone. *Only you weren't alone,* she reminded herself harshly. She pushed the laptop away, got to her feet, and paced the upstairs office.

Funny, the Internet opens the world to you, and it's easier to know what's out there. The possibilities. The choices. The problem is, it's out there. Not in your town. Not where you live. It doesn't make any of it feel any closer or more attainable.

When Kelli's key jingled in the door, Jules quickly closed her laptop.

"Hey," Kelli called tiredly.

"Hi." Jules hurried down the stairs to greet her. "Long day?"

"Mmm-hmm." Kelli smothered a yawn. "Have you eaten?"

"Yeah," Jules said. "Cooked up some chicken and rice. Want me to heat some up for you?"

"Oh, that would be wonderful," Kelli said. "I'll go shower."

Jules dished out a large portion of food and placed it in the microwave. *Are you going to tell her about Ronnie?* asked a voice in Jules's head.

She shrugged in irritation. *It's no big deal. There's nothing to tell yet. Ronnie's just a kid. She'll probably get bored and stop e-mailing any time now.*

You're keeping secrets. Again.

Jules stood, staring into space until the microwave beeped.

"Kell?" Jules called. "Dinner's ready."

When she received no answer, she went upstairs and found Kelli, her hair still damp, sound asleep on top of the comforter. Jules stood there for a long time, listening to Kelli's deep, even breathing. At last, she pulled the other side of the comforter over Kelli's prone figure and swung the bedroom door shut.

Back downstairs, she took the plate from the microwave. Holly meowed plaintively as she wound around Jules's ankles. Jules pinched a piece of chicken off and fed some to her, waiting just a moment for Mistletoe to appear for her bit. They always seemed to know when a treat was in the offing. Jules rewrapped the plate and put it in the refrigerator.

"We don't waste food in this house."

Jules smiled grimly as she heard Mae's voice uttering that phrase. She couldn't count how many times she had heard it while growing up. It didn't matter how hateful the food was—liver or lima beans or Brussels sprouts. Mae wouldn't let Jules up from the table until she had cleaned her plate. Many evenings, Jules had sat by herself long past dinnertime, eventually falling asleep at the table, her plate—still untouched—pushed aside. Pappy would come in and carry her up to bed while Mae grumbled about starving children in China.

"She's just as stubborn as you are," Pappy would point out, to which Mae would huff, "I am not stubborn. I just believe in right and wrong."

Hobie came to eat with them sometimes, though Jules was always surprised he came back after the first time. It had been soon after he and Jules had met, and Hobie eagerly helped himself to enormous portions of everything.

Mae glared at his plate. "You are going to leave some for the rest of us, aren't you?"

Hobie turned beet red and mumbled something about his mother always letting him have that much. He looked as if he might cry. Jules turned red, too, but in anger.

"Boy's just growing," Pappy said to cover the awkward silence. "It's a compliment to your cooking. You always say our string bean here doesn't eat enough to keep a mouse alive."

But that evening, Jules did eat a lot—to make Hobie feel better and to defy Mae. When at last Hobie went back next door with a mumbled, "Thank you, Miz Calhoon," Jules rounded on her grandmother.

"How could you say that to him? He was hungry."

"All of China's not that hungry," Mae said.

"What does China have to do with anything?" Jules asked with a stomp of her foot.

"That boy eats because he's sad," Mae said, scraping the leftovers into a bowl. "And his mother helps him stay that way. She's not doing him any favors."

Jules stopped, ready to sass back. She'd never considered that people might eat because they were sad. Maybe Mae was right. Hobie had a lot to be sad about.

After that, Hobie never ate as much when he had dinner with the Calhoons, but Jules knew he went home hungry on those nights.

"Food's not all he was hungry for," Jules murmured as she stood for a long time with her hand on the refrigerator door. Quietly, she went back upstairs, past the room where Kelli lay sleeping to the last room down the hall. She sat on the floor with her back against the guest bed and lowered the night-light off the bedside table. She clicked the switch, sitting in the amber glow, with the cowboy and his horse for company.

"Oh my gosh!" Carrie stopped, her mouth open in delight, when she and Jules stepped into the design showroom.

Jules looked around and spied Elaine with a customer over by the fabric swatches. Elaine gave a quick wave to acknowledge that she had seen them.

Turning to Carrie, Jules said, "Told you. Elaine can help you decorate your place or just help come up with ideas."

After Jules's first meeting with Carrie at Clearbrook, she had made a point of stopping by Carrie's classroom any time she was in the building to see how she was getting along. Carrie had eleven kids in her class, nine of them boys, all of them learning disabled and most of them hyperactive as well.

"Don't you feel like you need a Valium by the time you go home?" Jules asked one afternoon. Carrie laughed as Jules shook her head. "The energy level in here is off the charts."

"Today was an especially challenging day," Carrie admitted, dropping into her chair. "And," she glanced at the door to make sure no one was passing by her classroom, "there hasn't been a lot of support."

Jules nodded. "That's what I figured."

"I really appreciate your help with the intervention plans," Carrie said. "Do you spend this much time with all the special ed classes?"

A warm flush crept up Jules's neck, and she knew her face was turning red. "No. Not all. But I figured you might have been thrown in the deep end, and most of the other teachers have been doing this a long time. You said you were a reading specialist?"

"Yes," Carrie said. "I taught for three years and then took a reading specialist position in Newport News. So, it's been a while since I've had to deal with an entire classroom of kids."

"So, what prompted the move?" Jules asked.

All the looks and signs of mutual recognition had led to this moment. Carrie went to close the classroom door before answering.

"My girlfriend and I split up," she said.

"I'm sorry," said Jules. "How long were you together?"

Carrie doodled on the paper before her, drawing a series of concentric circles. "Four years. We worked in the same school, and then she met someone else, and... it was just hard being in the same building every day. Seemed like a good time to move."

"A fresh start," said Jules. "That can be a good thing."

Carrie nodded. "How about you?"

"Kelli and I have been together for five years," Jules said. "She's a nurse at Martha Jefferson. We'll have you over for dinner, introduce you to some friends. Where are you living?"

"I'm renting a duplex near Pantop," Carrie said. "It's very old, 1890s, the landlord said. It's really cute, but it looks pretty empty. I'm having a hard time deciding what to do with it. I'm kind of ready to move past Target chic."

"I know just the person to help you with that."

While they waited for Elaine, they browsed around the showroom. Carrie oohed and aahed over butter-soft leather chairs, richly upholstered couches, silk drapes, and fragile china.

"Okay, you're worrying me," Jules said. "Maybe I shouldn't have brought you in here."

Elaine joined them at that moment. "Hi, Jules," she said with a hug and kiss on Jules's cheek.

Jules made the introductions and said, "Carrie is a new teacher with us and has an empty duplex to fill."

Elaine's face lit up. "Really?"

"But," Jules said sternly, "remember, she's on a teacher's salary. I'm starting to think she has champagne taste on a beer pocketbook."

"What?" Carrie and Elaine said in unison.

Jules shrugged. "Just something my grandmother used to say."

Elaine tempered her excitement, but only a little. "Okay, let's start by walking around, and you just point out the things that you do and don't like. That will help me figure out which direction we should go."

Jules eased back into a poufy leather chair so deep and soft she wasn't sure she would be able to climb out. *Oh, this is heaven.* She let herself relax, the rich aroma of the leather enveloping her. Drowsily, she listened to the drone of Elaine's voice as she and Carrie wandered the studio.

"You don't have much furniture," Jules said, looking around Hobie's bedroom the first time he took her up there. In fact, the bed was the only piece of real furniture. Hobie's few clothes were folded into two cardboard boxes stacked on the floor—one for underwear and socks, the other for jeans and T-shirts. On another wall was a stack of old wooden crates filled with books—all the books Hobie always talked about.

"But that's good," she added, seeing the look on Hobie's face. "More room to play. My room has all kinds of stuff—two beds, a dresser, a chair. No room to spread out. This is better." She went to the crates. "You have lots of books."

Hobie brightened a little. "Here's all my Jules Verne books," he pointed out, and Jules heard the pride in his voice. "*Twenty Thousand Leagues Under the Sea*. And here's *Tom Sawyer* and *Robinson Crusoe*, but these aren't Jules Verne."

He pulled out some drawing pencils and blank paper, and they sprawled on the floor, copying illustrations from some of the books in his crates.

In halting bits, Hobie had gradually told Jules more about his family, how his father had died in a car accident with only a little life insurance from his job selling insurance—"that's not right," Jules said—how Hobie and his mother moved to Aldie to be near her sister's family in Chillicothe, how Hobie wore such a strange mix of clothes because he was wearing some of his father's old things and some of his own clothes from a few years ago.

"Lucky I'm so big, I guess," he said with a shrug, "because Mom couldn't afford to buy me new things. She's doing some baking and sewing to earn extra money, but it's not much."

Money was something that was never talked about in the Calhoon house except for when Mae complained about how expensive something was. Jules thought about Mae trying to make her wear her mother's old dresses and how upset Mae had been about the cost of the night-light. *Maybe she and Pappy don't have money to buy me things*, she realized.

Maybe, if I stop asking for things, stop them spending money on me, Mae will like me better.

Jules gave a scoff from her leather chair. *Didn't work, though, did it?* She roused herself as she heard Elaine saying, "I'll come by Thursday afternoon, then? About four?"

"That will be perfect," Carrie said.

Jules had to kick a little to pull herself out of her chair. "All done?"

"For now," said Elaine. She loved the challenge of decorating a blank canvas. "I have a good idea of what Carrie likes. Now, I just need to see her space. How's Kelli?"

"She's good," Jules said. "Working a seven to seven today." A thought occurred to her. "Are you and Donna available for dinner this weekend?"

"You're kidding," Kelli said a few hours later when she got home and Jules told her that they would be having three guests for dinner on Saturday.

"Do you mind?" Jules asked, realizing too late that maybe she should have checked with Kelli first.

"No." Kelli sighed, looking at the mail piled up on the kitchen counter—"how does it accumulate so fast?" she often asked in aggravation—and the tumbleweeds of cat hair rolling across the floor with the slightest stirring of the air, and the rugs that all needed vacuuming.

"I'll clean," Jules said hurriedly. "And we can grill something to keep it simple. Elaine will just have to make do with plain food that doesn't have foreign names and come with its own wine recommendations."

Kelli threw her hands up. "Okay."

Jules grinned and hugged her tightly. "You'll like Carrie," she said. "She's really nice."

Kelli wrapped her arms around Jules. "I just can't remember the last time you wanted to have people over."

Jules frowned. "I guess it has been a while. Have I been that bad?"

"Yes."

Jules pulled back to look into Kelli's eyes. "Why do you put up with me?"

Kelli studied Jules's face. She traced a fingertip, feather-light, over Jules's eyebrows, her lips. "Because I love you so very much," she murmured.

"I don't know what I would do without you," Jules said.

She chuckled as Kelli said, "I don't know what you'd do without me, either."

Jules response was a kiss, deep and slow as their bodies melted into one another.

"Oh." Kelli moaned. "You haven't kissed me like that in a long time. I'm about to hop into the shower." She nuzzled Jules's ear. "I'll be squeaky clean in a few minutes," she whispered seductively.

Jules stiffened. "You haven't had dinner yet, and I've got a few things I need to do this evening."

Kelli turned away.

Jules caught her hand. "I'll make it up to you. Soon."

Kelli nodded and headed upstairs.

CHAPTER 7

"Hey."

Donna looked up as Jules came into the classroom. "What are you doing here?" she asked.

"I need to do a couple of observations in your next class," Jules said. "Is this a good day?"

"Sure." Donna consulted her lesson plan. "We're covering the War of 1812. Exciting stuff."

"Can't wait," Jules said with a grin.

"Dinner the other night was really nice," Donna said. "Kind of felt like..."

"...like old times," hung in the air between them.

They didn't often go there. It was one of the awkward things about staying friends with an ex—the shared history, old stories about family, the intimate knowledge of each other's likes and dislikes....

Carrie had blended easily with the two couples, discussing the Newport News area with Elaine, who had grown up in Chesapeake. She had been to Carrie's duplex earlier in the week as planned and had brought fabrics and sketches with her, engaging the entire group in the decorating of Carrie's house.

"Be careful," Jules said to Carrie as she pulled a platter of burgers and a bowl of marinating chicken out of the refrigerator, "or who knows what you'll end up with."

She went out back to put the burgers on the grill. Donna joined her, perching on top of the picnic table.

"Carrie seems nice."

"Yeah, she does," Jules said. "I remember when we thought we were the only lesbians in the Charlottesville area. It's so hard to meet people."

Donna nodded, watching Jules place the burgers over the hot coals. The meat immediately began to sizzle. "Elaine will want to introduce her to all the single women we know," she said with a rueful smile.

Jules raised her spatula. "I'm not setting her up. I just wanted to introduce her so she wouldn't feel so alone. Where she goes from here is up to her."

She pulled some chicken breasts out of the marinade and laid them on the grill next to the hamburgers. "I don't even know that many single women anymore."

"Oh, we know several," Donna said. "It seems to go in waves of breakups, and then they shuffle and re-pair with someone else in the group. Elaine's old group of friends."

Jules chuckled. "I think I'm glad I don't know those people."

She flipped all the meat on the grill and went to the screen door. "Anyone who wants cheese or any weird stuff on their burger, come put it on in the next couple of minutes," she called.

Elaine appeared a moment later with a covered platter. Carrie followed her.

"I've got bleu cheese, Roquefort, pepper jack, and baby Swiss," Elaine said, sweeping the lid off the platter with a flourish.

"I've never tried Roquefort," Carrie said.

Elaine held the platter for her. "Try some." She took a slice of bleu cheese for herself. "Here's some pepper jack for you, sweetie," she said to Donna, peeling another slice of cheese off the platter.

"Donna doesn't like cheese—" Jules blurted before Elaine could lay the cheese on the burger.

Elaine looked up at her sharply.

"Um, I'm trying something new," Donna said quickly.

"But—" said Jules.

Kelli laid a calming hand on Jules's shoulder. "You don't know if you like it until you try it."

"Exactly," said Elaine with an edge to her voice.

Jules clamped her mouth shut and turned back to the grill.

"You mean," Jules said now, taking a seat in one of the front desks, "it was nice until I pissed Elaine off."

Donna laughed guiltily. "Well..."

"So how was that cheese?" Jules asked.

Donna snorted. "It was terrible."

Jules shook her head. "Why don't you just tell her? It's your food for Pete's sake!" She immediately held up her hands. "I'm sorry. It's none of my business."

"It was your business, once," Donna's eyes seemed to say, and Jules remembered what Kelli had said about Donna still being in love with her.

The bell rang, and the halls echoed with the thunder of hundreds of footsteps. Jules cleared her throat and stood to go take a seat at the back of the room.

"Anyway," Donna said. "Dinner was nice. We should try to do that more often."

"We will." Jules nodded, shuffling back as students began pouring into the room.

"What do you want to be when you grow up?"

Jules and Hobie lay side by side in the pile of leaves they had raked together under the oak tree out back, staring up through the branches at an impossibly blue sky.

"I want to be a writer," Hobie said without hesitation.

"Really?" Jules turned her head to look at him. "Like Jules Verne?"

"Yes." Jules heard more excitement in his voice than he had ever expressed before. "Jules Verne and Robert Louis Stephenson and Howard Pyle. And other writers," he said seriously. "Like Charles Dickens and John Steinbeck. They wrote really important stories, not just adventures."

Hobie sat up, his cheeks flushed with excitement.

"I'll be H.A. Fahnestock, like H.G. Wells."

"What's the 'A' stand for?"

Hobie made a face. "Alfred. It was my mom's dad's name. Hobarth Alfred. Why did they do that to me?" Then his face lit up again. "I want to write things that will change the way people think."

Jules frowned. "The way they think about what?"

Hobie hesitated, biting his lip. "The way they think about people—people who are different. People other people make fun of."

He waited, and Jules knew he expected her to laugh at him, but she didn't. He flopped back down. "What about you?"

Jules's fingers closed on an acorn. She tossed it in the air, catching it before it hit her in the face. "I'm going to be a jockey and win the Triple Crown," she said confidently.

"Don't you have to be near horses to do that?" Hobie asked.

Jules scratched her chin. That was an obstacle she hadn't quite figured out yet. "Well, whatever I do, I won't do it here."

"Where will you go?"

"Who cares?" she said. "As long as it's not Aldie, Ohio."

Hobie turned to look at her. "I wonder if that's how your mother felt."

———◆———

How many times did we have that conversation? Jules mused as she stared at a September calendar photo of brilliantly colored foliage thumbtacked to the wall of her cubby at the central office. *Hobie never wavered, never wanted to do anything else, while I went through a million choices. Let's see... I went from jockey to astronomer, to cowboy, to explorer—so practical. But Hobie never laughed or told me I was stupid.*

She raised a hand to her cheek and realized she was smiling. She couldn't remember the last time she'd smiled when she thought of him.

When Jules got home that afternoon, there were two bicycles in the front yard, tires pumped, water bottles in the holders, ready to be taken for a spin.

"Hi," she called as she entered through the front door.

"Hurry and get changed," Kelli said as she bounded from the kitchen. "Bikes are all set. I'm packing some snacks in case you're hungry."

She gave Jules a quick kiss and pushed her toward the stairs. Grinning at Kelli's contagious enthusiasm, Jules ran upstairs and reappeared a few minutes later, wearing bike shorts and a jersey.

"Take a windbreaker," Kelli said, holding one out. "It's getting a little chilly. All set?"

Within five minutes, they were pedaling out of their neighborhood along a county road that wound past open fields and orchards, wooden picking crates sitting ready for the apple harvest to begin. As traffic thinned, they were able to ride side by side for long stretches.

"Isn't it a beautiful day?" Kelli said, grinning back at her. Bicycling had become one of her outlets when she hurt her back, and she talked Jules into going with her whenever she could.

"Gorgeous," Jules agreed, enjoying the view of Kelli's hips on her bike seat as her legs churned up and down with her pedal strokes.

The crisp air smelled of apples and autumn. Many of the trees were starting to turn, their colors glinting in the slanting rays of the sun. They stopped to eat a bit and catch their breath and then completed a fifteen-mile loop that brought them back home.

"That felt good," Kelli said, her cheeks flushed, a slight sheen of sweat on her face.

"It did," Jules said. "Thanks for getting everything ready for us. You go shower and I'll start dinner. Ravioli sound good?"

"Everything sounds good," Kelli said, already halfway up the stairs. "I'm starving."

Jules put a pot of water on the stove and heard the shower start. She ran upstairs to the office and grabbed her laptop to finish reading the e-mail she'd seen in her in-box earlier that day.

You told me I should join sports teams and try to be more involved in school, but I'm only so-so at sports. I know some of those girls must be like us, but they all pretend to have boyfriends. They wouldn't give me the time of day, anyway. There is this one girl, Ashley Patterson. She's the best athlete in school—volleyball, basketball, track. They say she'll go to college on a scholarship for sure. She's nicer than the others. She talks to me sometimes, but she's so pretty, I get all stupid and tongue-tied and can't think of anything to say.

I guess I'm more of a brainiac, but the only other kids who join those kinds of clubs are the geeks who are more pathetic than I am. You asked me my favorite subjects and what I want to do. My favorite subject is English and literature. Don't laugh, but I want to be a writer.

*I don't know how that will happen, though. We don't
have money for college, even a state school, so my only
chance is a scholarship, but the counselors tell us not
to count on those. I'll probably end up working at
the mill after I graduate next year, like most people
around here.*

*You never said what you do or how you got out of
Aldie. Write back soon.*

"Work at the mill. Like hell you will," Jules muttered,
reading the message over again. She clicked the laptop shut
as Kelli came downstairs.

"Your turn," Kelli said.

"Water's just about at a boil and the sauce is heating
up," Jules said. "Be back down in a few minutes."

She returned to the kitchen just as Kelli was spooning
sauce over the cooked ravioli. "I was thinking," she said
as they sat down to eat. "I should probably check on Mae.
When I call her, all I get are one-word answers. I think I
might drive out this weekend."

"But I work Saturday," Kelli said.

"I know," Jules said. "But it's a long trip. There's no
need for you to come. I'll leave tomorrow after work, spend
a couple of nights, see how Mae's doing, and be home
Sunday."

Kelli reached for her hand. "I wanted to go with you
when you went back to see Mae. I wanted to be with you for
Pappy's funeral, if you remember."

"I know," Jules said again, frowning at her plate. "It
was stressful enough, Mae having to put up with having me

there. It would have been even harder to have a stranger in the house."

Kelli withdrew her hand. "A stranger."

Jules grimaced at her choice of words. "You know what I mean. From Mae's point of view, you're practically a stranger."

"And whose fault is that?" Kelli didn't say it, but she might as well have.

They ate in a strained silence for a few minutes.

"Is there anything else going on?" Kelli asked at last.

Jules glanced up at her. "What do you mean?"

"I mean," Kelli said, setting her fork down and placing both elbows on the table. "Is there anything else going on? You've been so distant and... different since you got back. At first, I thought it was just the funeral, but it seems like more than that."

She watched Jules's face, waiting as Jules struggled to respond.

"No. I mean... it's not just Pappy," Jules said. "Being in Aldie just dragged up a bunch of stuff. Old garbage, you know?"

"No, I don't know," Kelli said pointedly. "Because you never talk about it. This is as close as you ever come— referring to garbage from your past, but you never say what."

Jules stabbed a ravioli and popped it into her mouth before saying, "Maybe that's because I want to leave it in the past. If I wanted to talk about it, I would."

"Jules—"

"I've had enough." Jules rose from the table.

Kelli pushed her ravioli around her plate as Jules clattered around the kitchen, putting away the leftovers.

"I'm going up to pack," Jules said a couple of minutes later.

Upstairs, Jules sat on the floor in the gathering darkness of the spare room, her back resting against the bed as she twirled the illuminated night-light.

"Where would you fly if you could fly with the geese?" Pappy used to ask, and Jules, burrowed securely against his side, would say, "Everywhere. Over lakes and mountains. Way up north where there's always snow and then down where it's warm."

"And would you stop here on your way to see Mae and me?" Pappy would ask with a smile and a squeeze.

"I'd take you with me," Jules always declared. "We'd fly away together."

Jules blinked tears away as she stopped the light on the geese panorama. "You went without me," she whispered. "You both went without me."

CHAPTER 8

KELLI SAT AT HER wheel, the wet clay in her hands centering itself as she applied even pressure.

"You're still going to go?"

She pressed a thumb into the top of the lump to begin hollowing the interior.

"I already told Mae I was coming. It'll cause problems if I don't now."

"You could wait until next weekend when I'm off. Then I could come with you and share the driving."

"I can't."

The pot crumpled as Kelli's hand jerked spasmodically. She sat crying while the imploded lump of clay continued spinning, pulled farther onto its side by the centrifugal force of the wheel. She knew Jules must be on the road already—school had ended an hour ago—but there had been no phone call, no "I love you." Even this morning, their good-bye had been strained—a perfunctory kiss, "have a safe trip" and....

"Kelli?"

"Back in the studio," Kelli called, swiping her sleeve across her face.

Mary Anne came in, accompanied by the cats. "Hey—" She stopped when she saw her sister's face. "What's wrong?"

"Nothing."

"Liar." Mary Anne sat on the deacon's bench. Holly immediately hopped into her lap while Mistletoe wound around her ankles. "What is it? Did you and Jules have a fight?"

"I wish," Kelli scoffed. "Even a fight would be better than this."

Mary Anne sat silently, waiting.

"She left for Ohio today. Wouldn't wait for a weekend I'm off." Kelli sighed. "Ever since the funeral, she has just been so distant. She won't talk about whatever it is."

"Hasn't she always had times when she gets really quiet, though?" Mary Anne asked. "You used to think you had done something."

Kelli shook her head. "Not like this. Before, she would have those periods for a little while and then come back like herself, affectionate and talkative. But lately, it's like that Jules only pops in for a visit every now and then, and most of the time there's this moody stranger in her place."

She picked up the wet clay, pounded it back into a solid ball, and re-threw it onto the wheel, perhaps a little harder than necessary.

"And you think it's more than just her grandfather's death?"

"He was old and had been sick a long time," Kelli said, sniffing. "It's not like this was unexpected. I guess she could be taking it harder than I thought she would, but…"

Mistletoe jumped up onto the bench beside Mary Anne and swatted at Holly. The two kittens tumbled to the floor, wrestling. "You don't think maybe—?"

"What?" Kelli's head snapped up.

"Well, isn't she getting ready to turn forty?" Mary Anne asked. "You don't think she's going through some kind of mid-life crisis, do you?"

"I don't think so," Kelli said, frowning as she thought about this.

"Is there anyone else she would talk to?"

"No," Kelli said with a firm shake of her head, but then her eyes narrowed. "I wonder..."

It was after eleven when Jules got to the house. Way past Mae's bedtime. She pulled into the driveway behind Mae's Oldsmobile and paused for a moment on the porch before knocking, bracing herself for a surly welcome.

Mae opened the door and stepped back. "How was the drive?"

Jules, surprised not to be scolded, said, "It was pretty good. Not much traffic. It's just a long drive. Sorry to be so late." She set her suitcase down. "How are you?" She scanned her grandmother for any physical changes, but Mae looked exactly the same.

Mae went back to her chair—a gingham-checked thing older than Jules, covered by a crocheted afghan. Pappy's worn leather recliner sat where it had always sat—unused the last few years, but still in its place. Jules sat on the couch, the spot usually reserved for visitors.

The eleven o'clock news was on, the sportscaster talking about the Buckeyes' chances of winning tomorrow's football game.

"So, how have you been?" Jules asked.

Mae stared at the television. "I've been keeping busy," she said. "Working on the harvest festival down at the church, doing sick visits with some of the other ladies, trying to keep up with this place."

"Is there anything you need help with while I'm here?" Jules asked.

Mae pursed her lips and continued staring at the TV for a few seconds before saying, "Gutters could stand cleaning, if you're up to it."

"I'm up to it," Jules said. "I'll do it tomorrow."

Mae nodded but said only, "We should get to bed then."

She switched off the lamp as Jules retrieved her suitcase and headed toward the kitchen.

"Goodnight."

"Goodnight."

Up in her room, Jules suddenly missed her night-light, her first time up here without it in over thirty-five years. She left the overhead light off, undressing by the moonlight coming in through the window. She sat on the bed closest to the window, the one she had always used, still covered in the same quilt that had been there all of Jules's life. "Waste not, want not," Mae always said, and the quilt was part of that. It was made of bits and pieces of old sheets and shirts and pants and whatnot—not because Mae was sentimental about the memories tied to any of those things, but because it was practical. Perfectly good bits of material were still left, so why waste them?

Jules got up to open the window a crack and realized there were lights on behind the curtains of the house next door.

"What are you doing? Over."

The walkie-talkie gave a little burst of static every time the talk button was pressed and released.

"I'm reading. Over."

Jules rolled her eyes. "What are you reading?"

There was only a soft hissing sound for several seconds.

"You forgot to say 'over.' Over."

Jules looked at the walkie-talkie in her hand and shook her head. A couple of months ago, she'd seen an advertisement in a *Daredevil* comic book seeking kids willing to sell Christmas cards. "Look," she'd said to Hobie, showing him the ad. "We can win a pony, complete with his own saddle and bridle!" She signed them up, and they patrolled the neighborhood, selling Christmas cards until the neighbors started hiding behind closed curtains when they saw them coming, and still, "we only sold enough for walkie-talkies," Jules said forlornly.

"Maybe it's just as well," Pappy said with a sympathetic pat on Jules's shoulder. He bit down on the stem of his pipe to hide his smile. "Our yard is pretty small for a pony. And I don't think your grandmother would have been happy about letting him stay in the garage."

Once they got the walkie-talkies, they talked almost every night when they were supposed to be in bed. Most of their conversations on the walkie-talkies were nonsense. Jules wasn't sure why they could talk all day, but once they turned the units on at night, they suddenly couldn't think of anything to say.

She crept to the window so Mae wouldn't hear her out of bed and looked down at Hobie's house. "Why are the lights still on?"

"Over," she added before Hobie could say anything.

There was static as Hobie pressed his button. "My mom always used to leave a light on for my dad when he was coming home late. He said no matter how bad a day he had, it always made him feel better to have a light welcoming him home. And ever since he died... I think she doesn't like to be in the dark. Over."

"Oh." There was only the soft hissing of the walkie-talkies as Jules turned and looked at the soft glow of her night-light and the leaping fish while she thought about this. "I'm going to bed now. Goodnight, Hobie. Over."

"Goodnight, Jules. Over and out."

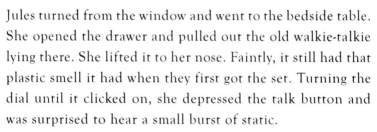

Jules turned from the window and went to the bedside table. She opened the drawer and pulled out the old walkie-talkie lying there. She lifted it to her nose. Faintly, it still had that plastic smell it had when they first got the set. Turning the dial until it clicked on, she depressed the talk button and was surprised to hear a small burst of static.

Raising the unit closer to her mouth, she whispered, "Are you there?"

She listened, but there was only a soft hiss in the dark.

Morning found Jules up on a ladder, scraping leaves and debris out of the gutters. She wrinkled her nose at the smell of the rotting leaves and helicopters from the maple trees.

"You be careful up there," Mae called up to her.

Jules paused and looked down at her grandmother standing in her slippers, a coat pulled over her housedress.

"My insurance will go up if you get hurt," Mae added, and Jules snorted.

"What did you expect?" Jules muttered with a shake of her head as she resumed scraping.

Methodically, she worked her way along the gutters, climbing up and down the ladder as she repositioned it every few feet. She was done by lunchtime.

Mae opened the kitchen door as Jules put the ladder back on its hooks in the garage. "Come inside now. I've got hot soup and biscuits."

Jules, chilled by the autumn bite in the air, came in and washed her hands, letting them run under warm water. "Smells good."

"Hmmph." Mae ladled a bowl of steaming soup and placed it and a plate of fresh biscuits on the table. "I've got a volunteer meeting this afternoon," she said, carrying a second bowl of soup to the table.

"That's fine." Jules buttered a biscuit. "I'll wander around town and see you back here later. Would you like to go out to dinner this evening?"

"Fool waste of money when I've got plenty to cook here," Mae said.

"But you cook every night," Jules said. "I'd be glad to take you out if you'd like."

Mae's gaze stayed on her soup bowl as she said, "I'll think about it."

Jules washed the lunch dishes while Mae went up to change for her meeting. "See you later," Jules called as she let herself out the kitchen door. It didn't matter if she got back home first; the kitchen door would be unlocked. "You should lock all your doors," she'd told her grandparents over and over, but Mae seemed to think crooks would only break in through the front door.

Jules pulled out her cell phone as she walked, knowing Kelli was at work, knowing she should have called last night, knowing Kelli would be feeling the same sick, hollow feeling Jules was feeling deep in her gut.

She called home and got the machine, as expected. "Hey, Kell. Sorry I didn't call last night. It was late when I got here." She knew as she said it how lame it was. "Just wanted to let you know I got here safe. Talk to you later." She paused. "Love you. Bye."

Kelli would hear that pause and wonder what it meant. Jules walked, scuffing at acorns and pebbles as she heard again the anguish in Stacy's voice when she'd cried, "Why are you doing this? Why are you walking away from us?" Donna had never done that, never asked for answers, never begged Jules to come back, but Jules could remember the look in Donna's eyes when Jules told her she thought they should split....

Jules clenched her jaw and quickened her pace. A few more minutes brought her to town. She stood, undecided for a moment, and then headed to the diner. As before, most of the counter seats were taken by locals catching up with one another. She slid into a booth—the same one she'd been in the morning of Pappy's funeral, she realized. She flipped her coffee cup and then groaned internally as she saw Trish coming toward her with a coffee pot and a big smile.

"Hi, Jules," she said as she filled the empty cup. "Guess who's here?" She turned to the counter. "Gil? Gilbert! Come on over here."

The forced smile on Jules's face froze as a man slid off one of the counter stools and approached her booth. She looked into a carelessly handsome face, blond wavy hair falling over his forehead. A similar pained expression crossed his features as he saw Jules.

"Hi, Gilbert," Jules forced herself to say, extending a hand.

He reached out for a peremptory handshake. "Jules."

"It's like a reunion!" Trish slid into the booth across from Jules, pulling Gilbert in beside her. "Have you two seen each other since graduation?"

"No," they both mumbled.

"Jules lives in Virginia now," Trish said. "And Gilbert teaches. Right here at Aldie High. Math. Can you believe it?"

"That's great," Jules said.

"What are you doing?" Trish asked.

"I'm a school psychologist," Jules said, feeling a hot flush creep up her neck at the expression that flashed across Gilbert's face.

"A psychologist." Trish giggled. "I bet everyone thinks you're trying to analyze them."

Jules gave a half-laugh.

"That's... that's good." Gilbert gave a small nod. He cleared his throat and gestured back toward the counter. "I gotta..."

"Yeah," Jules said quickly. "Good seeing you."

"You, too," he said with a quick search of her face before sliding back out of the booth and returning to the counter.

"Men." Trish shook her head. "Busy talking football. Can I get you anything?"

"Um... chocolate pie?"

"Coming right up."

Jules closed her eyes and turned to the window. *God, that was the last thing I expected. He hasn't changed at all.*

Trish returned with Jules's pie. "Here you go."

Jules smiled at her. "Thanks."

She ate a couple of bites and became aware of the feeling that she was being watched. Hesitantly, she glanced toward the counter, but Gilbert was deep in conversation with his neighbor. Visible between their heads, watching her from the kitchen, was a teenage girl wearing a hairnet and apron.

Ronnie. It had to be.

Jules gave her a small smile and a nod. A moment later, she went to the restroom. Ronnie came in a few seconds after.

"Hi," said Jules.

"Hi." Ronnie's face was flushed. Jules couldn't tell if it was from the heat of the kitchen or nervousness at their meeting.

"What time do you get off?" Jules asked.

"Two."

"Meet me at the Johnny Clem playground?" Jules said.

Ronnie nodded and went back to the kitchen.

Jules finished her pie, tipping Trish generously, and wandered across the street into the Five & Dime to poke around at the odds and ends stocked on the row upon row of shelves. *Nothing here like my lamp anymore,* she thought as she looked at the cheaply made lights sitting there.

Glancing at her watch, she saw that it was nearly two and headed toward the elementary school. The playground was again deserted. She sat on a swing and waited. After about fifteen minutes, a figure appeared around the corner of the school building. She grinned at the low-slung baggy guys' jeans, the butch swagger, the lank, unstyled hair—now freed of the hairnet—hanging not quite to the collar of a fleece jacket layered over an Ohio State T-shirt.

And you think people don't know?

Jules stood as Ronnie drew near, her gaze raking Jules's face as she breathlessly said, "Hi, Jules."

"Hi, Ronnie," Jules said, smiling.

"I can't believe you're here."

"Well, it was kind of a last-minute decision," Jules said. "I needed to check on my grandmother and..." She pulled a folded piece of paper from her jacket pocket. "This is a partial list of writing competitions for scholarships and some information on grants and loans. I want you to go to your guidance counselor and find out about these, all right?"

Ronnie's face lit up as she took the paper. "Thanks," she said, holding the list as if it were something precious.

"You can go to college," Jules said. "It won't be easy, but if you really want it, you can do it. I did."

Ronnie looked up from the paper. She was stockier than Jules, but about her height. "Where do you live? What do you do now?"

"I'm a psychologist in Virginia," Jules said, deliberately remaining vague as she guided Ronnie back toward the baseball diamond.

"Were you born here?" Ronnie asked. "Did you grow up here?"

"I lived here most of my life, with my grandparents," said Jules. "My grandfather worked at the mill. There was no way I was going to do that. And neither are you."

She stood on second base and looked around. Ronnie looked around, too, but the entire playground was empty save for the two of them.

"Can I ask you some things?" Ronnie asked hesitantly.

"Of course," said Jules.

"How... how did you know? You know, that you liked girls?" Ronnie stammered.

Jules tilted her head back, her hands stuffed in her jacket pockets. "I'm not really sure there was a specific moment. I was always out here, playing ball with the boys. I never had any close girlfriends." She scoffed. "They thought I was weird. But... I just never liked any of the boys. Not in that way. I already knew I liked girls when I was in high school, but I didn't have my first real girlfriend until I was in college."

"Do you—is there someone now?"

"Yes," Jules said. "We've been together for five years. Kelli. What about you? When did you first know?"

Ronnie blushed. "I saw stuff on the Internet. Books and movies about girls in love. And I just knew. I mean," she blushed even more furiously, "I've never read a whole one of those books or seen those movies. There's no place safe around here, and they're not in our library." She looked up, and her eyes burned with a feverish intensity. "But I've read the excerpts and watched the clips, and it was enough for me to know..."

Jules looked at her. "To know you're not alone?"

Ronnie nodded. "And then I saw you, and I just knew. I knew you were like me." She tilted her head. "You looked like you were crying."

Jules thought back. "Oh. I was here for my grandfather's funeral. That was a rough day."

"I was so scared, but I had to try and say something to you," Ronnie said.

Jules smiled. "I'm glad you did." *Liar. You were pissed as hell.*

Ronnie kicked at a clump of dirt. "I've just never had anyone else I could talk to about this. Did you?"

Jules turned away, looking back toward the school building. "No. I didn't."

CHAPTER 9

KELLI ANSWERED THE DOORBELL and stepped back to let Donna in. "Thanks for coming."

"Of course," Donna said. "I got here as quickly as I could. What's wrong?"

Kelli knew from the way Donna was looking at her that it must be obvious she'd been crying.

"It's Jules," Kelli said, leading the way into the kitchen. "Wine? Beer?"

"Oh, a beer would be great," Donna said. "We hardly ever have it in the house."

Kelli opened two bottles of Sam Adams and joined Donna at the kitchen island.

"What's going on?" Donna asked.

"I don't know exactly," Kelli said. She looked at Donna somewhat sheepishly. "I probably shouldn't have called you, but you're her oldest friend." Donna waited as Kelli took a drink of her beer. "It started about the time her grandfather died. She's just been pulling away more and more since. She brought home an old night-light he gave her when she was little. She spends hours sitting in the dark, staring at that light. She won't talk about whatever it is. She's distant with me. She won't—"

Kelli stopped and blushed.

"She won't be intimate?" Donna guessed.

Kelli stared at Donna, a chill stealing through her. As much as she'd wanted Donna's advice, it frightened her even more that Donna knew what she was talking about... because that meant—"This has happened before, hasn't it?" she murmured.

In answer, Donna took a long swig of her beer and then frowned as she picked at a corner of the label.

"Has she ever told you what happened between us?" Donna asked.

Kelli shook her head, not sure she really wanted to hear this. "She only said that you'd grown apart."

Donna's eyes glistened with sudden tears. "And what about Stacy?"

"When I met Jules, they were still living together, but sleeping in separate rooms." She thought. "I think she said the same thing, about the relationship just drifting apart."

Donna nodded. "It's what she does. She pulls away so by the time she leaves, she's right. There is only a shell of a relationship left, but she's the one who made it that way."

Kelli's heart ached—*for myself or for Donna?* "But why? Did you have a fight? Did something happen?"

Donna shook her head, wiping tears from her cheeks. "No. No fight. No anything. That's the hardest part. You don't know what you did. Or didn't do." She pressed her fingers to her eyes. "I have thought and thought about this, trying to figure out what went wrong. When it went wrong. The only thing I can remember is someone from her high school class trying to contact her about a class reunion—their tenth, maybe? I can't remember. But it was like someone put a wall up between us overnight."

Kelli listened, a sinking feeling making her almost wish she hadn't asked. All these years, she had secretly thought Donna must have done something and that Jules, being gallant and loyal, was protecting her by not revealing it. But every word from Donna's mouth was resonating deep within Kelli, as if she could feel the truth there. There was another question Kelli felt compelled to ask. "Did she... did she cheat on you?"

"With Stacy?"

Kelli nodded.

"I don't think so," Donna said. "But Stacy came into the picture just as Jules was pushing me away. I think it made the transition easier."

"And I did the same thing when she and Stacy were coming apart," Kelli said.

And now there's Carrie.

But neither of them said that out loud.

<hr />

Kelli's Tahoe was in the driveway when Jules got home Sunday afternoon. They had never gone this long without speaking, and Jules knew it was all her fault. She sat in her car, reluctant to go in.

At last, knowing Kelli had probably heard the car, she got out and pulled her suitcase from the backseat. Letting herself in through the front door, she called, "Kelli?" as the cats came to greet her.

"Hello, girls," she said, bending over to pet the meowing felines.

Kelli appeared in the kitchen doorway and waited, her arms crossed as she leaned against the doorframe, her face vacant. Jules stared at her, reading the guardedness in her eyes. "I'm sorry," Jules said, taking a step toward her.

Kelli moved into her arms, and they held each other tightly. "I'm so sorry," Jules said again, her voice muffled as she nuzzled into Kelli's neck.

Kelli moved her face so that her lips were at Jules's ear and whispered, "Please don't ever do that again."

In reply, Jules took Kelli's face in her hands and kissed her hungrily. Kelli responded, pulling Jules to her, slipping a thigh in between Jules's legs and applying pressure to her crotch. Breathlessly, they broke apart, and Jules led Kelli upstairs, where she closed the bedroom door and tugged Kelli's sweatshirt over her head. She bent to nuzzle the soft skin over her collarbones, down to the lacy edge of her bra. Kelli impatiently undid the bra and tossed it aside. Taking Jules's hands, she placed them on her breasts, the erect nipples pressing into her palms.

"I need you," Kelli whispered, drawing Jules to her for another kiss.

Jules backed Kelli up to the bed, unbuttoning her jeans and pulling them off for her. Kelli lay there, her bruised-looking eyes watching Jules questioningly. Jules pulled her own shirt and bra off and lay down on top of Kelli, kissing her everywhere while her hand slid down, inside Kelli's underwear to the heat waiting there. Kelli bucked as Jules's fingers slid inside, and she arched her back, drawing Jules's hand to the engorged clitoris demanding her touch. Almost as soon as Jules stroked it, Kelli gasped, her fingers raking Jules's back as she shuddered with her orgasm.

When Kelli's breathing slowed, she rolled Jules onto her back and began unbuttoning her jeans.

"Just hold me," Jules murmured, pulling Kelli back down to rest her head on Jules's shoulder. She kissed Kelli's forehead tenderly as she wrapped her arms around her. Kelli draped an arm across Jules's chest, her hand resting lightly against her neck and the pulsing artery there.

"Are you all right?" Kelli asked softly.

Jules pressed her lips to Kelli's forehead again. "I'm fine."

"And Mae?"

"She's good," Jules said. "I just had to see for myself."

They lay quietly for a long moment.

"Anything else going on?" Kelli asked.

Jules knew Kelli would feel the telltale surge in her heartbeat. "No," she said, her arms tightening around Kelli. "Nothing."

"Hi, Carrie."

Jules popped her head into Carrie's empty classroom, where she was grading papers. She looked up at the sound of Jules's voice.

"Hi," Carrie said. "What are you doing here?"

"I had a child study meeting," Jules said. "How's the redecorating going?"

"Oh, my gosh," gushed Carrie. "Elaine is brilliant! Thank you so much for introducing us. We've really only just started, but it feels like home already." She glanced at her watch. "Are you done for the day? You should come by and see it."

Jules considered. "Sure. Kelli works until seven. I've got time."

"Great!" Carrie shut her papers in a desk drawer and gathered her purse and jacket.

They walked together out to the parking lot. Jules followed Carrie's Mazda to a residential neighborhood in Pantop. The route took them right past the entrance to Martha Jefferson Hospital.

Immediately, a small voice in Jules's head said, *You shouldn't be doing this.*

Don't be ridiculous, she argued with herself. *I'm going to look at furniture. What harm can there be in that?*

Carrie squeezed into a tight parking space in front of a charming clapboard duplex with a double front porch. Jules had to drive on a few houses farther before she found a vacant bit of curb.

She followed Carrie up the porch steps and into the left side of the duplex.

"What do you think?" Carrie asked proudly.

"This is really nice," Jules said, taking in the unmistakable signs of Elaine's input. There wasn't a lot of furniture—only a sofa, coffee table, and what looked like an antique armchair positioned near a window with a spindle-legged table artfully set with a lamp and vase of flowers. On the walls were some framed art prints. The rug on the floor looked a little faded and slightly threadbare in places, but Jules had learned enough from Donna to recognize that it had probably been handmade in Iran and was very expensive. *This alone probably cost her half a year's salary,* Jules thought. Several large pillows were scattered about on the rug.

"Beauty should be a matter of the heart, not the head," Elaine often said, somewhat defensively.

"How about the wallet?" Jules longed to retort, but bit it back every time, obeying Kelli's look of warning. "I know," Kelli always said later, when they could talk privately, "but it's none of our business. Besides…" and Jules would chuckle sheepishly and say, "I know, I sound like Mae."

"Have a seat," Carrie was saying as she hung her things on a coat tree near the door. "Can I get you something to drink?"

"Uh, sure." Jules kicked her shoes off before treading on the rug. "A Coke would be good if you have it."

"I do," Carrie said from the kitchen. She emerged a moment later with two glasses. She handed one to Jules, who was sitting on one of the floor pillows.

"I feel like I'm sitting in a scene from *Arabian Nights*," she said.

"Just don't expect me to belly dance for you," Carrie said and then laughed awkwardly. "I know it was extravagant and probably foolish." She ran a hand over the jewel-toned threads, hand-knotted into intricate patterns.

"You don't have to justify it to anyone," Jules said. "As long as you're happy."

Carrie smiled. "Thanks. I keep expecting to be scolded for wasting my money. A leftover from my ex, I guess."

"Well, you're the master of your own destiny now."

"Yes, I am," Carrie said, nodding as she looked around.

"What else have you been doing with your time, besides letting Elaine spend all your money?" Jules asked.

"You just couldn't stop yourself, could you?" she could hear Kelli saying.

"Not much," Carrie admitted. "I mean, it took a while to feel like I knew what I was doing at work and then getting this place situated, so I haven't done much around here yet."

"You haven't been to Monticello or Montpelier?" Jules asked.

Carrie shook her head.

"We'll have to go," Jules said. "You can't live around so much history and not go see it. Maybe we can do Monticello sometime in the next couple of weekends in October and then Montpelier in November for their Hunt Race weekend."

"That sounds like fun," Carrie said.

"Good. I'll talk to Kelli, and we can see if Donna and Elaine would like to come along."

"Sure," Carrie said, her dark eyes focused intently on Jules. "But I'd still like to go even if they don't."

"Gosh, Mrs. Fahnestock, this is good!" Jules exclaimed as she wolfed down her dinner. "We never have homemade bread."

Mrs. Fahnestock beamed. "I like to make dinners special for my Hobie," she said, her eyes shining. "It's not every day he turns twelve."

"Will you come?" he had asked a couple of weeks previously.

"Are you having a party?" Jules asked. She had never been invited to a birthday party, but she had heard about them.

Hobie sniggered. "Who would I invite? Joey Reynolds? You're my only friend."

Jules thought about this. "We don't need anyone else."

Mrs. Fahnestock had outdone herself, even if it was only for Hobie and Jules, with all of Hobie's favorites: fried chicken and mashed potatoes and green beans and fresh bread.

Jules ate until she felt as if she would bust. Just when she was sure she couldn't eat another bite, Mrs. Fahnestock went into the kitchen, emerging a moment later with an enormous chocolate cake lit with twelve candles. She and Jules sang "Happy Birthday," and Hobie blew all the candles out. Mrs. Fahnestock cut large pieces of cake for each of them, and, somehow, Jules managed to make hers disappear.

"Time for presents," Mrs. Fahnestock announced when they were done.

Jules laid her present on the table in front of Hobie while Mrs. Fahnestock did the same with a larger, heavier package. Eagerly, Hobie tore the wrapping paper off Jules's present.

"It's a blank book," she said. "For writing your stories."

"Gee, thanks." Hobie smiled at her, and she was struck again by how pretty his eyes were.

He turned next to his mother's package and opened it to find a boxed set of Jules Verne books. Jules gasped, but Hobie's face darkened. Mrs. Fahnestock's smile faltered.

"Don't you like them?" she asked tremulously.

Hobie sighed. "Yes, I like them, Mom," he said. "But they cost too much money. You shouldn't have done it."

"Oh," she said, sounding relieved. "But all your other books are yard sale books. I wanted you to have some nice ones."

He reached out to run a finger down the spine of one of the books in the set. "Thanks, Mom."

"I'm glad you like them," she said, gathering up the cake plates.

"Can we help?" Jules asked, remembering Mae's stern warning that she'd better offer to help with the dishes.

"That's sweet of you," said Mrs. Fahnestock. "But I'll do these. You two go play."

Hobie carried his presents upstairs, where he immediately put his new books in one of his crates.

"What are you going to write in this?" Jules asked, gesturing to the blank book she'd given him.

Hobie bit his lip. "If I show you something, you swear you won't tell? Ever?"

Jules held up a thumb wrapped in a strip of white adhesive tape. "Blood brothers."

"Even if you're my blood sister." He grinned and held up his thumb, also sporting a bandage, courtesy of the ritual bloodletting Jules had talked him into two days ago.

"There has to be blood to be blood brothers," she'd said as Hobie warily eyed the pocketknife in her hand.

"Yeah, but that thing is rusty," he protested. "We'll get lockjaw."

Jules didn't know what lockjaw was, but when she pried open the one remaining blade in the pocketknife—an old one of Pappy's—she had to admit it was pretty rusty. "Well, what would you use?"

In the end, they used a pin that had been held in a match flame to sterilize it and pricked their thumbs. Hobie had to close his eyes and let Jules do it, but she had to poke his thumb three times before she drew blood because he kept jerking his hand away. They managed to squeeze enough drops of blood to draw crude initials on a fragment of old bone Jules had. "I've been saving this for something important," she said. Then they swore to be blood brothers forevermore—"and die before we reveal our secrets to anyone," she added for dramatic effect. Hobie's eyes got big, but he swore the oath. They dropped the bone into a hollow tree to seal the pact.

Pressing their bandaged thumbs together now, Hobie said, "Okay. I'm going to show you something I've never shown anyone else."

He pushed his bed away from the wall a bit and squeezed into the gap. There, he prized up a loose floorboard and lifted out from the gap beneath it a sheaf of papers.

"These are the stories I've written," he said, and Jules noticed he sounded proud, something she'd never heard in his voice before.

"Wow," she breathed. "That's a lot. What are they about?"

"Different things," Hobie said with a shrug. "But now, I can write them in here." He held up the book she'd given him. "Maybe I'll let you read them someday."

CHAPTER 10

Sunshine glinted off the brilliantly tinted leaves still on trees, while those that had fallen swirled in golden tornadoes in the wake of the cars winding their way up the mountain toward Monticello.

The Tahoe, crammed with Kelli, Jules, Donna, Elaine, and Carrie, followed the queue of cars already headed toward their destination, even at such an early hour.

"We'll eat at Michie Tavern when we're done," Jules said, pointing to the inn they were passing. "The food is fantastic. We'll work up an appetite with all the walking we'll be doing."

Donna, who was possibly the most excited of all of them, had been reading aloud from the updates she had printed off the Internet about Monticello's recent archaeological work on Mulberry Row, where some of the slave quarters had been.

Kelli looked in the rearview mirror. "We brought our own tour guide."

Donna flushed but defended herself, saying, "It never hurts to have more background. Makes the tours more interesting."

"Yes, sweetie," said Elaine, patting Donna's knee, "but you're ruining the suspense."

Carrie laughed, but Donna lowered her papers and sat silently between them. Jules caught Kelli's eye. *Don't say anything,* Kelli's glance said, and Jules turned to look out the windshield again.

"It's a good thing we came early," Jules said, noting that the visitors' parking lot was rapidly filling.

They retrieved camera bags and bottles of water from the SUV's cargo section and made their way to the visitors' center, where people were lining up for shuttles to take them up to the house.

"Let's walk up," said Jules. "It's not far, and it'll be gorgeous with the leaves."

Elaine shifted her purse strap higher up on her shoulder. "We'll take a shuttle and meet you up there."

Donna gave an apologetic shrug and turned toward the shuttle queue. Carrie stood undecided for a moment as the two couples moved in opposite directions.

"Wait for me," she called to Jules and Kelli, hurrying after them.

They followed marked trails through the woods, leading them up to the top of the mountain. "It always cracks me up when people call these mountains." Carrie laughed. "Compared to the Rockies—"

"Oh, that's a sore subject," Kelli said. "Don't let Donna hear you say that."

Jules laughed at Carrie's questioning glance. "Or you will be subjected to an hour-long lecture on how these mountains would have dwarfed even the Himalayas when the earth was young, many gazillions of years ago. Be respectful, grasshopper."

Their path brought them up past the family cemetery, many of the old limestone grave markers so weathered and pitted that the names and dates were barely discernible behind their cast-iron fence. They found their way to the shuttle drop-off, where Elaine and Donna were sitting on a bench as tourists queued, waiting for their house tours to begin.

Kelli looked at her watch. "Our tour doesn't start for an hour," she said, peering at her map. "We have time to wander Mulberry Row, just over there. Since we did bring our own expert." She smiled at Donna.

Elaine slipped off one of her shoes, rubbing her foot—"Heels," Jules growled to Kelli a few minutes later when they were out of earshot. "She wore heels!"—and said, "We'll stay here and wait for our tour."

Donna glanced at Jules and stood. "You can wait here and rest. I've been wanting to see what they excavated. I'll be back for our tour." She moved off before Elaine could protest.

"You're going to pay for that later, aren't you?" Jules whispered to Donna, who didn't respond.

Between Donna's research and overheard bits from Monticello's tour guides, they learned a lot as they moved down the excavated row of old slave cabins, work sites, and gardens, taking in the history of the place.

"It's fascinating," Carrie said as they circled around to where their house tour would start.

"It's humbling," Donna said, turning to look back.

Elaine was fuming by the time they got back to her. "It's a good thing I stayed here to keep our place in line!"

"What's she complaining about? She's still sitting on the exact same bench where we left her," Jules said in an undertone to Kelli, who snorted but said placatingly, "We were probably gone too long."

"You mean, Donna went with us instead of sitting with her," Jules muttered, choosing a spot in line a few feet away from Elaine.

She made sure she kept others between herself and Elaine as their group was called and their tour began, but there was no need. Elaine's bad mood seemed to have evaporated as they began to tour the rooms of Monticello. She pointed out to Carrie various architectural features and design elements. "Jefferson was a visionary in his use of natural light," she whispered loudly, causing their tour guide to shoot her an irritated look as he raised his voice to be better heard over Elaine's running commentary.

Their tour finished at the North Pavilion, shaded by an enormous pin oak towering over them. Elaine sat down again on one of the many benches while Kelli moved off to take some photos of the flowerbeds bordering the house.

"I want to go look at the kitchens and breweries underneath," Jules said. "Anybody want to come?"

"I'll come," Donna said, jumping up.

"I'll rest here with Elaine." Carrie took a seat beside her on the bench.

Jules and Donna found their way down to the rooms on display below. Jules watched Donna's bright eyes as she read the placards and took in the tiny spaces where the plantation's slaves had cooked and prepared the house's food and drink.

"It's amazing they preserved all this," Donna said.

"It was elaborate, for its time," Jules said. She glanced around, but there were no others nearby. "Are things okay with you and Elaine?"

Donna turned to her. "Why?"

Jules gave a small shrug. "She just seems on edge. More than usual, I mean."

"Well," Donna said, "things have been slow for her lately—no big projects coming in, so she's decided we should redo our living room."

Jules looked at her. "Didn't she do that when you moved into the house—what?—two years ago?"

"Which I reminded her," Donna said. "I don't see the point. The paint is fine. The furniture is still brand-new. She changes rooms when she's bored like other people change clothes. Except her way is more expensive." She flushed.

"Sorry," Jules said, kicking herself. "I didn't mean to pry. You'll figure it out."

Donna nodded and moved along to the next display. "What about you?"

"What about me?"

"You seemed like you were having a hard time after Pappy's funeral," Donna said. "How are things now?"

Jules turned away, pretending to read another placard. "Everything is fine," she said emphatically. "I don't know why everyone keeps asking that."

Donna placed a hand on her shoulder and made her turn. "Maybe," she said, searching Jules's eyes, "they keep asking because it doesn't seem fine."

"Oh, that was fun," Kelli said, flopping down on the couch and kicking her shoes off. The kittens immediately jumped up and began walking over top of her, meowing their displeasure at having been left alone all day.

"It was... interesting." Jules lifted Kelli's legs and placed them in her lap as she sat down.

"Okay," Kelli amended. "Monticello was fun. The rest, not so much."

"Elaine can be a real pain," Jules said.

Kelli stroked Mistletoe, who had settled on her chest, purring loudly. "Well, her studio is struggling. You know... the economy is tight right now, and people don't have money for expensive home projects. Just the necessities. I'm not sure, but I think she borrows a lot to stock her studio with expensive furnishings and then counts on selling them in her designs to make the money back."

"Seems like a risky way to live," Jules said.

"I think maybe that's part of the appeal," Kelli mused. "Kind of like a financial adrenaline rush. There's the reward when everything goes well..."

"...and the crash when it doesn't," Jules finished for her. "I don't think Donna is comfortable living that way."

Kelli shook her head. "I wouldn't be, either. I like stability. Steady partner, steady paycheck, planning for the future." She smiled, reaching for Jules's hand.

Jules's brow furrowed as she looked down at Kelli's hand in hers. "What were you and Donna talking about?"

"When?"

"When we were waiting to be seated at the Tavern," Jules said. "You two had your heads together off by yourselves."

"Oh, it was nothing." Kelli sat up and swung her legs to the floor. "She just needed to vent a little about Elaine. I need a drink. Can I get you anything?"

"No," Jules said, staring after her as she disappeared into the kitchen.

"Hey," Kelli called. "Remember the girls need to go the vet for their checkups on Monday. You can still take them?"

"Yes, but you know they'll be pissed at us for days."

―――◦✕◦―――

The air on Monday afternoon was filled with the pitiful yowling of two anxious cats in their carriers in the back of the Subaru.

"Oh, it's all right," Jules crooned, trying to soothe them. "You like Dr. Barbara. She always gives you too many treats."

She drove carefully, taking turns more slowly than normal to avoid shifting the carriers around in the cargo area.

Please don't be dead.

As she drove, Jules tried to block the memory of the limp lump of feathers lying in the bottom of the cage, but she knew it was no good. It didn't hit often, but when it did....

"You know what's going to happen, don't you," Mae had snapped when Jules and Pappy came home with a parakeet in a shiny new cage. "I'll be the one expected to feed it and clean its cage."

"No, you won't," Pappy said, his hand resting on Jules's shoulder. "Jules will take care of him. She promised."

Jules beamed up at him, nodding. She and Hobie had fun playing with Pauly, teaching him to step onto their fingers, and letting him perch on their shoulders up in her room with the door and windows securely closed. She diligently cleaned his cage and kept his food tray full of birdseed and his water bottle filled with clean water. He slept in his cage up in her room and woke her in the mornings with his cheerful chirping as he hopped about his cage, rattling the little bell Jules had bought at the pet store and playing with the toys she hung inside his cage.

But then spring came, and she and Hobie played outside nearly all the time.

"When was the last time you cleaned that bird's cage?" Mae asked often. "I'll do it later," Jules said, pausing only briefly to peer into the cage as she passed by on her way in and out of her room. The food tray looked full of seed. *Mae must be feeding him,* she thought as she ran down the stairs.

Then one day, "How's the bird?" Mae asked, looking up from the stove as Jules came in, sweaty and out of breath from playing army with Hobie.

"He's fine," Jules said. "Why?"

Mae didn't answer. Jules ran upstairs to find Pauly lying in the bottom of his cage. As Jules reluctantly approached, she whispered, "Please, don't be dead." The newspaper on the bottom of his cage was completely covered with droppings. She hadn't cleaned the cage in weeks. Gingerly, she picked him up, his little head drooping as she held the still, cold body, her eyes filling with tears.

"He starved to death," came Mae's voice from behind her.

Jules jumped. "No." She shook her head. "No. His tray has seed. You've been feeding him."

"I told you I wouldn't feed him or clean up after him," Mae reminded her curtly. "That tray has nothing but empty seed shells. That poor thing starved to death. And you said you would take care of him."

Jules began crying in earnest, sitting on the floor of her room, cradling Pauly, stroking his feathers, no longer sleek and iridescent as they used to be, but dull and bedraggled. Mae went back down to the kitchen. After what seemed like a long time, she came back upstairs with an empty Kleenex box.

"You can bury him in this," she said, a little more gently.

Jules looked up at her with red-rimmed eyes.

"I know you're sorry now," Mae said. "But there's no going back from this. You can't play with another creature's life. It's hard, but you have to learn."

More tears spilled from Jules's eyes. "Does Pappy have to know?"

Mae looked down at her, a curious expression on her face. She cleared her throat. "I don't suppose he has to. Birds are delicate. They die sometimes for no reason." She turned back toward the stairs. "But don't you forget."

Jules took a deep breath and wiped away the tears coursing down her face as she pulled into the vet's parking lot. "Damn," she muttered, looking into the rearview mirror at her puffy eyes and red nose. "It's been almost thirty years," but she knew, thirty or sixty or ninety—no matter how many years—"I won't forget."

CHAPTER 11

I've been writing for information on the scholarships and grants you gave me. My guidance counselor asked me where I got the list, but I told her I did some research and found them on my own. I don't want her to know about you.

It was so great to meet you! I've been saving all my money to buy a car. Maybe, if I do, I could come and visit you and Kelli someday–

"What are you reading?"

Jules jumped at the sound of Donna's voice and clicked shut the e-mail on the computer screen. "Nothing. Just catching up on e-mails," she said.

Donna scrutinized her face. "Well, you look like you just swallowed something that made you sick. You okay?"

"Yeah." Jules turned from the computer.

"Are you testing today?"

"Uh, yes." Jules consulted a folder. "A triennial on a tenth grader who was labeled learning disabled in second grade and has never been retested."

Donna shook her head. "Don't you love it when that happens?"

Jules shrugged as the bell rang. "Anyway, I'd better go find her and get started. Talk to you later."

Damn, damn, damn. She made her way through the halls. *This is what you get for responding to that fucking note. Come to visit. Just what I need. Some sixteen-year-old deciding she doesn't want to be at home anymore and making up some fantasy relationship with me and there goes an entire career.* Jules paused and leaned against a corner locker, feeling nauseous. *What was I thinking?* She stood there, swallowing the bile rising in her throat, willing herself to calm down. *She doesn't know where you are. She doesn't even have a car yet. You can deal with this.*

She took a deep breath and went on to find the student she was supposed to test.

Two hours later, she walked out of the building, feeling as if she were going to explode. The girl she'd tested was definitely still in need of special ed services. Her processing was so agonizingly slow, it had been all Jules could do not to scream, "Just give me an answer!" She threw her briefcase into the backseat of the car and got in. *It's not her,* she knew. It was Ronnie and lies and secrets and... "Why didn't I tell Kelli a long time ago?" she moaned, pressing her forehead to her steering wheel. "Tonight. Tonight, I tell her."

About everything? asked a sly voice in her head.

She turned the ignition, her jaw clenched tightly. "Everything."

"Where were you after school? I waited for you. Over."

Jules waited, her walkie-talkie hissing emptily in her hand.

"Hobie? Are you there? Over."

"I'm here."

Jules looked out her window. "You didn't say 'over.' Come to the window."

It was still twilight, but "Bedtime is bedtime," Mae insisted, so Jules was often in bed while June daylight lingered, making it impossible to go to sleep.

"Come to the window," she repeated.

Hobie appeared at his window, his head turned to one side.

"What happened?" she asked. "Look at me."

Reluctantly, Hobie looked over at her, and, even in the twilight, she could see he had a black eye.

"What happened?"

"Nothing," Hobie said into his walkie-talkie.

"Well, something happened," Jules said. "You didn't give yourself a black eye. It was Joey, wasn't it?"

"You can't say or do anything. It'll only make it worse."

"Why did he do it?" Jules asked.

"The usual," Hobie said resentfully. "Making fun of my weight. Making fun of my clothes. I'm sick of it. I can't wait for this school year to be over next week."

Jules had never heard him talk like this.

"I went to the newspaper office after school," he said into his walkie-talkie. "They're going to give me a newspaper route. Then I'll have money. I can help Mom and maybe have some left over to buy new clothes before we start junior high next year."

"That's good," Jules said. "Which route, the morning one or the afternoon one?"

Hobie looked over at her guiltily. "The afternoon one. I won't be able to play after school anymore. I'll have to come straight home and get the papers out."

"I could help you," Jules said.

There were several seconds of silence, then Hobie said slowly, "No, I think it would be better if I did this on my own."

It was Jules's turn to be silent.

"But we could still play after dinner," Hobie said quickly. "Jules?" he whispered when he got no response.

"Sure," she said at last. "I've got to go to bed."

"Good night," said Hobie. "Over and out."

But Jules had already clicked off her walkie-talkie.

———◆━◇◆◇━◆———

Jules sat in the driveway, her hands tightly gripping the steering wheel. She closed her eyes, swallowing that lump, burning as it rose in her throat again. "You can't sit here forever," she whispered and opened the car door.

"Kelli?"

Jules stood inside the front door, listening, but there was no answer. She called again, peeking into the pottery studio, but it was empty. She opened the door to the garage. The Tahoe was there. "Kell?" she called as she went upstairs to the bedroom and stopped short.

Kelli was sitting on the bed, hugging her knees to her chest.

"What is it?" Jules asked, sitting down to face her.

Kelli sat like a statue, her face impassive, eyes staring straight ahead.

"Kelli?" Jules laid a hand on her knee.

"Mary Anne called," Kelli said at last, her tone flat. "I thought she was calling to make plans for Thanksgiving. But... Mom has had some abdominal pain. I thought it was her gallbladder. They did a CT yesterday." Her voice cracked, and she had to pause. Jules waited, her heart pounding. "It looks like pancreatic cancer," Kelli whispered.

Jules felt as if someone had punched her in the gut. Her mouth was dry, and her tongue felt like sandpaper. "Are they sure?" she managed to ask.

Kelli's chin quivered. "They're going to do a biopsy to verify, but they're pretty sure."

Jules slid closer, wrapping an arm around Kelli's shoulders. "I'm so sorry," she said as Kelli leaned into her and began crying.

When Kelli could talk, she said, "I've got the next couple of days off. Mary Anne and I are going to go home. They've already got Mom set up to see a team of specialists at Hopkins. We'll see what they have to say. If I have to, I'll get her in to see someone down here."

"But..." Jules hesitated. "Isn't pancreatic cancer usually...?" The question hung in the air as Kelli pulled away.

She stood. "We'll see what the specialists have to say."

The remainder of the evening was spent helping Kelli get packed. What conversation there was was forced and artificially casual. Jules, feeling helpless to do anything really useful, stayed near, holding Kelli's hand as they went to bed. She could hear Kelli sniffling next to her, but couldn't think of anything to say.

The next morning, Mary Anne was there early. The three of them had a silent cup of coffee before Kelli hugged Jules tightly and said, "I'll call you later."

Jules nodded and waved them off before going back inside to get ready for work. She spent the morning at the central office, scoring and starting to write the report on the girl she had tested yesterday.

"Damn," she muttered, as she realized she'd made another mistake—her third one in the past hour. She kept looking at her cell phone, willing it to ring but dreading when it would. She didn't see how any team of oncologists could offer much hope with pancreatic cancer.

"You know I wouldn't mind if you ever want to spend the holidays with your grandparents," Kelli had said when she and Jules first moved in together.

"I know," Jules said, kissing Kelli's hand. "But I don't want to go to Aldie for the holidays. I'll see Pappy and Mae other times."

She had gladly spent the holidays with Kelli's family. The Warrens were nice people, and Kelli's mother, Carol, had always made Jules feel like one of the family—"not like Mae would have been with Kelli," Jules reminded herself whenever she felt brief twinges of guilt about not being with her own family at Thanksgiving or Christmas.

But now, with this diagnosis right before Thanksgiving... She knew nothing would be the same for Kelli's family.

Finally, the phone rang mid-afternoon.

"How did it go?" Jules asked.

She could hear Kelli crying. "About like you thought it would. Mom told them to give her the odds straight up, no whitewashing. Dad wants her to try chemo, but I don't think she's going to do it. They said the tumor is inoperable and has less than a five percent chance of responding to chemo. She asked us why we would want her to spend the time she has left in hospitals and doctors' offices when she could be spending it with us." Kelli gave a hiccup of mirthless laughter. "She's right. I can't ask her to go through that and for what? A couple of extra months? Maybe? And they'd be horrible months. If it was any other kind of cancer..."

Jules nodded as she listened. "False hope is the worst thing," Mae had said more than once. "Better just to face up and be grateful for what you have." *She's wiser than I give her credit for.*

"How's Mary Anne?" Jules asked.

"Not good," Kelli said. "She's angry."

"At your mother?"

"At everything," Kelli said, lowering her voice. "Let me walk farther away from the house so she doesn't hear. She told me on the way down that she and Brian aren't getting along. He's spending all kinds of extra time at the insurance office and less and less at home."

"They're not going to split, are they?" Jules asked.

"I don't know," Kelli said.

Jules could hear a dog barking as Kelli walked by a neighbor's house.

Jules expelled a slow breath. "This situation with your mom could either bring them back together or—"

"—or push them over the edge," Kelli finished that thought. "I know." She walked on for several seconds as they both thought about what might be coming. "I'm so glad I have you, Jules."

CHAPTER 12

Central Virginia ground to a halt, as it always did at the first sign of snow. A storm, moving up the coast overnight, dumped five inches of light, fluffy snow on the region, and all the area school districts had cancelled for the day. Stores had been cleaned out of eggs, milk, and toilet paper. "People act like they won't be able to get out for a week," Jules always said. Every winter, she was grateful for Pappy's driving lessons in the snow. "Turn into the skid," he would say calmly, taking Jules out to an empty parking lot and letting her deliberately set the car to sliding so she could learn what it felt like and how to correct it without panicking. Sometimes, they took Hobie along—"but don't tell my mother," he pleaded. "My dad was killed in a car accident. She'll have a heart attack if she knows we're doing this."

Jules smiled as she remembered those times, taking turns doing donuts in Pappy's old 1969 Dodge Dart. She sighed and resumed her shoveling of the driveway. Kelli wasn't due back until the next evening, but she wanted to have everything cleared away in case she came home early. Just as she got the last of the snow removed from where the plow had blocked in the driveway, her cell phone rang. Expecting to hear Kelli's voice, she was surprised when Carrie was on the other end.

"My first snow day in years," she said, sounding like a little kid. "We had more hurricane days than snow days in Newport News."

"What have you done with your snow day?" Jules asked, leaning against her shovel and catching her breath.

"Well, of course, I was already up getting ready for work when they called it," Carrie said. "I hadn't even looked out my window. I've been shoveling my car out and just came in to get warmed up. What about you?"

"I'm shoveling, too," Jules said. "Just finishing up."

"Is Kelli at work?"

"No," Jules said. "She's in Maryland, visiting her family. She should be home tomorrow."

"Oh. Would you like to get something to eat?" Carrie asked.

"Why don't you come over here?" Jules said. "Kelli made a big pot of chili before she left. It's a good chili day."

"Are you sure?" Carrie asked. "I wasn't trying to invite myself over."

Jules laughed. "I'm sure. I've got more than enough. You remember how to get here, right? And don't forget to save your parking space with a trash can, or you will lose it."

A short while later, Jules answered the doorbell to find Carrie standing on the porch, bundled up in a down jacket, hat, and scarf.

"Come in," Jules said, stepping back to let her in. "You can leave your boots there with mine on that rug."

"Your house is so nicely done." Carrie looked around as she left her snowy boots near the front door and padded into the living room in thick socks.

"All Kelli," Jules said. "Did we get to show you around the day you came over for the cookout?"

"No."

"Come on, then." Jules led the way and showed Carrie the rest of the house.

"Oh, this is wonderful," Carrie said as they entered the pottery studio. "What does she do with all these?"

"Well, she sells them through a few shops in town," Jules said. "And Elaine always takes a lot of them."

"Have you guys known Elaine long?" Carrie asked, picking up one of Kelli's vases and admiring the glazing.

"No. We met Elaine when she and Donna got together," Jules said.

Carrie looked up. "So you knew Donna?"

Jules flushed. "I've known Donna since college. We... were together for a while."

Carrie's eyes opened wide. "Donna is your ex? And Kelli and Elaine are okay with you all being friends?"

Jules shrugged. "It was a long time ago. Just because you're not with someone now doesn't mean you can't still be friends."

Carrie snorted. "I can't imagine being friends with my ex."

Jules considered. "I think that depends on why you parted. You said something about there being someone else...?"

"Someone she was screwing for months, only I was too stupid to realize it," Carrie said bitterly. "I don't see us ever being friends again."

Jules nodded sympathetically. "I'm sorry it ended badly. I guess I was lucky. Donna and I stayed friends and she and Kelli like each other."

Carrie turned to look at her more closely. "What about you and Elaine?"

"Oh," Jules said with a self-conscious laugh, feeling herself turn red again. "Well, three out of four ain't bad."

Carrie tilted her head. "You don't like Elaine?"

Jules let out a slow breath, stalling as she weighed her words. "I didn't say that. It's more... I get the feeling sometimes that Donna doesn't get much say about a lot of things, but..." Jules held up her hands. "If Donna's happy, I'm happy." She stepped toward the door. "Let's continue the tour."

By the time they finished looking around upstairs, the house was filled with the aroma of the chili simmering on the stove and fresh corn bread baking in the oven. The oven timer went off just as they entered the kitchen.

"Perfect timing," Jules said. She pulled the baking pan from the oven and set it to cool.

Holly and Mistletoe, deciding Carrie was safe, emerged from wherever they had been hiding to let her pet them while Jules dished out bowls of chili and carried them to the table. She came back to put the corn bread on a platter. "Hungry?"

"I'm starving."

"Me, too. Let's eat," Jules said as they sat at the table.

"Oh, this is good," Carrie said after taking her first spoonful of chili. "I feel like a bottomless pit today."

Jules grinned. "Shoveling snow and being out in the cold always does that to me."

"You said Kelli is from Maryland?"

"Yes. Hagerstown. Her folks still live there."

"What about you?" Carrie asked.

Jules swallowed before saying, "I'm from Ohio."

"Do your parents still live there?"

"I was raised by my grandparents," Jules said. "My grandmother still lives there in the same house I grew up in."

"Where are your parents?" Carrie asked, then immediately looked abashed. "I'm sorry. Just tell me if I'm asking too many questions."

"It's okay," Jules said. "My mom was unmarried, ran away, dropped me off with her parents when I was three. Not much to tell."

Carrie's mouth fell open. "You haven't seen your mother since you were three? Don't you miss her? Wonder where she is?"

Jules shook her head as she stirred her chili. "She never came back. Never wrote. I have no idea where she is or what name she might be using." She looked up. "So, it doesn't really matter if I miss her or wonder where she is."

Jules used her T-shirt to wipe away the sweat running into her eyes. She pried open the flaps of the next box and began sifting through the things inside it. More Christmas decorations, boxes of Christmas lights. She heard the side door of the garage open, and she froze.

"Jules?"

She breathed again. It was Pappy. "Up here."

He climbed the ladder to the storage space over the garage. "What in the world are you doing up here? It's like an oven."

"I know." Jules panted. "I... I wanted to see if I could find some pictures of my mother. I want to see what she looked like."

Jules couldn't read his expression in the shadows and didn't know if she was in trouble.

"I can't ask Mae," she said.

"No." He thought for a moment. "They're not up here. Come on down before you have heat stroke."

She closed up the box she had opened and followed him down the ladder. She wiped her sweaty face again with her T-shirt.

"You wait by my chair," he said. "I'll meet you there in a little bit."

Jules went around to Pappy's smoking chair, grateful for the shade and the breeze after the steamy closeness of the air in the attic. She was just beginning to wonder what was taking Pappy so long when he appeared around the corner of the garage, carrying a shoebox.

"Here we are," he said, sitting down in his chair and propping Jules on one thigh as she gazed curiously at the box. He laid a gnarled hand protectively over the box lid. "I hid this away. I thought you might want to see them someday, and... well, your grandmother might want to see them, too, even if she doesn't know it yet."

He lifted the lid to reveal dozens of photos, many of them curled and yellowed. Jules picked a handful out and shuffled through them as Pappy provided background. "That one was taken when your mother was a year old, down at Mae's parents' house in Dayton," and "We took this one the day we moved in, here in this very house. This is your mother and Mae sitting on that old tree swing."

Jules peered, fascinated, at a girl who looked just like her, except she wore dresses in all the pictures. "She looks like me," she said.

Pappy smiled. "Yes, indeed. Sometimes you are the spitting image of your mother." He chuckled. "Especially when you're mad."

Jules looked at him. "Was she wild like Mae says?"

Pappy scratched the cleft in his chin. "She was independent," he said slowly. "She liked to do things her way, and that didn't always sit so well with your grandmother."

"But she ran away with a boy."

Pappy's face got sad. "Yes." He sighed. "She might not have done that if—Maybe if we'd let him come around, let them court here at the house... but Mae didn't like him. He was a mill boy from Chillicothe. Didn't think he was the right boy for Joanie..."

Jules put the photos back in the box and replaced the lid firmly. "I won't do that," she said, looking into Pappy's eyes. "I won't leave you."

He blinked fast and sniffed, rubbing his hand roughly over his face. "Good. I don't know what I'd do without my Jules."

"I'm sorry," said Carrie. "I didn't mean to drag up sad memories." She reached a hand out and laid it on Jules's forearm. "I'm sure your grandparents loved having you."

Jules glanced down at Carrie's hand. "One of them did." She reached for the platter, her arm sliding away from Carrie's hand. "More corn bread?"

CHAPTER 13

JULES WENT TO THE pottery studio, a wooden Santa in each hand. "Do you want the carved Santas on the mantel again this year?"

Kelli sat at her wheel, her head bowed as she worked the clay in her hands. "I don't care. Put them wherever you like."

Jules sighed and walked back out to the living room, which was littered with open boxes. The dining table was covered with stuffed Santas, carved Santas, Santas riding cows, Santas being pulled by dogsleds. The cats were busily batting about Styrofoam peanuts that had fallen to the floor and jumping in and out of the open boxes. Kelli always insisted on decorating the house the weekend before Thanksgiving. "That way, we're all geared up and ready," she said every year. She never seemed to lose her enthusiasm for the holidays.

"You knew this year would be different," Jules muttered as she looked around helplessly.

Carol Warren's diagnosis had been confirmed, and the pancreatic cancer was progressing rapidly. Kelli's dad, Jerry, had taken leave from his work to be home with her. Kelli and Mary Anne had been driving up to Hagerstown every week on Kelli's days off. When Kelli was home, she was quiet, spending hours and hours in the studio, working in solitude. She didn't want to talk, which was most unlike her. Jules tried to ease her stress—making dinners, doing the laundry, vacuuming—taking over all the household chores Kelli would normally have helped with.

"Thank you," Kelli murmured sometimes, her eyes filling with tears. "Mary Anne says Brian is making things tough for her. He says he's busy at work and keeps asking why she isn't cooking dinners and taking care of the kids more. He says he's tired of it. I can't believe he's doing that now... I don't know what I would do without you."

Jules sighed again, looking at the two carved figures in her hands. "Whatever," she said, placing the Santas in what she hoped was an acceptable display on the mantel. She put out some of the other Santas on the sideboard, on the bookshelves, on the desk but then decided that they didn't all have to go out this year. She closed the flaps on the boxes, nearly shutting Holly inside one of them, and carried them back up to the attic before bringing down the boxes of ornaments. By late that afternoon, the tree was up and decorated. She stepped back and surveyed the house. She knew it wasn't up to Kelli's usual standard, and Elaine would have rolled her eyes, but, "it's as done as it's going to be."

Guiltily, she glanced at her laptop as she passed where it was plugged in. Her recent e-mails to Ronnie had been brief, peremptory—and Ronnie had noticed. *Are you okay?* she wrote. *Are you mad at me?* Jules's replies had been vague at best, but "I just don't have time for her right now," Jules reasoned. "I have to concentrate on Kelli."

It had been decided to have Thanksgiving dinner at their house this year. "I can't," Mary Anne had said fretfully. She wasn't handling the cumulative stress very well. "It's all right," Kelli had said. "We can do it. Mom and Dad can stay with us, and then you and Brian and the kids can just come for dinner." Together, they had arranged who would cook what and plans had been made for Carol and Jerry to drive down to Charlottesville on Wednesday.

Jules put away the last of the Christmas boxes and sat down to look at the grocery list. With a frustrated sigh, she went back to the studio. "Kell, I hate to interrupt, but I really can't do the grocery trip by myself. If I get the wrong stuff..."

Kelli sat up, and Jules realized she'd been crying. She wiped her nose with the back of her hand. "Okay." She sniffed. "Give me a few minutes to clean up here."

"The house looks nice," Kelli said a few minutes later as Jules drove them to the grocery store.

Jules reached for her hand. "Not as nice as when you do it."

"It looks fine," Kelli said, forcing a smile. "I want it to look nice for—" Her voice caught, and she couldn't continue.

Jules squeezed her hand. "We'll make it a nice Thanksgiving and Christmas."

A little while later, they were in the middle of the produce section, picking out cranberries and sweet potatoes when Jules's cell phone rang.

"It's Mae," she said, looking at the screen.

"Don't you think you should answer it?" Kelli said, her hand suspended in mid-air, holding a scoop full of cranberries.

"Mae?" Jules answered. "What's wrong?"

"Who said anything's wrong?" came Mae's voice. "I just wondered what you were doing for Thanksgiving."

Jules's guard immediately went up. "We're having dinner here. Why?"

"No reason," said Mae. "I just wondered if you were heading this way, so I know if I need extra food."

Jules looked up at Kelli, who was watching with a perplexed expression. "Mae, I haven't been to Aldie for Thanksgiving in forever. Why would I be coming there now?"

"Why do you do that?" Mae asked.

"Do what?" Jules frowned.

"Say 'coming to Aldie' or 'going to Aldie.' You never say 'coming home,'" Mae said.

Jules blinked. "Are you all right?" she asked.

"Of course I'm all right," Mae said. "Since when do I have to not be all right to ask my granddaughter if she's coming home for Thanksgiving?"

Since you never gave a damn before if I came back. Jules took a deep breath. "Well, no. I am not coming to—I am not coming home for Thanksgiving. We already have plans here. As a matter of fact, we're at the grocery store buying what we need."

"Oh."

Kelli started mouthing something.

Jules's eyes widened in horror as she read Kelli's lips. She shook her head violently.

Kelli dropped the cranberries and snatched the phone. "Mae? This is Kelli. Would you like to come out here for

Thanksgiving? My parents are coming, so it may be a little crowded, but you are more than welcome."

Jules leaned close, listening to the silence.

"Well, thank you, Kelli," Mae said at last. "That is very nice of you to ask. I'll... I'll think about it and let you know."

"Just know you're welcome," Kelli repeated before Mae hung up.

"What are you doing?" Jules demanded as she put her phone back in her pocket.

Kelli turned to look at her. "I'm inviting your grandmother out here for her first Thanksgiving without your grandfather," she said pointedly. "She's never called about Thanksgiving before. Don't you think maybe she's hinting that she's lonely? And I would hope that you would do the same thing for my father once—" She jammed the scoop into the cranberries again and stuffed them into a plastic bag.

Jules pushed the shopping cart silently as Kelli wandered through the bins of produce, gathering green beans and potatoes.

⋅——◆◇◆——⋅

A heavy frost made the grass crunch underfoot as Jules and Hobie walked to school, their breath puffing out in front of them like locomotive steam in the cold air.

"Only one more week," Hobie said, grinning.

Jules had never known anyone who looked forward to Thanksgiving more than Hobie did.

"Turkey and ham and sweet potatoes and mashed potatoes and gravy and cranberry sauce and rolls." He had been ticking the list off every morning for the past few days until even Jules's mouth watered in anticipation. "And then for dessert, pumpkin pie and pecan pie and ice cream and whipped cream."

Jules felt full just thinking about all the food. Mae usually made a lot of food for Thanksgiving, but not as much as Mrs. Fahnestock.

"Are you having Thanksgiving with your aunt and uncle and cousins again this year?" Jules asked.

Hobie frowned under his knit cap, pulled low to cover his ears—"I don't want you getting an ear infection," Mrs. Fahnestock worried—and said, "I'm not sure. Mom hasn't said anything about going there like we usually do, and I think she was going to ask your grandmother if you guys want to come and have dinner with us."

"Really?" Jules lit up. It was always just her and Mae and Pappy for Thanksgiving, and it seemed to her that the only thing special about it was all the extra special china and silverware that had to be washed after.

That afternoon, when they got home from school, Jules found to her surprise that Hobie's mother was in the living room, talking to Mae.

"Now, Bertha," Mae was saying, "You know she was just talking off the top of her head."

"Maybe," Mrs. Fahnestock said. She sounded as if she had a cold. Jules closed the back door quietly and tiptoed through the kitchen to listen in the hall. "But she said it to be mean and spiteful."

"Oh, I don't know," said Mae. "She might be wishing she was in your place."

"What?" exclaimed Mrs. Fahnestock. "How could anyone wish for this?"

"Well, I don't know," Mae said again. "Maybe the way she sees it, you've only got the one boy to worry about, and he's a good boy. You say your sister's boys are wild, and between them and her husband, she's got five to worry about. I don't think she really meant it. She's just tired and worn out and spoke without thinking."

Mrs. Fahnestock sniffed. "You think so?"

"I do," said Mae. "Now you call her and say you're coming anyways."

"You're sure?"

"I'm sure," said Mae. "You call her this very evening. It'll work out. You'll see."

Mrs. Fahnestock thanked Mae and went home. Jules stormed into the living room as Mae closed the front door.

"You mean we're not having Thanksgiving with them?"

"I expect not," Mae said, going back to the ironing board she had set up in front of the television where *As The World Turns* was playing.

"But me and Hobie were counting on it," Jules said.

"Hobie and I," corrected Mae.

"Why'd you tell her to go to her sister's?"

"They had a spat, that's all," said Mae.

Jules, who had never had a brother or sister to have a spat with, didn't think this was a very good reason to gyp her out of a good meal. "So what?" she said. "They could have skipped this year, and we could have had dinner with them."

Mae's iron slammed down heavily on Pappy's undershirt—"I never understood why she thought she had to beat the wrinkles out with the iron," Jules would recall as an adult—and she said, "You're too young to understand, but when family lets something split them, especially if it happens around a holiday, it makes it harder to put it behind them and find common ground again. Better to heal the wound when it's fresh and not let it fester and grow."

Jules tilted her head. "You make it sound like an infection."

"It can be." Mae jutted out her lower lip. "It can be."

Jules pulled into the driveway. "She's never driven farther than Dayton," she mumbled. "I'd have to go get her. It's a fourteen-hour round-trip to go out there and get her and bring her here. And then I'll have to do it all again in a few days to take her home."

Kelli turned to her as she pulled bags out of the back of the Subaru. "She hasn't even said she wants to come. Relax."

Sullenly, Jules followed Kelli into the house, grocery bags swinging from her hands. She deposited them on the counter and went back outside to get the rest.

"Would you take these out to the garage freezer?" Kelli asked, holding out bags of frozen rolls as Jules placed the last of the grocery bags on the counter.

Jules looked up. "What?"

"Take these out to the garage, please," Kelli repeated.

Jules snatched the rolls and stalked out to the garage.

"What is wrong with you?" Kelli demanded when she came back into the kitchen.

Jules glared at the floor. "You have no idea what you've done."

"I invited your grandmother for Thanksgiving," Kelli said, perplexed.

"No," Jules said, her nostrils flaring. "You set me up for seven hours alone with her in the car."

Kelli threw up her hands. "Fine. I'll go get her if she wants to come."

"And how—?" Jules realized she was nearly yelling. Lowering her voice, she said, "And how is that going to look? You had no business—" She broke off and stormed out, slamming the front door behind her.

Jules wandered aimlessly through the neighborhood, her balled-up fists shoved deep in her jacket pockets as she walked, her heels slamming into the pavement with each footfall. Inside her head, a continuous stream of arguments, counterarguments, and yet more arguments played in a continuous loop, her lips moving as she muttered to herself. She had no idea how long she'd walked when she pulled up.

"This is the last thing Kelli needs right now," she reminded herself and, reluctantly, she turned for home.

By the time she got there, Kelli had finished putting the groceries away and was seated at the kitchen table, looking through a few recipe books.

"Sorry," Jules mumbled as she hung her jacket on a peg in the laundry room.

Kelli didn't look up. "You should be glad you still have a grandmother," she said softly.

"You don't understand!" Jules almost retorted but bit the words back. Instead, she said, "I'll go clean the bathrooms."

CHAPTER 14

"You can't put this off," Kelli said. "We need to know. Mom and Dad get here tomorrow."

Jules had avoided calling Mae, hoping against hope that she would call to volunteer that she was staying in Ohio. "I guess," she said, retrieving her cell phone.

She pressed the buttons and went into the family room, where Mistletoe was batting at an ornament on the tree.

"Mae?" Jules said. "We were wondering what you decided." She stood with her eyes screwed shut, waiting.

"Well, I sure would like to come," Mae said, and Jules grabbed for the back of a chair to steady herself, "but I ran into the pastor yesterday, and he told me Bertha Fahnestock isn't so good. Not that she ever is these days, but he figures this holiday season is going to be a bad spell for her. So, I think I'd better stay here. She won't come for dinner, but I can bring something over and check in on her."

Jules blinked. "Oh. That's probably a good decision." She could feel her heart start back up again.

"But you be sure and tell Kelli I appreciate her invitation," Mae added, and Jules flushed at the subtle reprimand. "If you change your mind and want to come this way, you'd be welcome."

"Thanks, but..."—"why don't you ever tell her anything?" Kelli had asked more than once. "How is she supposed to be part of your life if you never share anything with her?"—"... but Kelli's mom was just diagnosed with cancer," Jules said.

"Goodness," said Mae. "No, you stay there. Tell Kelli I'll ask the pastor to raise her mother up in prayer."

"I'll tell her."

"Good-bye, then."

"Bye."

Jules went back into the kitchen. "She's staying in Aldie to keep an eye on... on a sick neighbor."

Kelli looked up from the mixer, where she was adding spices to the pumpkin pie filling. "See? All your worry was for nothing."

Jules stood staring out the kitchen window. "Hmmm? Oh, yes. For nothing."

Mr. Walburn—he's my English teacher—he's been helping me apply to writing competitions I can enter to maybe get a scholarship offer. I know I won't get a full scholarship, but he says a lot of colleges offer partial scholarships, which could still help. He says my writing is really good and is encouraging me to go into journalism, but I don't know. I think I want to write fiction, but he says it's easier to get paid for journalism.

I'm so glad you told me about Kelli's mother. I was afraid I did something to make you mad at me. I hope she gets better, but I know she might not. My grandfather had cancer, and it was awful. He got so skinny and weak before he died.

I hope your Thanksgiving was good. We went to my gran's like we always do. And, like every year, I had to answer a bunch of stupid questions about boyfriends—why don't I have one, am I keeping him a secret, I'd have all kinds of boys after me if I dressed more like a girl. They think they're funny, but it's not funny to me. I want to shout at them and tell them off. But I don't. I just smile and pretend I think it's funny, too.

Did you go through that? I hate it, but I just keep thinking, one day I'll be gone from here.

Write back soon,
Ronnie

"Who's Ronnie?"

Jules whipped around from the copier. "What?"

Donna pointed to the computer screen where Jules had left her e-mail open. "Who's Ronnie?" she repeated.

"Just some kid I met in Aldie when I was there," Jules mumbled, feeling her face grow hot as she turned back to the copier.

"You're e-mailing a kid you met in Aldie?" Donna asked. "Why?"

Jules shrugged with her back to Donna. "She's bright. Wants to get out of Aldie. We hit it off." She could feel Donna's gaze boring into her back, but she refused to meet her eyes.

Donna waited. When Jules didn't offer anything further, she asked, "How was Thanksgiving?"

Jules's shoulders relaxed just a bit. "Carol looks awful," she said, finishing her last copy and reaching for a stapler. "She's probably lost thirty pounds. I just hope she makes it to Christmas."

"You'd better hope she doesn't die on Christmas," Donna said sympathetically. "I don't know how families cope with that kind of reminder every year. How's Kelli?"

"She puts on a brave face for her parents," Jules said. "And for her sister. Her husband is being a real jerk. He's pissed because Mary Anne's attention isn't all on him and he has to help out more." She glanced up. "How about yours? Did you go home?"

"Yes," Donna said. "We have a new teacher who thought I meant Paris, France. I laughed and told her, no, it's Paris, Virginia. Not quite the same thing."

"But more beautiful," Jules said with a fond smile. "At least I think so. How are your folks?"

"They're good," said Donna. "Same as always. Dad has a new black lab he's training for field trials, so he's happy. Mom said to say hi to you. She always asks about you."

"I miss her cooking," Jules said. "And her hugs. She's a good hugger." She slid the copies she had made into a folder. "Did Elaine go home with you?"

"God, no." Donna rolled her eyes. "She'd die in a place like Paris, even for a couple of days. No, she went to visit a cousin in New York City."

Jules shuddered. "Okay, *that* would kill me."

"Me, too," Donna said, and again, there was that look in her eyes—the one Jules had noticed ever since the night of the party when Kelli had said....

Jules turned away. "Well, I have to get ready for an eligibility meeting."

"Okay. See you later."

"See you," Jules said as Donna left. She went to her computer. "You idiot," she whispered, cursing herself for leaving the screen up. She glanced over Ronnie's e-mail again. *I had to answer a bunch of stupid questions about boyfriends... did you go through that?*

Even Jules had to admit she wasn't looking forward to starting junior high school. She and Hobie had both heard how the seventh and eighth graders hazed the sixth graders. "No one's doing any of that to us," Jules bristled, but Hobie wasn't so sure.

"If they gang up on you, there's nothing you can do," he said.

The night before their first day of school, they had talked late into the night on the walkie-talkies, hashing over the same worries they'd been fretting about for weeks. Finally, Mae had hollered up the stairs, "If I have to come up there, young lady," and they quickly got off the walkie-talkies.

When they got to the building, an intimidating modern structure with huge plates of mirrored glass, Hobie consulted his schedule. "My homeroom is that way," he said, pointing left.

"And I think I'm this way," Jules said, looking down the right-hand hallway. "See you."

"See you," Hobie said as if he were on his way to his execution.

Jules turned right and scanned room numbers as she walked, getting jostled by older, bigger kids.

"Who's the new boy?"

"Huh?" Jules turned to see Amy Curry walking beside her, wearing what was surely a new dress, with her hair done in ribbons. She never talked to Jules. "What new boy?"

"The boy you were walking with, silly," Amy said.

Jules laughed. "That's not a new boy. That's Hobie Fahnestock."

Amy turned and looked back. "No, it isn't."

Jules turned, too, and realized she could see Hobie's head bobbing along, taller than most of the other kids around him.

"He's changed," Amy said, and there was a weird tone in her voice that made Jules frown. "I should have known better," Amy added, peeling away from Jules. "Like you would have a boyfriend."

Jules suffered through homeroom and then Ohio history and math. Junior high was different; they had to change rooms for different classes, and she got lost twice. Finally, it was time for lunch. She got to the cafeteria and sat at a table in the back, saving a seat for Hobie, wanting to tell him how she had tried to find her way to math and ended up in woodshop instead. Anxiously, she waited, her stomach growling. Minutes went by, and she began chewing on her peanut butter and jelly sandwich, still keeping an eye out for him. A small group of four or five students entered the cafeteria, and she saw with a start that it was Hobie walking with four girls. She stared at him, and it was a shock to realize how much he had grown. He was skinnier, too, not skinny the way she was, but he wasn't fat anymore. All those hours pedaling his bike on his paper route. And he was wearing jeans and a shirt that fit him. How had she not noticed these things before? She caught his eye and waved. He began making his way back to her, and the girls followed. They all sat with Jules. Three of the girls she knew from elementary school, though they had never said more than "hi" to her before. The fourth girl was new this year.

"So, you're Jules," the new girl said, sitting next to Hobie. "I'm Valerie Dickson. We just moved here from Columbus."

"Hi," said Jules grumpily. She wanted to talk to Hobie alone, not with all these silly girls around them chattering away about which boys were cute and what other girls were wearing.

Joey Reynolds came by, accompanied by several of his usual gang of boys. "Hey, Jules," he called. "We're going to play catch. Wanna come?"

"I didn't bring my mitt," she said, wishing she had so she could escape.

"We have an extra," Joey said. "Come on." His eyes glinted maliciously in Hobie's direction. "You don't want to waste lunchtime sitting with—" He bit off whatever he'd been about to say. "—sitting inside when we could be playing ball."

Jules looked back at Hobie, who said, "Go ahead."

Jules stood, cramming what was left of her sandwich in her mouth. "I'll catch you after school," she said, her words muffled by a mouthful of peanut butter.

When the bell rang at the end of the day, Hobie was waiting for her on the sidewalk. They walked in silence for a couple of blocks.

"So, what was up with all the girls today?" she asked at last.

Hobie shrugged. "Dunno. They just started talking to me. They never did before. And I'm sorry about lunch. They just followed me. I couldn't tell them to go away."

Jules had her mouth open to tell him *she* could have told them to go away, but she stopped. Hobie had never had anyone want to talk to him before. She felt like a heel about leaving him. "Sorry about lunch," she mumbled. "I shouldn't have gone off with Joey."

"It's okay," he said. "I know you like to play baseball with them."

They walked along, sneakers scuffing the sidewalk. "Not as much as I like being with you," she said.

He grinned. "Valerie asked if you were my girlfriend."

Jules snorted with laughter. "Your girlfriend? What'd you say?"

"Well, you're a girl and you're my friend—my best friend—so I said yes," he admitted sheepishly.

Jules thought about this. It kind of made sense, even if it felt weird to think of Hobie and her that way. "Okay."

Kelli placed the last pot in the kiln, carefully closed the lid, and set the controls. Glancing at her watch, she hurried to the sink to wash up. *Just enough time to get the meatloaf made and baking before Jules gets home.* She went into the kitchen and remembered her laptop was upstairs in the office. The last time she was home, she had e-mailed herself her mother's meatloaf recipe—one of Jules's favorites.

"She's been so wonderful," Kelli had said to Mary Anne over Thanksgiving. "She decorated the entire house by herself; she's been doing all the cleaning and cooking."

Mary Anne scoffed. "I can only wish. Brian acts like the world is coming to an end if he has to cook or do a load of laundry." She looked at her sister. "Is she talking about whatever was bothering her?"

"No," Kelli said. "But it doesn't seem quite as bad lately. The weirdest thing was when I invited her grandmother here for Thanksgiving, Jules went bonkers."

"Really?" Mary Anne asked. "Maybe there's some history there you don't know about."

"There's something," Kelli said darkly.

Hurrying now, she went to Jules's laptop, where it was plugged in at the kitchen desk. After flipping it open, she hit the power button and—"What?" A password prompt had come up on the screen. Jules had never used a password before. Kelli stared at the screen for several seconds before closing the lid and going upstairs for her own laptop.

The meatloaf was baking and potatoes were boiling when Jules got home.

"Mmmm." She sniffed appreciatively as she entered the kitchen. "Oh, that smells wonderful."

"Good," Kelli said. "I was hoping you'd come home hungry."

"I'm starving," Jules said. "What do you want me to do?"

Kelli pointed to a pile of lettuce and vegetables sitting on the counter. "You can make a salad."

"Done."

Kelli stirred the potatoes while Jules washed her hands and started chopping carrots and tomatoes.

"How have you been?" Kelli asked. "I feel like I've hardly seen you lately."

"I know," Jules said. "You've been a little busy. I've been kind of crazy at work, trying to squeeze kids in before they're off for Christmas break."

"Have you talked to Carrie or Donna lately?"

Jules turned to glance at her. "Well, I saw Donna at school last week. She's fine. And I saw Carrie the week before at her school. Why?"

Kelli shrugged. "Just wondered." She opened the oven and stuck a thermometer in the meatloaf. "Almost done. Should be ready in about fifteen minutes."

In a little while, they were seated at the table. "So," said Kelli, "what else has been going on? I've been so preoccupied with Mom, I feel like I don't know what's happening in the real world."

"Um..." said Jules as she chewed a bite. "Really, not much else. This is good." She pointed at her plate with her fork. "I still need to know what you'd like for Christmas."

Kelli exhaled. "Christmas. I can't believe it's just a couple of weeks away. I haven't done anything—no shopping, no decorating, no cards."

Jules reached for her hand. "You've got other things to worry about this year."

Kelli looked down at their linked hands, her eyes filling with tears. "I really don't know how I would have gotten through this without you."

Jules lifted Kelli's hand to her lips. "You won't have to get through it without me. I'm here, always."

CHAPTER 15

"WHAT DID YOU ASK for for Christmas?"

Jules and Hobie were sitting in Hobie's living room with the lamps off, watching the flashing lights on the little white plastic Christmas tree they had. "We have a real tree, too," Hobie had said the first year that Jules came over, but for some reason, they liked watching this one, blinking its random colors from the bulbs inside, while they sat watching for the all blue or the all red or the multi-color every few seconds.

"I asked for a new bike," Hobie said. "I'm getting too big for my old one. My knees are up to the handlebars, but..."

Jules knew he had been about to say his mom couldn't afford a new bike. "Maybe Santa will bring you one," she said with a grin. It had been a couple of years since they had admitted they no longer believed in Santa, but Jules wished sometimes that they still did.

He grinned back. "Maybe. What about you?"

"A new baseball mitt," she said. "But Mae will probably say it's too unladylike for me to keep playing baseball.

Everybody's getting weird about 'acting our age' and me 'being a lady' lately. Have you noticed?"

Hobie nodded. "Yeah. Mom said a couple of times—" He stopped abruptly.

"What?"

He looked as if he wished he hadn't said anything.

"What did she say?" Jules prodded.

"She said I should make other friends," he said. "Play with kids other than you."

"Why?"

He shrugged. "She thinks I should have guy friends. Like that's going to happen. You know what Joey and those guys are like. They'll make sure I never have any other friends. Even if I wanted to," he added quickly.

"Why can't everybody just leave us alone?" Jules said as the tree cast a blue hue over them.

———— ◆◁◇▷◆ ————

"The first Noël, the angel did say..."

Jules sat in the dark living room of the Warrens' house, lit only by the lights of their Christmas tree, listening to the music playing on the stereo and the low hum of voices coming from the kitchen.

In the weeks since Thanksgiving, Carol's cancer had progressed at a frighteningly fast rate, so that she was too weak to travel for Christmas. "We'll have to call hospice soon," Kelli had said after her last visit home. So they had all come to Hagerstown. It was crowded, with Mary Anne's husband and two children in addition to Kelli and Jules. Mary Anne kept shushing the kids.

"Let them be," Carol said from her recliner, padded with extra pillows to make it more comfortable for her emaciated body. "It's Christmas. They're supposed to be excited."

Jules wondered what Mae was doing this first Christmas Eve without Pappy. She reached for her phone and called.

"Merry Christmas," she said when Mae answered.

"Merry Christmas to you," Mae said, sounding surprised. "How's Kelli's mother?"

"Not good," Jules said in a low voice. "We're up here with them for the holiday."

"Well, it's good you're there. The pastor keeps remembering her in the prayer roll."

"Thanks. How are you doing?" Jules asked.

"I'm fine," Mae said. There were a few seconds' silence, and then, "It's different this year, even though he wasn't home the last few years..." She cleared her throat. "I spent part of the day with Bertha. She had her photo albums out. Fool idea if you ask me, just makes it worse. But she had a picture of you and Hobie next to that bike you and Carl fixed up for him. Remember?"

Jules closed her eyes.

"Jules?"

"I remember."

Mae cleared her throat again. "Well, things change. And all the wishing in the world can't undo it. Course I didn't say that to Bertha."

"No," Jules said. "I've got to go. I just wanted to call and wish you a Merry Christmas."

"Oh, well, all right, then," said Mae. "Be sure to tell Kelli Merry Christmas for me."

"I will."

Jules clicked the phone off and sat there. *Why did I call?* She could remember that Christmas, that bike. When Jules had said something to Pappy and Mae about Hobie needing a new bike, Carl had looked around Aldie until he found a used one in need of fixing up—"just don't you spend an arm and a leg," Mae had warned him—and then Jules and Pappy had spent hours cleaning and fixing and painting it for his mom to give him. "He doesn't need to know we had anything to do with it," Pappy had said to Jules. "Let him think it was all his mother."

"But why?" Jules asked, tilting her head as she looked at him, dark green paint dotting her forearms where she was painting the frame and getting as much on herself as on the bike.

"Because not having money for things makes folks feel bad," Pappy said. "It makes 'em feel beholden, and we don't want that. We did this as a gift, and a gift it shall be. Just between us. And then our enjoyment will come from watching him enjoy it."

He did love that bike, Jules recalled with a smile.

Kelli came in at that moment. "What are you doing sitting here in the dark?" she asked, sitting next to Jules.

"I like the lights," Jules said. "You can enjoy them more in the dark."

"You and your lights." Kelli smiled and leaned against Jules's arm. "We're going to get dressed for the Christmas Eve service. Mom says she wants to go." Kelli reached for Jules's hand. "Will you come?"

Jules raised Kelli's hand to her lips. "I'll come."

"Hey," Jules said, popping her head around the door of Donna's classroom. "I got your note. What's up?"

"Hi," Donna said. "Elaine wanted me to ask you guys about getting together now that the holidays are over. We're always so crazy in those weeks leading up to Christmas and New Year's."

"Oh." Jules sighed. "That sounds nice, but... Kelli's taken family leave for a few weeks. Her mom is getting hospice care now."

"I'm sorry," Donna said. "Is there anything we can do?"

Jules shook her head. "I don't think so, but thanks. I'm just glad we got through Christmas."

"How was it?"

"It was nice, actually. I think Carol mustered all of her energy to do as much as she could, because she seemed to decline really fast right after," Jules said. "Thanks for looking after the girls while I was away."

"How's Kelli?"

Jules shrugged. "She's having to hold it together for her dad and sister right now. She's the medical one, so they keep depending on her to make all the decisions. I know she doesn't mind being there, but I think she's going to collapse once this is over."

"This sucks," Donna said, shaking her head.

"What?"

"Getting to the age where our parents and grandparents are dying."

"Yeah, it does kind of suck," Jules said. "Since none of us had kids, it feels like we skipped from college to this with no warning."

"Are you going to go back?"

"I will when Kelli says it's closer to time," Jules said. "I hope the administration doesn't give me any grief about why I need time off. I can't say my mother-in-law is dying."

"I haven't thought about how I'd deal with that," Donna said. "You could just use your personal days instead of bereavement leave. They don't usually ask questions about those."

Jules looked at her watch. "I've got to get to a meeting. Thank Elaine for us, but we'll have to wait a while before we can plan anything. See you."

"See you."

When she got home that afternoon, Jules was surprised not to be greeted by two yowling cats. Peeking into the family room, she smiled when she saw them both sleeping on opposite ends of the couch, Holly with her tail curled over her face and Mistletoe on her back, all stretched out.

"Must have played hard today," Jules said, turning to the kitchen to get a snack and check her e-mail, something she hadn't done since before Christmas. "I'll probably have a hundred new messages," she mumbled as she flipped open her laptop and suddenly stopped with her finger poised over the power button. The password prompt had come up immediately.

"Shit."

She took her laptop to the kitchen table and dropped heavily into a chair. "I didn't leave you asleep," she whispered. "I know I didn't."

Kelli. There was no other explanation. They'd never had any rules about using each other's computers, no secrets to hide—"until now," Jules said, grimacing at how this must have looked to Kelli.

145

She pushed up from the table and began to pace the kitchen. "Damn. I should have told her about Ronnie right from the start," she muttered. She stopped abruptly. *She was asking about Donna and Carrie,* Jules recalled. *She thinks I'm cheating.*

She reached for her phone but stopped. "You can't do this over the phone." She sat down again. "You need to think about this," she said, trying to calm herself. She typed her password and opened her e-mail. As expected, there were a ton of messages, three from Ronnie. The first was just an update on her grades and a few responses she'd received to her queries about writing competitions, the second was basically a Christmas card, wishing Jules and Kelli a Merry Christmas, but the third made Jules's heart stop.

> *...our pastor wanted to meet with me. I thought it was about being in a stupid Christmas play or something, but he got me in a room alone and started talking to me about sex and how it's God's plan for men and women to be attracted to each other and how it's against God's law to be attracted to girls—for me to be, I mean. He wants to meet with me every week to counsel me. It was so humiliating. And creepy. He made me nervous. I don't know what I'm going to do. People are coming into the library. I've got to go.*

That message was dated December 23rd, and nothing since. Jules scrolled through her e-mails again to be sure. She felt torn in ten directions at once—she couldn't bear the thought of Kelli thinking the password was to keep an affair secret, and this was not the right time to burden her with Ronnie's situation, but now something was happening to Ronnie, something that sounded wrong—"but there's no way I can go out to Ohio now," Jules said, talking out loud to herself as she thought.

She typed a quick response to Ronnie, asking her to reply as soon as she could and let Jules know if she was okay. She closed her laptop and sat back, rubbing her forehead, trying to think of what she could do from Virginia....

Jules sat up. There was someone, someone right there in Aldie, who could help. She reached for her phone and waited breathlessly as she listened to the rings on the other end. Seven, eight rings with no answer. "Why don't you get an answering machine?" Jules had asked a hundred times. "Why?" Mae always replied. "You're the only one not in Aldie who calls, and if I'm not home, I can't talk to you anyway. So just call back."

In frustration, Jules hung up and went to feed the cats, who immediately woke at the sound of a cat food can popping open. Meowing, they trotted into the kitchen and wound themselves around Jules's ankles as she dished out their food.

"Here you go," she said, setting the bowls on the floor. She turned her attention to her own dinner, but her stomach was so agitated, she didn't have much of an appetite. She pulled down a box of corn flakes and poured some into a bowl. As she sat to eat, she tried Mae again. Still no answer.

She calmed down a bit as she ate. *You can't send Mae into the diner asking questions,* she thought with a wry smile at the image of Mae barging in, handbag swinging. *Wait and see what Ronnie writes back.*

As she spooned the last of her cornflakes from the milk in the bottom of the bowl, she murmured, "Kelli is the one I need to concentrate on for now."

CHAPTER 16

KELLI SAT WATCHING HER mother sleep. A hospital bed and bedside commode had been set up in the living room soon after the new year when her mother became too weak to go up the stairs to her bedroom. Nearby, the sofa still held the rumpled sheets from last night. Jerry insisted on staying nearby through the nights.

"I don't want her to be alone—" he had started to say but then stopped as his voice cracked. He hadn't left the house in days.

"You go, get out of the house for a bit," she'd said to her father that morning. "Go get a haircut, go see the guys at the hardware store, just take some time for yourself. I'll stay with her."

"Well," Jerry said reluctantly, "we do need some groceries. I won't be long."

Kelli pulled an armchair up next to the bed and sat, her knees drawn to her chest. There hadn't been time—or energy—to think about Jules these last days. Every time those thoughts tried to push their way to the forefront, she shoved them back so she could focus on her parents, but now, with the house quiet and still, she couldn't help herself. *Why in the world did she need a password on her computer? What was she afraid I'd find?* Questions ran amok inside her head, leaving her with a tangle of emotions, none of them good. *We need to talk,* she thought, *but when?* She pressed her forehead to her knees, trying not to think about the things Donna had told her about her breakup with Jules, the distance that had sprung up, seemingly out of nowhere. "It's not the same," she whispered.

Carol stirred, and her eyes fluttered open.

"I didn't mean to wake you," Kelli murmured, leaning forward to take her mother's skeletal hand in her own.

Carol smiled. "I don't mind. I don't want to sleep too much." She looked down at their hands, and her eyes opened wide. "I didn't realize I've turned so yellow," she said, looking at the contrast between Kelli's rosy skin and her own jaundiced hand. She looked up at Kelli. "How long have you been sitting here?"

"Not long."

Carol shook her head. "That's what you always said when I had one of my migraines and would wake up to find you sitting in the bedroom."

Kelli smiled tenderly. "Just had to keep an eye on you."

"And you still are." Carol's eyes shone with sudden tears, and Kelli had to fight to keep her own emotions under control. "Where's your father?"

"He went to the grocery store. He'll be back in a bit." Kelli leaned forward. "Can I get you anything?"

"No." Carol squeezed Kelli's hand. "There's nothing I need now."

Kelli looked into her mother's eyes, and unspoken understanding passed between them. Kelli nodded, her throat painfully tight. "Get some rest. I'll call Mary Anne and Jules."

Kelli waited until her father returned from his grocery trip to tell him it was probably time. "You go sit with her," she said. "I'll put the groceries away." She dialed her sister while she emptied bags. "Hey," she said when Mary Anne picked up. "If you can get up here today, you probably should."

"Oh, God," Mary Anne whimpered.

"Calm down," Kelli said, trying to maintain her own composure. "You cannot go to pieces. I need you up here. Pack enough clothes to be here for a couple of days and... you should probably bring what you want to wear for the funeral." She could hear her sister crying. "Just get here safely. Maybe you and Jules can drive up together, unless you want Brian and the kids to be here."

"No," Mary Anne said quickly. "Brian wouldn't be of any use anyhow, and I don't want the kids to see..."

"Okay," said Kelli. "I'll have Jules call you."

<hr />

A tense silence filled the car as Jules drove. She'd called Mary Anne as soon as she got Kelli's text.

"Who's taking care of the cats?" Mary Anne asked as they drove through Front Royal.

"Donna said she would," Jules answered. "Brian and the kids are okay for a few days on their own?"

"They'll have to be. They'll come up if—" Mary Anne gave a small hiccup as she swallowed a sob.

Jules drove on, letting Mary Anne cry in the passenger seat.

"Was it like this, when you went for your grandfather's funeral?" Mary Anne asked unexpectedly.

Jules thought. "Well, he'd been in a nursing home for about five years, and I hadn't been home much," she said.

Mary Anne turned to her. "Did you get to say good-bye?"

"I said my good-byes a long time ago," Jules said flatly.

She could feel Mary Anne's eyes boring into her.

"Don't hurt her," Mary Anne said softly.

Jules turned to her sharply. "What?"

"I don't know what happened back there in Ohio," said Mary Anne, "but I can see what Kelli has been talking about—it practically spills out of you when you think about or talk about that place. But don't hurt Kelli. Please."

Jules swallowed the lump in her throat and kept driving, each lost in her thoughts as the miles to Hagerstown rolled by.

When they got to the house, Kelli met them at the door. "The hospice nurse is here," she said. "Mom is conscious, but just barely. I just wanted to give you a warning."

Mary Anne's hand flew to her mouth as she entered the living room, and Jules covered a gasp. In the week or so since they'd last been there, Carol had wasted away even more, her skin stretched tightly over prominent cheekbones, her arms stick-thin on top of her covers.

"Hi, honey," she said hoarsely when she saw Mary Anne, her eyes closing again as Mary Anne knelt next to the bed and took her mother's hand.

"Talk to her," Kelli whispered as she stepped back from the bed. Jules stood next to her, laying a hand on Kelli's shoulder. Kelli reached up and squeezed Jules's hand as she watched her mother's shallow breathing. The nurse was seated in the corner, ready to be of assistance if she was needed, but trying to stay out of the family's way. They pulled dining chairs around the bed and sat, wanting to be near as Carol's breathing slowed and became more sporadic, eventually stopping altogether. Kelli looked back at the nurse, who came to the bed and placed a stethoscope on Carol's chest.

"She's gone," she said softly, stepping away to fill in the time of death on the papers she had with her.

Kelli held Mary Anne as Jerry leaned forward, sobbing, with his arms flung around his wife. Jules stepped out onto the front porch, her arms wrapped around her against the February cold.

———◆◦◆———

Jules and Hobie walked along a street Jules had only been down a few times. Hobie was collecting for his paper route and Jules was helping carry the papers. She had a heavy canvas bag slung across her shoulder, just like the one Hobie was wearing. Almost all the snow had melted from a big snowstorm that had hit the area the week before, cancelling school for two whole days.

"I got almost all of my newest story written," Hobie was saying as they walked.

"What's this one about?" Jules asked, folding a paper for him.

"It's about a boy who has to go live with his grandparents after his father dies," he said with a sheepish grin.

Jules looked at him. "Uh, sounds kind of familiar, almost like two stories blended together."

Hobie's ears turned pink. "Yeah. I thought, between the two of us, we have an interesting situation."

Jules waited while Hobie went up the walk of the house they were at and knocked. The lady who answered had his money waiting for him and waved to Jules, who waved back.

"So," said Jules when Hobie rejoined her, "what happens—"

She stopped suddenly.

"What?" Hobie asked.

"Listen."

From somewhere nearby came a strange combination of sounds—several sharp cracks, laughter, and what sounded like a dog yelping. Jules and Hobie took off running toward an abandoned lot that still had a rusty chain-link fence around it. There, Joey Reynolds and his gang of boys were throwing firecrackers at a skinny German shepherd, who was running in a blind panic every time one went off near it.

"Stop it!" Jules hollered, launching herself onto Joey, one arm wrapped around his neck, the other hand punching him as hard as she could. Hobie, now taller than most of the other boys, had pushed a few of them down and was stamping all the firecrackers he could get to, mashing them into the wet, snow-sodden turf. Three of the boys jumped him, pummeling him with their fists.

Joey threw Jules off, and she landed heavily against the ground. "What are you doing?" he yelled back.

"You stop it!" She got up from the ground. "Why are you torturing that poor dog?"

"We're just having fun," he said, wiping his nose to check for blood. Jules was happy to see there was some.

"It's not fun to scare an animal," she said hotly. "It's cruel. You leave it alone."

"Or what?" he sneered.

"Or I'll go get my grandfather and he can tell your parents what you were up to," Jules said. She looked around. "He's the foreman over all your dads at the mill."

Joey thought about this. "C'mon," he said to the other boys, who had gotten off Hobie. "We had our fun. Let's go." They made a point of shoving Hobie roughly on their way out the gate in the chain-link fence.

Only then did Jules turn her attention to the dog, who was cowering in a far corner of the fence, looking for an escape.

"Come here," Jules said, speaking in a low voice. "I won't hurt you." She crept closer, but the dog whined and tried jumping the fence. It tumbled backwards, landing heavily. Jules stopped where she was.

"Do you think it's hurt?" Hobie asked anxiously, wiping his jacket sleeve across his bloody lip.

"She's a female. I don't know," Jules said. "She's so scared, she won't let anyone near her right now."

"She looks really thin," Hobie said. "I wonder how long it's been since she had any food."

He was right. Her fur was matted and muddy, and her ribs stuck out, but her eyes as she watched them were bright. Jules slipped her canvas bag off her shoulder. "I'm going to stay and try to calm her down so we can check if she's okay. You finish your route and see if you can get some food from your mom and come back here, okay?"

"Okay." Hobie slipped Jules's bag over his shoulder and left, closing the gate behind him.

Jules sat on the ground, ignoring the cold and damp, talking softly to the dog and holding her hand out, but not trying to get any closer.

By the time Hobie got back, dusk was falling.

The dog had huddled next to Jules, licking her face, but when Hobie opened the gate, she skulked to the far corner again, cowering and whining.

"I brought some bologna," Hobie said. "And a rope."

"Good thinking," Jules said. She took both from him. "Go stand by the gate again, will you?"

He went back and waited while Jules walked slowly toward the dog, talking to her in a calming voice and holding a piece of bologna out. The dog came to meet Jules and meekly took the meat from her hand. She allowed Jules to tie the rope around her neck, holding back only briefly when she felt the tension as Jules tried to lead her.

"Come on," Jules crooned. "It's all right."

Hesitantly, the dog followed until she got near Hobie. Whining and pulling back, she refused to go any nearer to him. Jules handed Hobie a piece of bologna. "Kneel down, make yourself smaller."

Hobie did as she said, and cautiously, the shepherd crept nearer to him until she could reach out and take the dangling meat.

"Good girl," Jules said.

"What are you going to do with her?" Hobie asked.

"Take her home," Jules said.

"You think your grandmother will let you keep a dog?" Hobie asked, looking at her as if she were crazy.

Jules shrugged. "I don't know. I wish I could find a way to ask Pappy first," but she knew this would be between her and Mae.

When they got home, Hobie wished her luck and went inside where his mom had dinner waiting. Jules put the dog inside the garage and took the rope off. "Please be good," she whispered, giving the dog a kiss on the head.

"Where have you been?" Mae said from the stove where she was stirring something in a pot while Pappy sat at the table, looking over the headlines in the paper. "You know dinner is at six sharp." She took a second look at Jules. "What have you been into?"

Jules looked down. She hadn't realized how muddy and messed up she was after her tussle with Joey. She took a deep breath and out spilled the story of what Joey and his friends were doing to the dog. Pappy lowered the paper, and Mae's lips got thinner.

"Where's the dog now?" Pappy asked.

Jules swallowed. "In the garage."

Mae turned sharply.

"Well, let's go take a look," Pappy said. Mae moved the pot off the burner, and they all went out to the garage.

When they opened the door, the dog cowered as far away as she could. Pappy squatted down and called to her. Her ears pricked, but she didn't come. Jules stepped forward, talking to her, and the dog belly-crawled to her, wagging her tail as she let Jules pet her. Jules turned to look at her grandparents.

Pappy grinned up at Mae, but his grin faded at the expression on her face. "Mae, the girl has a way with the dog."

157

But Mae wasn't looking at the dog. She was looking at Jules, and Jules was looking back. Jules stood and said, "I know it's a big responsibility to have a dog. I promise. I will take care of her if you let me keep her."

Pappy looked back and forth between them, puzzled.

Mae stood there a long time before finally saying, "If I have your word, then you can keep the dog."

CHAPTER 17

"WE'RE SO SORRY."

"Our thoughts and prayers are with you."

Jules's head pounded—from the repetition of the same words of condolence, over and over, and from the overpowering smell of the many flower arrangements set around the room—*and probably just from having to be in another damned funeral home*, but she didn't voice this thought to Kelli.

Dutifully, she stood next to Kelli for over an hour as the people in the reception line came by to speak to the family. The line snaked around the room, so that people kept passing each other, giving them a chance to visit and catch up. Both Carol and Jerry were retired schoolteachers, so it seemed the entire city of Hagerstown knew them. Kelli kept a worried eye on her father, but Jerry seemed to be taking strength from the outpouring of support.

"Go sit down for a while," Kelli said in a low voice. "We're fine here."

"Are you sure?" Jules asked.

Kelli nodded, turning back to shake the hand of the person in front of her.

Jules went to a small grouping of chairs in a corner of the viewing room and sank into one, rubbing her forehead.

"Want to get some fresh air? It'll help."

Jules looked up, startled to see Donna. "Hi," she said, standing to give her a hug. "I didn't know you guys were coming."

"Just me," said Donna. "Elaine's got a thing with a client tonight. Some soirée she decorated for and wants to be there."

Jules chortled. "A 'soirée'? She can't just say 'party' or 'get-together'?"

Donna gave a little shrug. "'Soirée' sounds more expensive, so she could probably charge more. How about a breather?"

"I would love to get some fresh air," Jules said with a grateful sigh.

They walked out a side door of the funeral home, avoiding the crush of people still coming in the main entrance, gathered around to sign the guest book. The cold air felt refreshing to Jules as she breathed deeply.

Donna reached up to massage her shoulders. "God, you are strung tighter than a banjo. No wonder you've got a headache."

"Been a lot going on." Jules groaned as Donna's fingers found a particularly tight muscle.

"How are you doing?"

"I'm fine," Jules said. "It's Kelli I'm worried about. She's had to hold everything together for her whole family. Jerry was almost incapable of making decisions about the casket, the service. Mary Anne hasn't been much better. They're just so torn up."

"Kelli must be, too," Donna said.

"She is, but she won't let herself deal with it until later, after everything is taken care of," Jules said. "Thanks." She stretched her neck as she turned to face Donna.

Donna's hands dropped to her side. "When are you coming home?"

"Tomorrow evening, after the funeral and burial," Jules said. "I've got to get back to work." She looked at Donna more closely. "You drove all the way up here, alone? And you're going back tonight? That's a long trip."

Donna looked at her in the orange glow from the outdoor lights illuminating the funeral home's exterior. "I wanted to be here."

"I know Kelli will appreciate it."

"I came for both of you."

Jules turned away.

"You just lost Pappy," Donna reminded her unnecessarily. "And now this. It's got to be hard."

"I'm fine." *How many times have I said that in the last few months?*

"Okay," Donna said. "I'm going to go see Kelli."

Jules nodded and remained where she was, looking out at the traffic driving by—ordinary people doing ordinary things with their evening, their lives undisturbed by a death in the family, a gap, an empty place at the table... *How I wish it could be like that again.*

* ❦ *

"I thought I heard one of the secretaries say you were down here."

Jules looked up as she gathered her testing materials, placing blocks and story cards back in their case.

"Hey, Carrie. How are you?"

"Hungry. Have you had lunch yet?"

"Uh..."

"I know," Carrie said, laughing. "Elementary lunches. But today is pizza and tater tots. Can't get any safer than that."

Jules narrowed her eyes as she tried to remember. "Tater tots. I haven't had a tater tot in forever."

"Well, come on, then," Carrie said, waving Jules to follow her. "I owe you a lunch. It won't be as good as Kelli's chili, but food is food."

Jules closed her testing kit and accompanied Carrie to the cafeteria. A few minutes later, they were seated in the staff lunchroom. "I never eat in the cafeteria unless I'm on lunch duty," Carrie said with a shudder. "Nothing like being in the middle of a hundred kids eating to make you lose your appetite." She squirted ketchup on her tater tots. "So, how is Kelli doing?"

Jules glanced at her. "How did you know?"

"Elaine," said Carrie. "I went by the studio last week, looking for a lamp." At the look on Jules's face, she added, "No, I didn't pay next month's salary for it."

Jules grinned. "Sorry. It's none of my business. Kelli is doing okay." She ripped the crust off her pizza to save for later. "She's home now. She'll be going back to work this weekend."

"How old was her mother?"

"Sixty-six," said Jules. "She'd only been retired for three years. All those years working and you think you've got time to enjoy things and travel and... BAM. Your whole world falls apart."

She looked up at Carrie as three other teachers came in and settled at another table. "What about your parents?"

Carrie swallowed and said, "My parents split up when I was in high school. They're both remarried now. Everyone's healthy as far as I know. Knock wood."

"Any siblings?" Jules asked.

Carrie nodded. "Two older brothers. One went into the navy, and the other works at the shipyard."

"Are they married? Any nieces or nephews?"

"Both married and five nieces and nephews."

Jules smiled. "I always wondered what it would be like to have a big family, lots of people and noise at the holidays. Ours were usually pretty quiet."

Carrie looked over, but the other teachers were absorbed in their own conversation. "Have you guys ever talked about having kids?" she asked in a low voice.

Jules looked up, startled. "Hell, no." She shook her head. "Kelli has never expressed any desire to be a mom, and I sure don't want to."

Carrie tilted her head, a probing expression in her dark eyes. "Was your childhood that bad?"

Jules popped a tater tot into her mouth and thought as she chewed. "There were happy moments," she said. "I just don't feel very maternal. I never had good examples of mothers when I was growing up, not in my house anyway."

"But when we have children," Carrie said, "they *are* wanted most of the time. We have to work so hard to get them."

Jules eyed her. "You want kids, don't you?"

Carrie nodded. "Yeah. A couple would be perfect."

"Do you want to be pregnant?"

Carrie shrugged. "I wouldn't mind."

Jules smiled and picked up her pizza. "I hope you find someone to make a family with."

<hr/>

I haven't met with the pastor again. I keep coming up with excuses. I asked Sandy for all the hours she can give me at the diner, and even if I'm not working, I'm telling them at home I am. I just hope no one finds out. I've been hanging out at the public library, trying to get all my homework done from the nights I am working, but they only stay open till eight, so then I just hang out until nine or ten before I go home.

I wish we could stop going to that church completely— we used to be Methodist, but when my mom married Steve, we started going to his church with him and his three kids. All the women and girls have to wear dresses. Don't laugh, but I actually have to wear a dress on Sundays. The one I have is getting a little tight and worn out, but I don't want to go shopping for a new one. I just keep wearing sweaters over top, but that won't work once it warms up.

I've still got to get through one more year here before I can get out of Aldie and never come back. I don't know if I'm going to make it.

Jules read through Ronnie's e-mail with some relief. She wasn't happy, but she was okay. She wondered if Ronnie and her mom used to go to Mae's Methodist church—it was the only one in Aldie, but there were a million Yoders in that part of Ohio, so the name wouldn't mean anything. *Wouldn't that be a hoot?*

She closed her laptop, password-free now, though she couldn't tell if Kelli had tried it again. "If she finds out about Ronnie, we'll talk about it," Jules had told herself firmly. As for the other things, well... they hadn't talked about those, either.

Kelli was home now, kind of. She and Mary Anne were driving up to Hagerstown on at least one of her days off each week to spend the day with Jerry. "He's so lonely," she said to Jules in bed one night when she got home late. "I think he just wanders around the house when we're not there."

"He probably is, for now," Jules agreed sleepily. "Is he ready to go back to work at the hardware store this spring? Or teaching or tutoring? He was a great teacher. I'm sure there are tons of kids who could use extra help in math."

"We suggested that," Kelli said. "And he may soon, but he's not ready yet."

"Mae was already involved in a lot of things," Jules said. "But she had the in-between years when Pappy wasn't home anymore. She kind of got used to being on her own. Your dad is having to adjust to everything at once."

Kelli rolled over and rested her head on Jules's shoulder. "I know I've said this before, but I can't thank you enough for everything you've done the last couple of months."

Jules held Kelli closely. "I haven't minded. Anything to make this less stressful for you."

Kelli gave her a little squeeze. "How are you doing? Have you talked to Mae lately?"

"Not lately," Jules said. "I should probably give her a call. And I'm fine. Busy at work. Lots of testing."

"It was so good of Donna to come to Mom's viewing," Kelli murmured. "She's a good friend."

Jules nodded. "She is."

"I'm glad you were able to stay friends with her."

Jules squeezed her eyes shut. "Me, too."

"Sit. Stay."

Jules was patiently training Friday to obey commands. "Well, we found her on a Friday," Jules said when Mae scoffed at such a silly name, and "It's just like Robinson Crusoe," Hobie added as if that settled it. He had finally gotten Jules to read the book, and she'd been devouring all his other books since.

Bathed and brushed and fed, the dog turned out to be beautiful. "She was an expensive dog," Pappy said, puffing on his pipe as Jules brushed and brushed her outside near his smoking chair.

"But no one answered my ad," Jules reminded him quickly.

"It's only fair you give her owner a chance to claim her," Mae had said, and so Jules had run a one-week ad in the Aldie Gazette, hoping against hope that no one would call.

Friday was proving to be highly intelligent and already knew basic commands. "That dog would jump over the moon if Jules asked her to," Pappy said to Mae. "She knows who saved her."

Pappy and Hobie were the only males Friday would allow near Jules. She never barked or snapped, but Jules could tell when her ears pricked and her eyes focused whenever they passed other men or boys that she was getting defensive. She and Hobie took Friday with them everywhere—playing in the woods, down to the creek, even out to the dump. They'd never found stuff as good as the day they found the army gear, but Jules kept hoping.

Upstairs at night, Friday slept on a dog bed next to Jules's. "I will not have that dog getting dirt and hair on my sheets," Mae had said, but Friday didn't seem to mind. Several times a night, she would nuzzle Jules's hand, and Jules would sleepily scratch her ears, reassuring her enough to curl up on her bed and go back to sleep.

The only place Friday couldn't go with Jules was to school. Middle school really was worse than elementary; Jules didn't care what anyone said. There was no more recess, only twenty minutes after lunch for them to play outside, and "everybody's getting weird," she said to Hobie with a shake of her head. "The girls were always stupid, but they're stupider now when boys are around." And the boys were just as bad. Even boys like Joey Reynolds seemed to always be looking to see if girls were around and watching them. "I don't get it," Jules said.

She was in the bathroom after lunch one day when some girls came in. They were whispering excitedly. "I saw Billy Hamilton looking at mine today," one girl was saying, and "Andrew Scott snapped mine to see if I was wearing one," said another.

"Well, we've all got to wear them now," said a third girl.

"All except Jules Calhoon," said the first girl, and they all giggled. "We'll be in high school and her titties will be hanging down to her waist before she gets a bra."

Jules looked down, pulling her shirt tight. She'd been pushing at the painful swellings on her chest for weeks, trying to mash them back flat the way they used to be. When that didn't work, she'd started wearing an extra undershirt, hoping no one would notice. She stayed in the stall until the girls had left and then slunk to her next class, rounding her shoulders and stooping to make her shirt baggy in front. After school, she ran home, glad that Hobie had to do his paper route.

When Jules got home, Friday greeted her, wagging her whole body and whining happily. Jules ran upstairs and put on a sweatshirt. Together, they headed out to the backyard, where Jules sat under a tree, her face buried in Friday's neck.

"I can't tell Mae," Jules murmured to Friday, her face burning with shame at the mere thought of having to tell her grandmother she was getting boobs and needed a bra. Friday whined and licked her cheek.

She and Friday went for a walk, practicing the "heel" command. It was hot in her sweatshirt, but at least with it on, she could be herself, until dinnertime.

"Take that thing off," Mae said. She'd set up a floor fan to move the air in the kitchen. "It's hotter than an oven in here, and you're wearing a sweatshirt."

"I'm cold," said Jules defensively. "You have that fan blowing right on us."

"Nonsense," Mae said. "Your face is all red. Go take it off."

Jules got up from the table to pull the sweatshirt off and toss it onto the steps up to her room. Pappy glanced up from his plate and did a double take as she came back to the table. Clearing his throat, he turned back to his roasted chicken and mashed potatoes.

Jules never heard what was said between her grandparents, but the next morning, three bras were lying at the foot of her bed, wrinkled and musty-smelling, and she knew they must have been old ones of her mother's. She'd sworn she would never wear another thing of Joan's, but "at least I didn't have to go to a store with her," Jules muttered to Friday as she held one up, trying to figure out how it worked.

CHAPTER 18

Kᴇʟʟɪ ꜱᴀᴛ ᴜᴘ ꜰʀᴏᴍ her wheel, inspecting her handiwork. Gently, she molded the lip of the pot to form a spout and then began rolling a rope of clay to fashion into a handle. She glanced at the clock and saw that it was four-ten. Of its own accord, her mind ticked off another day, another little landmark in a life that would never feel the same. It seemed impossible that tomorrow would be a month.

Yesterday at this time, Mom was dying.

Three days ago, I was calling Mary Anne and Jules to come home.

A week ago, we were at the funeral home, picking out her casket.

And now, *tomorrow will be a month....*

She closed her eyes and shook her head. "How long before you don't do that anymore?" she asked herself.

She spent several minutes positioning and shaping the handle and then carefully set the pot aside to dry and went to wash up. The aroma of the pot roast she had cooking in the Crock-Pot drifted into the studio. Smiling as she scrubbed the clay off her hands, she imagined Jules's reaction to coming home to find dinner ready for a change—and one of her favorites, too. She went into the kitchen and stirred the vegetables simmering in the broth. After turning the oven on to pre-heat, she got dinner rolls out of the freezer.

"Yeah, right," she grunted, tugging on the plastic bag. "Tear here. They never tear here." She went to the desk to get some scissors and stopped as she saw Jules's laptop lying there, plugged in. She retrieved the scissors, went back to her rolls, and placed four of them on a baking sheet. She put the remainder of the rolls back in the freezer and returned the scissors. Biting her lip, she stood over the laptop. She lifted the top and was reaching for the power button when the front door opened and Mary Anne called out.

Jumping as if she'd been bitten, Kelli slammed the lid of the computer closed. "In the kitchen," she called.

Mary Anne came in. "Mmmm, smells good." She lifted the lid of the Crock-Pot and sniffed appreciatively.

"What are you guys doing for dinner tonight?" Kelli asked.

"Nothing," Mary Anne said. "Brian said he has to work late at the office, and the kids both have games tonight, so they'll eat on the road with their teams."

"Stay and eat with us, then."

"You sure?" Mary Anne asked. "This isn't a romantic special occasion?"

Kelli laughed. "Not romantic, but special because it's been ages since I cooked anything for her."

She put two more rolls on the baking sheet and placed it in the oven. "Pour us something to drink and let's sit while these cook. Jules should be home any minute."

Mary Anne poured two glasses of peach tea and joined Kelli at the table.

"So, how are things with you and Brian?" Kelli asked.

Mary Anne shrugged. "Better, I guess, now that I'm home more. I think he was really overwhelmed by being a single parent while I was away so much."

Kelli glanced at her sister. "Well, did he have to do anything you don't normally do by yourself? He's just not used to being the one to do it."

"You're right," Mary Anne said with a chuckle. "Even the kids are more appreciative. Clean uniforms, lunches made, dinners made, clean house."

"They don't appreciate you. Not like they should." Kelli shook her head. "They got just a taste of everything you do because you weren't there to do it."

"Oh, I know it won't stay like this," Mary Anne said. "I'm just enjoying it while it lasts." She glanced toward the entryway. "Quick, before Jules gets home. How are things with you guys?"

"Mostly normal," Kelli said. "She never has talked about whatever was bothering her. It doesn't seem as bad as it was, but..."

Guiltily, she glanced toward the laptop.

"What?"

"It's nothing," Kelli said quickly. "It's just... before Christmas, I tried to get on Jules's laptop to look for a recipe I had sent myself, and it had a password on it. It never had a password before."

Mary Anne sat up straighter. "Why do you think she did that?"

Kelli took a sip of her tea. "I honestly don't know. We've never had secrets from each other, nothing we couldn't let the other see." She looked at the laptop, frowning. "I just don't know."

"Let's turn it on and see if we can figure out her password," Mary Anne said.

"What? No!"

"Why not?" Mary Anne asked. "If I thought Brian was cheating on me or keeping—"

"Who said anything about cheating?" Kelli instantly regretted having said anything.

"Why else would she need to put a password on it? Except to keep you from reading something she didn't want you to see."

Kelli shook her head again. "Maybe it's work stuff and she has to lock it to protect confidentiality."

Mary Anne gave her a skeptical look. "Has she ever put work stuff on her home computer before?"

Reluctantly, Kelli shook her head.

"See?" Mary Anne said. "She's hiding something."

"Even if she is, I'll wait for her to tell me," Kelli said.

They heard the front door open.

"Hey, hon," Kelli called out, getting up from the table with one more warning glance at her sister.

"Hey, Mary Anne," Jules said as she entered the kitchen. "Oh, my gosh, that dinner smells wonderful!" She inhaled deeply.

Kelli gave her a quick hug and kiss. "Wash up and—" the oven timer went off at that moment—"we'll eat." She laughed, and Jules paused on her way to the sink.

"I haven't heard you laugh in ages," she said, soaping up her hands.

Kelli turned from the stove and smiled at her.

Mary Anne set the table while Kelli dished out three bowls of vegetables and Jules cut the roast. In a moment, they were seated, eating ravenously.

"Oh, this is good," Jules mumbled through a full mouth.

"It is." Mary Anne reached for a roll and the butter. "So, Jules, how's work been?"

"Um." Jules swallowed. "Medium busy. Lots of meetings, testing load is picking up. It always does the second half of the school year."

"Do you ever have to bring work home?" Mary Anne asked innocently, pulling her shins out of Kelli's reach under the table.

Jules shook her head. "I could bring my work laptop home if I needed to, but we're not allowed to put kids' files or test results on our personal computers. Confidentiality. Why?"

"Oh, just curious," Mary Anne said with a half-glance toward Kelli while Jules was looking down. "I've been thinking about putting a password on our computer at home," Mary Anne continued, despite the glare coming from Kelli's direction. "The kids have been getting on some websites I'm not too sure about. What do you think?"

Despite her irritation with her sister, Kelli couldn't help glancing at Jules to see what her reaction was. Her heart sank as Jules stopped chewing and her face drained of color. No longer hungry, Kelli poked at a chunk of potato while Jules took a long drink from her water glass.

Keeping her eyes on her dinner, Jules said, "I think most parents should be keeping a closer eye on where their kids go on the Internet. A password is a good idea. And I usually counsel parents to not let kids have computers in their rooms, but they don't listen."

Mary Anne gave a half-laugh. "Of course, maybe I should put a password on it to keep Brian off the porn and gaming sites. I don't think he's smart enough to cheat on me online. I check his e-mails regularly."

The silence at the table was deafening.

"Look—" Jules started to say, but "I need seconds," Kelli interrupted, scooting her chair back to stand. "Can I get anyone anything while I'm up?"

She passed behind Jules and gave Mary Anne a look that clearly said, "I will kill you if you say another word."

Mary Anne glanced at the expression on Kelli's face and said meekly, "No. I'm good. I should get home." She finished her last couple of bites and carried her bowl to the sink to rinse it, saying good night to Jules.

Jules sat at the table, her appetite gone, while Kelli saw her sister out. She could hear a muffled hissing from the foyer before the door opened and then closed again. Kelli came back to the kitchen, and Jules stood.

"I'll clean up, since you did all the cooking," she said. "Why don't you go sit and rest?"

She put away the leftovers and got the dinner dishes loaded in the dishwasher before feeding the cats, who were noisily reminding her it was their dinnertime as well.

Squaring her shoulders, she went into the family room, where Kelli was watching television. She sat next to her on the couch and waited.

When Kelli didn't say anything, Jules said, "The password is off the laptop."

Kelli bit her lip and nodded but kept her eyes glued to the TV.

"I'm not cheating on you," Jules added quietly.

CAREN J. WERLINGER

"Then why did you lock it?" Kelli asked, turning the volume down on the television.

Jules closed her eyes. "It was stupid. There's this kid, a girl I met in Aldie. She's gay but can't tell anyone there. She passed me a note when I was there for Pappy's funeral, a kind of plea for help. I've been e-mailing her."

Kelli turned to Jules. "Why didn't you tell me about this?"

Jules shook her head. "I don't know. I should have, right from the start. But I didn't know at first how much of a leech she might be, and then your mom got sick. It was just never the right time."

Kelli laughed—a shaky, relieved laugh. "I was just... I couldn't imagine why you've been so weird since the funeral. Well, actually, I could imagine, and everything I imagined was terrible. I was afraid..." She leaned over and pressed her face to Jules's shoulder. "I'm so glad you told me."

Jules kissed her hair. "I should have told you earlier. I'm sorry."

Kelli lifted her face, and they kissed, a gentle kiss at first, and Jules could feel Kelli's hesitation, the unspoken question in her lips.

"Yes," she murmured, turning to take Kelli in her arms, kissing her deeply, feeling her and tasting her in ways she hadn't in a very long time. She ran her hands through Kelli's silky hair and pulled away from her mouth to kiss her forehead and her eyes and her ears. Kelli pushed her back onto the sofa, unbuttoning Jules's shirt and loosening her bra, lying down on top of her and kissing her slowly, all the while allowing her hands to explore Jules's body.

Jules responded with another whispered "yes," as she arched her back, urging Kelli on.

"She's ended up with a very eclectic look," Elaine said as she drove to Carrie's house in Pantop. She glanced back at Kelli and Jules in the backseat of the Mercedes. "I think you'll love what she's done with her place."

You mean what she let you do with her place, Jules nearly said. She actually had her mouth open when she felt Kelli's hand squeeze her thigh in warning, and she remained quiet as Kelli quickly said, "I'm sure it will be beautiful."

"It's nice of her to have us all over," Jules added as Kelli nudged her to say something—"something nice," she could hear Kelli imploring silently.

"Well, I helped with that, too," Elaine said. "She wasn't really sure what to serve, so I shopped for her and gave her some tips."

Jules immediately regretted not having eaten beforehand. If Elaine had chosen the menu, it wasn't a good night to be hungry. "Everything she makes has some weird, stinky cheese or sauce all over it," Jules often complained. Donna, as if she knew what Jules was thinking, turned around and smiled sympathetically.

Elaine drove two extra blocks before she found a parking space large enough to suit her, and they walked back to Carrie's duplex. Only a few piles of dirty snow remained on the curbs, though winter's cold was hanging on. They walked up her porch steps where the front door was open.

"Hello," Elaine called, pulling open the storm door and slipping her shoes off as she walked in. The others followed suit. Jules, sniffing tentatively, was pleasantly surprised by the aroma filling the air.

"Hi, everyone." Carrie emerged from the kitchen, her cheeks flushed, a spatula in hand. "Hang your coats on the hall tree, and help yourselves to wine," she said, pointing to what looked like an Indonesian teak buffet set with a tray holding several wine bottles.

"I'll pour," Kelli said while Elaine followed Carrie into the kitchen to see how things were going.

Jules and Donna accepted glasses and wandered into the living room, which wasn't vastly different from the last time Jules had been there except for a new wall cabinet that looked like a Chinese antique, modified to house a television. Donna, too, must have recognized how expensive the Persian rug on the floor was because she stepped around it.

"This is nice," Kelli said, joining them.

"It is," Jules said grudgingly.

Donna chuckled. "Not everything she does is way out there."

"Am I that transparent?" Jules asked.

"Yes," Kelli and Donna replied simultaneously.

They were left on their own for only a few minutes before Carrie called them to the table for the first course, a butternut squash soup. Jules took a tentative spoonful and looked up.

"This is good," she said.

"You don't have to sound so surprised," Elaine said with an edge to her voice.

Kelli choked a little on her soup. "Did you make this from scratch?" she asked Carrie when she could talk.

"Yes." Carrie beamed from Jules's other side. "My first attempt at a homemade soup."

"It's delicious," Donna said.

Soup was followed by rack of lamb served with a blueberry sauce and roasted zucchini as Carrie, Donna, and Jules talked school and upcoming mandatory standards of learning testing, and Kelli and Elaine talked about the studio.

"I don't know why you don't just do the pottery full time," Elaine was saying, and Jules's attention was caught.

Kelli shook her head. "I think the enjoyment would go out of it for me if it turned into my livelihood. I'd have to worry about what's selling and what's not, instead of just doing what I like. Besides I like getting to use both sides of my brain."

Jules leaned over. "And knowing there's a steady paycheck and health insurance and retirement."

"You can have so much security, you're like a tree," Elaine said icily. "Never moving or stretching. Just rooted in one place your whole life."

Jules's eyes flashed. "A lot of trees spread their roots and branches across broad expanses and cover a lot of ground from their one place. It's the ones with shallow roots that get blown over by the first big storm that comes their way. Maybe you're more like a tumbleweed."

"More lamb?" Carrie asked quickly, leaning across Jules as she passed the platter.

"Thank you." Kelli accepted the platter and passed it on to Elaine, whose lips were pressed into a thin line, her nostrils flared.

Kelli reached for Jules's hand under the table and squeezed it.

"I wish you would try a little harder not to antagonize her," Donna said a little while later when Elaine and Carrie were huddled in the kitchen, putting the finishing touches on the dessert. "She really is a good person."

Jules gave a resigned nod. "I'll try. She just knows how to push my buttons."

"I'd say it's mutual," Kelli said.

"Probably." Jules looked at Donna. "Okay. Okay. She can't be all bad. She had enough sense to pick you."

CHAPTER 19

"PASS ME THE NINE sixteenths socket, will you?"

Jules lay on her back next to Pappy under their Dart, Friday lying just beyond the car with her head resting on Jules's foot.

Jules loved helping Pappy fix things. Mostly, she passed tools or was the second set of hands to hold stuff, but she learned by helping and could do some things by herself now, like take spark plugs out, adjust the gap, and reconnect them—in the right order. And she could take the lawn mower blade off and sharpen it on Pappy's grinding stone and put it back on. "Nice and sharp," he would say, nodding approvingly, his large hand patting her shoulder.

"Girls should be doing other things," Mae used to grumble, but she had long ago given up hoping that Jules would take any interest in household tasks, beyond her required chores of cleaning and doing dishes. "I could teach her how to sew and cook," but Jules had no interest in any of those things.

Her time with Pappy wasn't just time to learn how to fix things. They talked. "About what?" Hobie asked sometimes.

"All kinds of things," Jules would say. "His time in the war—he was in Korea, but he doesn't talk about that, only his training at Camp Lejeune. What it was like growing up on his daddy's farm with five brothers. We talk about what I want to do when I'm grown-up."

"What do you tell him?" Hobie asked curiously, as Jules still tended to change her mind every other month.

Jules pursed her lips. "I'm thinking about being a vet."

"You'd make a fine Marine," Pappy said now as she told him her latest career choice.

"No," Jules said. "A veterinarian." Pappy chuckled, and she realized he was teasing. "Like James Herriot. I think I'd like to take care of animals." As if she understood, Friday gave a small woof of approval.

Pappy grunted as he struggled to loosen a stuck bolt. "That's a fine thing," he said. "You can do anything you set your mind to, Jules. Of that, I have no doubt."

"What did my mother want to be when she was my age?"

The wrench slipped, and Pappy skinned his knuckles. "Ouch!" He dabbed his bloody knuckles against his pants, and Jules knew that was that. Don't make a fuss about little hurts. Or big ones. It was an unspoken rule in their house.

"As I recall, she wanted to study music, be a music teacher," Pappy said.

"Really?" This was something Jules had never considered. Other than Pappy singing along to musicals on the television and dancing his little jigs, there was never music in their house. Only church hymns on Sundays.

"How old is she now?"

"Twenty-eight next Thursday," Pappy said so immediately that Jules knew Joan must have been on his mind already.

She lay on her back, staring up at the drive shaft of the Dart. "Do you miss her?"

"Every single day," Pappy said. "Pass me the grease gun."

"Does Mae?"

Pappy didn't answer for a few seconds as he dabbed grease onto the threads of the bolt. "I expect so," he said. "She doesn't talk about it, but I expect she does."

"What would you do if she came home?" Jules asked.

He glanced sideways at her. "What would you do?"

Jules scratched her chin, as Pappy always did when he was thinking. Her greasy finger left a smudge. "I don't know. I don't miss her. Not like you. I don't know her. But I don't think I'd trust her not to go away again, and I wouldn't want to see her hurt you and Mae all over again like the first time." She thought some more. "So I think it would be best if she just didn't come back."

Pappy was quiet for a long time as he worked. "I expect," he said softly, "that would be best."

"I love Virginia in the spring." Kelli looked around happily at the dogwoods blooming in pink and white and the redbuds with their purply-pink blossoms sprinkled along the edges of the woods bordering the interstate. "Does Ohio have these trees?"

Jules thought. "I don't know. I never remember seeing trees in bloom like this, but maybe I just didn't pay attention."

Kelli reached over to Jules's thigh as she drove. Jules raised Kelli's hand to her lips, kissing it tenderly. Ever since the evening Jules told Kelli about Ronnie, there had been a new intimacy between them.

"Not new," Kelli would have said. "Old. Like we were in the beginning."

They had made love more often in the past few weeks than in the prior six months. Lying in a tangle of arms and legs one night, their bodies still covered in a light sheen of sweat from their lovemaking, Kelli had felt bold enough to say, "Can we go together to Ohio soon? I'd like to meet Ronnie and see Mae."

Jules had lain quietly for a few seconds, long enough for Kelli to wonder if she'd pull away again, but she hadn't.

"We'll go the next weekend you're off," she said.

Now, in the car, Kelli said, "I'm really glad we're doing this trip together."

Jules opened her mouth to reply but closed it again. She squeezed Kelli's hand.

Kelli seemed to sense what Jules couldn't say. "It'll be okay."

Jules forced a smile. "I know Ronnie will be glad to meet you, and Mae asks about you and your father every time I talk to her."

"Has Ronnie written anymore?"

Jules shook her head. "Not since someone wrote 'dyke' on her locker in red nail polish a couple of weeks ago. I wrote to her and told her to report it to her principal and guidance counselor, but I don't know if she did."

"She knows we're coming?"

Jules nodded. "I sent her an e-mail this past week."

"What about Mae?"

"I just told her we wanted to see how she was doing," Jules said.

"And you're sure I'm welcome?" Kelli asked.

"You're probably more welcome than I am," Jules said wryly.

"And I'll stay with you up in your room?"

Jules laughed. "There are two twin beds, remember? Besides, it's the only other bedroom in the house. If Mae even knows enough to wonder whether we sleep together, she won't talk about it."

"So you never talked to her or Pappy about me or Donna or... anything?"

Jules glanced over. "Are you kidding? To Mae, we are friends and housemates. Maybe she suspects more, but she's not asking and I'm not telling."

As she had the past autumn when Jules came for a weekend visit, Mae was waiting up for them.

"How was the drive?" she asked as she settled back in her chair with the crocheted throw.

"It wasn't bad at all," Kelli said, sitting with Jules on the couch and looking around curiously.

"You stopped to eat?"

"Yes, we're fine," Jules said.

"Well, we should get to bed. I'm sure you're tired after such a long trip," Mae said, clicking the television off with the remote.

"She only got a color TV with a remote when her old black-and-white set finally died and she couldn't find a new one with channel dials to click," Jules had told Kelli when they first met. "She didn't believe the television salesman that they didn't make that kind anymore. She was certain he was just trying to sell her a more expensive model."

"I think that television is the only thing in the house not left from the sixties," Kelli whispered to Jules once they were alone in the kitchen.

"Doesn't matter," Jules whispered back. "She still watches the same three channels."

Upstairs, Jules flipped on the overhead light, once again missing her old night-light. She and Kelli pulled pj's out of their one suitcase. Jules retrieved the bathroom bag from the suitcase while Kelli changed.

"We'll have to brush our teeth in the bathroom downstairs," she apologized.

"No problem," Kelli said.

"Be back in a minute."

A few minutes later, Kelli had finished in the bathroom and come back upstairs to find that Jules had turned out the light and was standing at the window.

"Who lives there?" Kelli asked, peering down at the little house next door, lights glowing through the curtains.

"Just an old lady now," Jules said. "I was friends with her son, but... he doesn't live there anymore."

The next morning, they were awakened early when Mae began clattering around the kitchen, making breakfast.

"Welcome to the Calhoon house." Jules yawned, reaching a hand across to Kelli in the other bed.

They dressed quickly and went down to the kitchen.

"I'm going to show Kelli around Aldie," Jules said as they ate. "We'll be back later today. If there's anything you need help with at the house, we can take care of it. And we'll go out to eat tonight if you'd like."

"No need to do that," Mae said over her bacon and eggs. "I laid by a big pot of beef stew, and we'll have homemade rolls."

The morning was chilly, so they wore light jackets for the walk to town. Jules couldn't help glancing over at the Fahnestock house as they walked past. One of the curtains was pulled aside, and a pale face was visible, watching them. Jules quickened her pace.

They went straight to Sandy's, where Jules ordered coffee and chocolate pie. Kelli shook her head and ordered wheat toast and a cup of tea.

"And why are we eating a second breakfast?" she asked in a low voice.

"Because it's Saturday morning and Ronnie should be here working," Jules replied, watching the kitchen, glad to see that Trish was nowhere in sight.

Sure enough, Ronnie's hair-netted head slid into view as she gave a small wave. "I'll be right back," Jules said and slid out of their booth to go to the bathroom. She was back in a few minutes as their waitress brought their food. "She gets off at noon," she said, digging her fork into her chocolate pie. "We'll meet her then."

Jules and Kelli finished their food, paid the check, and wandered around Aldie. Jules took her into the Five & Dime.

"This feels like a step back in time," Kelli said, looking at the miles of shelves loaded with all kinds of merchandise.

Jules picked up a foot-long stick of bubble gum. "I think this might be the same stick I decided not to buy when I was thirteen," she joked. The woman behind the counter frowned at her, and they ducked out of the store, laughing.

They wandered in and out of Aldie's few stores, then spent the remainder of the morning at the public library. Jules read restlessly, checking her watch every few minutes until, "It's time."

"Where are we going?" Kelli asked as Jules led her away from the main drag.

"The elementary playground," Jules said. "It should be deserted so we can talk without being overheard."

As expected, the playground was empty. The swings oscillated gently in the spring breeze carrying the smell of the mill in their direction. They had barely arrived when Ronnie jogged around the corner of the school, wearing her usual baggy guys' jeans and a sweatshirt.

"Hi, Jules," she said breathlessly as she approached.

"Ronnie, this is Kelli," Jules said.

"Hi, Ronnie," Kelli said, holding her hand out.

Ronnie ran her gaze over Kelli's features as she shook her hand. "I've so wanted to meet you," she said shyly.

Kelli glanced at Jules. "And I've wanted to meet you."

Jules led them back to the baseball diamond, and they sat on one of the bleachers. "So, tell us what's been happening."

Ronnie shook her head. "I don't understand why stuff is starting to happen now. I haven't done anything. I don't hang out with anyone. I don't go to parties or anything like that."

"Have you met with the preacher again?" Jules asked.

Ronnie shook her head again, angrily this time. "No. I get out of that church as soon as I can. I've avoided being anywhere around him."

"Good," Kelli said. "That doesn't sound like a good situation."

"What about school?" Jules asked.

"There's a gang of girls—not the athletes—other girls, the popular ones, probably popular because they do whatever the boys want," she added scathingly, "but they're suddenly aiming at me. I don't know why. I'm sure it was them who wrote on my locker, but I can't prove it."

"How do you know it was them?" Jules asked.

Ronnie laughed. "Because they're so stupid, they spelled dyke wrong," she said. "D-I-K-E."

Kelli chuckled, but Jules frowned. "What did the school do about it?"

Ronnie looked down at her hands. The nails were chewed to nubs. "They gave me a bottle of nail polish remover and said it was nothing to be concerned about. 'Just a juvenile prank,' they said."

Kelli gave a gasp of indignation, but Jules laid a quieting hand on her arm. "What about your guidance counselor? Did you go to her?"

Ronnie's face burned scarlet. "I tried, like you said, but..."

"What?"

"She asked me if it was true. What they wrote." Ronnie looked up, her face a mixture of distress and anger.

"What did you say?" Jules asked.

"I asked her what difference that made. It was them and what they were doing we should be talking about."

"Good for you," Kelli said.

Jules's eyes narrowed. "What did she say?"

Ronnie's eyes filled with sudden tears, which she quickly wiped away. "She said if it was true, then there was nothing she could do." She sniffed. "So I stood up and said, 'Well, I guess there's nothing you can do,' and I left."

"I'm proud of you," Jules said quietly. "She hasn't gone to anyone—like your mother—has she?"

Ronnie shook her head. "No. At least not that I know of. That was just last week."

"Has your mother ever said anything?" Jules asked.

"When I was little, she used to tease me about being more boy than girl," Ronnie said. "But now, she's so busy with her job and Steve and his kids—they're little, elementary and middle school—we just don't talk."

They sat in silence for a few minutes, watching some crows squabble over a piece of food dropped from some child's lunch.

"What about the scholarships and grants?" Jules asked. "How are those going?"

Ronnie's expression brightened. "I sit for a writing competition next month," she said. "I won't know the results until this summer, I think. But…" Her face fell again. "I've looked at the financial aid forms. They ask for all kinds of information about your parents' income and taxes and stuff. I know Steve won't give that information. He doesn't think college is worth it. You should hear him go off about the Democrats bailing out all the people with their big college degrees who got the country into such a mess in the first place. What happens if I can't get them to fill out that form?"

"Where's your father?" Kelli asked.

Ronnie shrugged. "I don't know. I haven't seen him since I was little. He's supposed to send Mom child support, but he hasn't for a long time. She used to complain about it before she married Steve." She paused. "I think that's part of why she married him and does most everything he wants. It's better than being a single mom again."

Jules scratched her chin as she thought. "How much money do you have saved?"

"Almost two thousand dollars," Ronnie said. "But I don't know how much I'll need."

"Well, keep saving every penny you can," Jules said. "Don't buy a car. If you go to school in a place like Columbus, you won't need one anyhow. Just keep saving."

"What do I do about school?" Ronnie asked.

Jules looked at her sympathetically. "I'm not sure what to tell you about that. Most school systems have plans in place to deal with bullying, but knowing Aldie, they haven't bothered. I'll see what I can do, but in the meantime, keep your head down and deal with it as best you can."

Kelli reached into her purse and pulled out a scrap of paper and a pen. "Here's our phone number, so you don't have to rely on e-mail all the time. Do you have a cell phone?"

Ronnie shook her head. "Steve says who would I call, so Mom won't get me one."

"Then reverse the charges," Kelli said. "Call us if you need us."

Ronnie held the paper reverently. "Thanks." She pulled a worn nylon camo wallet out of her back pocket and tucked the paper securely into one of the pockets before placing the wallet back in her jeans. Jules smiled and reached into her own pocket, pulling out her wallet and retrieving a worn, crinkled piece of paper from within.

"Remember this?" she asked.

"My note!" Ronnie gasped. "You still have it?"

Jules nodded and said a little sheepishly, "It's been crumpled up, thrown away, put through the washer—it just wouldn't go away." She looked up at Ronnie. "There has to be a reason for that. You just hang in there like this note did. Somehow, some way, you will get through this."

CHAPTER 20

"Wow, I hadn't realized how good you were getting." Donna held up one of Kelli's vases, admiring the glazing and the form.

"Thanks," said Kelli modestly. "They have gotten better. At least the walls are uniform in thickness now."

Donna shook her head. "It's more than that. The form is really pleasing, kind of feminine," she said, running her hand over the sensuous curve of the vase.

Kelli blushed at the compliment, deciding not to share that it was the curve of Jules's naked hips she'd been remembering as she made that particular vase. "I appreciate your coming over to pick these up for Elaine."

"I don't mind. I wanted to talk to you anyhow." Donna placed the vase carefully in a box, tucked a kitchen towel around it for padding, and reached for another. "How have things been?"

"Better," Kelli said. "It's almost like the old Jules is back."

"Almost?"

"Well, there are still moments when she seems like she's brooding about something," Kelli said.

"How was your visit to Aldie?" Donna asked.

"Surprisingly good." Kelli carried over some miniature vases to place in another box. "I wasn't sure what kind of welcome to expect, but Mae was really nice. I think even Jules was surprised."

"And Jules seemed okay, being back in Aldie?"

"Mostly," Kelli said. "We met a high school girl Jules has been e-mailing."

Donna looked up sharply. "You met her?"

"You knew?"

Donna nodded. "I saw some of the e-mails on Jules's computer at school. She acted all flustered when I asked who Ronnie was. I..." Donna paused and turned back to a box.

"You thought she was cheating?"

Donna shrugged. "She'd been acting so strangely again. I didn't believe her when she said it was a girl from Aldie. She's never wanted any kind of connection to there. I shouldn't have suspected her. I'm sorry."

"Don't be." Kelli remembered her own distrust. "She put a password on her laptop to keep me from reading the messages accidentally, and... I hate to admit it, but that's where I went, too."

Donna studied Kelli's face for a moment and then smiled. "Well, I'm glad we were both wrong. So, what's the story with the girl?"

"She's lesbian. Can't tell anyone—her family's strictly religious—but she's starting to be picked on at school, and they won't do anything. She wants to go to college. Jules has been helping her with scholarship and grant information."

"Did you like her?" Donna asked, looking up from the box.

Kelli nodded. "I did. She seemed like a good kid. She's working hard, saving her money to make a better life for herself. I give her credit."

Donna finished packing one box and reached for some tape. "And the visit with Mae went well, too?"

"Yeah. I mean, she's not warm and fuzzy." Kelli chuckled. "But she welcomed me. Asked how my dad is doing." She placed more pots in a box. "There was one thing, though."

"What?"

"Well, there's a neighbor woman—I don't know exactly what happened. I think her son might have run away..."

"I've been looking in on Bertha Fahnestock more regular since Christmas," Mae had said Saturday afternoon when Jules and Kelli got back from meeting Ronnie. "Making extra when I make my dinner and taking some over to her. I don't know how much cooking she does these days."

She'd handed Jules a casserole dish, still warm inside the towel wrapped around it. "Take this over to her."

"No, Mae," Jules said. "I can't—"

Mae's sharp features softened a bit at the panicked look on Jules's face. "Please. It would do her good to see you."

Kelli looked back and forth between them, puzzled, as Jules reluctantly carried the casserole dish next door.

She was back in a few minutes, looking strained, but said only, "She said to tell you she appreciates it."

"I'm not sure what that was all about," Kelli said now as she and Donna carried the boxes of pottery out to Donna's car. "Thanks again for taking these to the studio."

"No problem," Donna said as she backed out of the driveway. "See you soon."

———◆◇◆———

Jules sat in the teachers' section of the elementary parking lot, waiting out the vicious storm that had hit as she drove there. The wind howled and the rain slashed as lightning forked the sky and thunder rolled. These sudden, violent storms were not unusual in this part of the state, but they usually blew through quickly. The crab apple and cherry trees, packed with pink blossoms an hour ago, were being stripped before her eyes. The grass under the trees was now littered with petals like a layer of pink snow.

Her eyes slid out of focus as the rain streamed down her windshield, distorting her view, but Mrs. Fahnestock's face came more sharply into focus in her mind's eye. She had answered Jules's knock by peering first through the curtains pulled across the windows to check who was on her porch. Jules's heart was pounding as she heard chains and bolts slide before the door was opened a crack and one pale, distrustful eye peered out at her.

"Hi, Mrs. Fahnestock," Jules said. "My grandmother made extra of our dinner for tonight and asked me to bring some over to you."

Bertha opened the door wide enough for Jules to enter and stood hidden behind it. "Come in."

Reluctantly, Jules stepped inside the dimly lit house as Bertha closed the door behind her and shot one of the bolts home. She shuffled into the kitchen, her slippers scuffing on the worn carpet, leaving Jules no choice but to follow. She glanced around the living room and recognized all the same furniture, sitting exactly as it had been the last time she'd been inside the house. She averted her eyes from the photos of Hobie perched on the fireplace mantel as she hurried through into the immaculate kitchen. A loaf of freshly baked bread cooled on the stovetop.

Jules set the casserole dish down on the table and turned to find Bertha wrapping the bread in one of her own towels.

"How are you, Jules?" Bertha asked, her voice sounding slightly hoarse, as if it wasn't used too often.

"I'm fine," Jules said. "How... how have you been?"

Bertha looked at Jules and said, "Next week is his birthday."

Jules realized with a shock that Hobie's birthday was coming up next week, April 29th. "Oh, right," she said awkwardly.

"Forty. I'll make his special dinner," Bertha said. "All his favorites." She nodded. "All his favorites." She handed the bread to Jules. "Take this to Mae and tell her thank you for me."

"I will, Mrs. Fahnestock," Jules said, turning back toward the front door. She twisted the bolt and opened the door. "Bye."

Bertha closed the door, and Jules could hear the locks and chains sliding and rattling again....

A bolt of lightning struck nearby with an almost simultaneous clap of thunder so loud it made Jules jump. "Damn, that was a close one."

Within a few minutes, the rain began to lessen and the intervals between flashes of lightning and the rumbles of thunder began to lengthen again. Jules reached for her briefcase containing notes for her meeting, pulled her hood up, and made a dash for the school entrance.

"Did you drown?"

"What?" Jules threw her hood back.

Bob Manzella was standing there. "I asked if you drowned," he repeated, pointing to the dwindling deluge outside.

"Not today," said Jules, turning to hang her dripping raincoat on a hook in the office.

"We're meeting in the library conference room," he said.

"Be right there."

When she got to the conference room—a small converted audiovisual closet that she usually used for testing—there were already a few people seated around the table, including Carrie, as this meeting was in reference to one of her students. Bob was seated at the head of the table, the student's file in front of him. Carrie smiled and indicated the seat next to her. Jules had to squeeze to get to the seat, as the conference room was not really large enough to accommodate this many people.

Bob cleared his throat and began, "We're here to—"

"Excuse me," Jules said, standing and reaching a hand across the table. "I'm Jules Calhoon, the school psychologist. I tested Luís."

The older woman sitting there smiled and shook her hand. "I remember you," she said with a strong accent, but good English. "I'm Josefa Rivera, Luís's grandmother."

The woman sitting next to her also shook Jules's hand. "I'm Victoria Ryan, the interpreter, just to make sure Mrs. Rivera understands everything that is said."

Bob cleared his throat loudly. "Yes, well, as I was saying, we're here to discuss Luís and the recent trouble he's been getting into."

"He's a good boy," Mrs. Rivera said.

"Well, he's been getting into fights lately, his grades are slipping, and he talked back to me when I called him into the office last week," Bob said sternly.

"He was doing fine," Carrie said, leaning toward Mrs. Rivera, her thigh pressing against Jules's. "His grades were good until this last grading period. Now, he's not turning work in, he picks fights with the other boys, and he won't answer questions in class. I've tried talking to him, but he just sits there. Has something happened at home?"

"¿Le entiende?" Victoria asked.

Mrs. Rivera nodded as her eyes brightened with tears. "Is his father. He is in jail for the last three years, but he is out now. He come around and make promises to Luís that he spend time with him, take him places, but then he don't come. Two weeks ago, they were supposed to go to movie on Saturday night. Miguel don't come, but Luís, he wait up all night for his papa." She dabbed at her eyes with an embroidered handkerchief. "I tell Miguel, he no can do this to his son, but he meet with friends—" she said this last with an expression of distaste—"and he get drinking and then he forget about his son. And poor Luís, he don't say so, but it hurt him." She tapped her chest. "He is a good boy."

"Can you talk to Luís, Mrs. Rivera?" Jules asked. "Will he talk to you?"

Mrs. Rivera dabbed at her eyes again. "I try. Sometime, he talk. He is angry with his papa, but then he feel bad to say he is angry."

"Well, we have to do something," Bob said. "If he gets into another fight, he's going to find himself suspended."

"Uh, probably not," Jules said. "Because he's got a special ed label, we'd have to call a meeting, and I would guess that the consensus would be that his disabling condition is contributing to his lack of impulse control, which means legally we can't suspend him. We need to find another solution."

"Maybe Miss Calhoon and I could talk to Luís," Carrie said. "Unofficial counseling to see if we can get through to him."

Victoria Ryan translated this last for Mrs. Rivera, whose eyes lit up. "Oh, would you, please? I would do anything to help Luís, but I don't know what to do."

"I don't do individual counseling," Jules started to say, but at Mrs. Rivera's pleading expression, she exhaled. "But maybe we could try and see what happens."

Mrs. Rivera reached across the table for her hand. "Oh, thank you. Thank you so much."

When the meeting ended, Jules fumbled with her file papers as the room emptied. When only the two of them were left, she rounded on Carrie. "I would appreciate it if you talk to me before you volunteer me for extra things. My meeting schedule and testing load is picking up, and I really don't have time for this."

"I'm sorry," Carrie said. "But you already know him. I think he'll talk to you. He really is a good kid, and if we can get through to him, maybe we can turn things around before he fails the year."

"I can't pull him out of any classes. Doesn't he have to catch the bus after school?" Jules asked hopefully.

"He doesn't take a bus," Carrie replied. "Their house is just around the corner. We could meet with him after school once a week."

With a resigned sigh, Jules nodded. "Wednesdays work best for me."

"Great!" Carrie said. "What have you been doing outside of work? Spring around here is gorgeous."

"Well, usually, Kelli and I do a lot of bike riding, but with her mom's illness and now going to spend time with her dad, we haven't really done much this year."

Carrie turned to her. "I've always wanted to get into bicycling, but in Newport News, the traffic was so heavy. It seemed like you'd be taking your life in your hands if you rode around there."

"Well, the county roads around here are great for riding. Light traffic, rolling hills," Jules said as she clasped her briefcase. "I could take you out if you want, see how you like it."

"Oh, would you?" Carrie said, laying a hand on Jules's arm. "That would be great. Let me know when."

<hr />

"So what do you want to do this last summer before we start high school?" Jules asked as she and Hobie walked down the dirt road toward the dump, little dust clouds rising with each footfall. Friday trotted ahead, stopping every now and then to check on their progress, jumping playfully at squirrels and rabbits she scared out of the undergrowth, and chasing them a short way before reappearing in the lane, waving her tail proudly.

"Not think about high school," Hobie said emphatically. "It's going to be bad enough. I don't want to spend all summer talking about it. I'm just glad we made it through middle school."

Jules laughed. "It wasn't that bad."

"For you maybe," Hobie said, his voice slipping into a higher octave as it still did sometimes.

"But you made lots of new friends the last couple of years," Jules said, a little jealously.

Hobie shook his head. "Only girls. No guys."

Jules looked up at him. She only came up to his shoulder these days, he had grown so much. He still had the prettiest eyes she'd ever seen, and he had had a lot of attention from the girls at school. His voice, when it settled into its new low register, made him sound awfully grown-up. "What difference does that make?"

"A lot," he said darkly.

"Well, look who's here," said a mocking voice, and Joey Reynolds appeared ahead of them in the dirt lane, surrounded by five of his buddies. "It's the girls, out for a morning walk."

The other boys laughed.

"Shut up, Joey," said Jules.

"Or what?" Joey asked. "You and your girlfriend will beat us up? We're six to two, Calhoon."

"What's the matter?" Jules threw at him. "You want us to wait while you round up some more for your side?"

Hobie groaned next to her, but she didn't care. She clenched her fists, ready to fly at them, but at that moment, Friday leapt out in front of Jules and Hobie, her ears erect and hackles up as she growled menacingly.

Joey and the others quickly backed away. "You keep that dog back," he said, his own voice slipping into a soprano squeak.

"I think she remembers you." Jules made no motion to grab hold of Friday's collar.

Joey continued backing up, his eyes glued on Friday's bared fangs. "You keep it back," he repeated.

"Friday," said Jules quietly. Friday immediately ceased growling and came to sit next to Jules, but her alert eyes stayed focused on Joey. "I think it would be a good idea for you to go away and leave us alone," Jules said.

Joey's mouth twisted into a snarl. "Saved by your girlfriend again, faggot," he shot at Hobie as the guys turned back in the direction from which they'd come. "She won't always be around to save your fairy ass."

Hobie spun around and began walking toward home. Jules trotted to follow, Friday guarding their rear.

"I thought we were going to poke around the dump," Jules said.

"You go."

"What's the matter?" Jules asked. "Are you mad at me?"

Hobie walked on, not answering.

Jules grabbed his arm. "Why are you mad at me?"

Hobie turned on her, and tears glittered in his eyes. "Don't you see?" He flung his arm back toward the site of their confrontation. "It's never going to end with them! And he's right. I don't always have you around to save my ass. I'm the one who gets beat up, not you!"

He started walking again.

"So, you want me to just shut up and let them say stuff to us?" Jules asked from behind him.

Hobie stopped. "No," he said, looking down at the gravel as he ground a pebble into the dirt with the heel of his shoe. "I just want it to stop. I'm sick of them. I'm sick of... everything. I want it to stop."

Jules caught up to him. "I know," she said as they walked on. "Why did he call you a faggot?"

Hobie's face burned red. "Never mind. Let's go."

CHAPTER 21

JULES WAS STRETCHED OUT on the sofa, watching television with Holly curled up on her chest and Mistletoe snuggled between her thigh and the back of the sofa, when the front door opened with a bang. Jules jumped up so suddenly that both cats leapt away hissing, their fur on end.

"Hello?" came a voice from the foyer.

"Mary Anne?" Jules called. "I'm in the family room."

Mary Anne rushed in, tears streaming down her face.

"What's wrong?"

"Where's Kelli?" Mary Anne looked around dazedly.

"She's not home yet," Jules said. She glanced at the clock. "She should be here any minute. Can I get you anything?"

"A drink," Mary Anne said flatly. "Anything with alcohol."

"Okay," Jules said. "Wine?"

"Fine." Mary Anne dropped into the recliner and reached for a tissue.

Jules went into the kitchen and opened a bottle of Merlot. To her immense relief, she heard the garage door open, and she poured a third glass of wine. A moment later, Kelli came into the kitchen, looking around cautiously.

"What's up?" Kelli asked. "Why is Mary Anne's car in the driveway?"

Jules shook her head. "Not sure yet. She just burst in here, crying and demanding a drink," she said, handing Kelli a glass. She picked up the other two glasses of wine.

Kelli took a big gulp. "Okay." She took in and expelled a big breath. "Let's see what this is about."

Together, they entered the family room. Jules handed Mary Anne a glass, which she drained in one. With a shrug, she handed Mary Anne the other glass as well.

"What is going on?" Kelli asked as Mary Anne's eyes filled with tears again.

In answer, Mary Anne held up a cell phone. "That bastard," she said, choking as she began crying again.

Kelli and Jules glanced at each other.

"I had to drive his car to pick the kids up from practice," Mary Anne said when she could speak. "I found this in the glove compartment." She brandished the phone. "It's not his regular phone. And when I—" Her sobs choked her. "When I turned it on... the texts and photos that are on here... He's got a lover. Has had for months according to these." She manically began poking and swiping the screen.

"Oh, crap," Kelli muttered. She went to kneel next to her sister's chair, wrapping an arm around her shoulders. "Are you sure? You might be reading something—"

"Read them!" Mary Anne said shrilly, pushing the phone into Kelli's hand.

"I don't want—" Kelli started to say, but "Read them!" Mary Anne commanded, sounding almost hysterical.

Kelli took the phone and glanced at a few of the texts. Jules could tell by the expression of distaste on her face the nature of what she was reading.

"These are—"

"Pretty disgusting! I know." Mary Anne grabbed the phone back and scrolled through more of the texts. "And they go on like that, like they're sixteen years old or something."

"Stop," Kelli said, placing her hand over the phone's screen and tugging it out of her sister's hand. "Stop reading. This is just going to torture you more."

She got up and set the phone down on the coffee table as she took a seat next to Jules on the sofa. "What are you going to do?"

"I'm going to kick his ass!" Mary Anne exploded. "I'm going to kick it right out the door. And then I'm going to take his sorry ass for every penny he has!"

Kelli held up a hand. "Stop and think about this."

Mary Anne's head jerked up. "What's to think about?"

"Well, the kids for one thing," Kelli said. "It's almost the end of the school year. Do you want to do this to them right now?"

Mary Anne sat silently as her brain slowed down enough to consider what Kelli was saying.

"This could be a good time for you and Brian to go to counseling together," Kelli said.

Mary Anne's chin jutted out mulishly. "I don't want—"

"Listen, you've both been through a lot," Jules cut in. "Your mom's illness and death and now your dad needing a lot of your time. I'm not excusing Brian cheating," she added at the expression on Mary Anne's face. "It's just that you've had a lot of things driving a wedge between you. Before you end it, maybe you need to see if there's anything worth saving."

Mary Anne's eyes filled with tears again. "And to think I practically accused you of cheating. Talk about paybacks."

Kelli finished her yoga DVD, grunting a little as she rolled up her mat. She pressed her fists into her lower back. The past two days had been tough at the hospital. They had a morbidly obese patient in the ICU, and rolling him in bed, even with help from other nurses, was taking a toll on her bad back.

"Maybe a walk," she said to herself as she looked at the crystal clear blue sky outside. The mountains in the distance often disappeared in a summer haze once the heat and humidity picked up in the central Virginia region, but this early in the season, everything looked bright and new and clean.

"Oh." She moaned as her knuckles found a tender point in her right butt cheek. "Maybe a bike ride would be better," she said. Holly looked up at her and meowed.

She changed into bike shorts and shoes and filled a water bottle. Out in the garage, she frowned as she realized her bike was against the garage wall, and Jules's was leaning against it.

"That's weird," she muttered as she rolled Jules's bike farther along and went back to check her tire pressure from her last ride a couple of weeks ago. Jules hadn't been out yet this season.

Her tires were okay, but when she swung a leg over the saddle, she realized her seat was in a different position. Looking closely, she couldn't see the marker line she had drawn on her seat post where her seat height was typically set. She raised it back up to the correct height and tightened the quick-release lever.

Twenty miles later, she coasted back into the driveway to find Jules's Subaru parked there. She used the keypad to open the garage door and leaned her bike against the wall. When she stepped into the kitchen, Jules was at the stove, stirring something in a saucepan.

"Hey, there," Jules said, smiling. "Good ride?"

"Mmm hmm." Kelli went to the sink to rinse out her water bottle. "Funny, though. My seat was in a different position. Have you been out?"

"Oh," said Jules. "I forgot to tell you with all the Mary Anne and Brian drama the last few weeks. I took Carrie out for a ride last week. She's been wanting to try cycling, so we did the Frog Eye loop. I figured twelve miles was all she should do for a first ride."

Kelli turned from the sink. "You let someone else ride my bike?"

Jules glanced at her. "No. I rode your bike, and she rode mine. What's the big deal?"

Kelli turned back to the sink, her jaw muscles clenched.

"What? You're pissed because I rode your bike?" Jules asked.

Kelli turned and glared at her. "I'm pissed because you took her out on our bikes and didn't tell me."

Jules threw her hands up. "They're bikes for crying out loud. It's not like I let her use your pottery wheel or sleep in our bed." She immediately saw the look in Kelli's eyes and hastily said, "I didn't mean it like that. I'm just saying, it's only a bike."

"Maybe this is only a bike," Kelli flung at her, "but underneath that, it's much more. And if you can't see that, then we do have a problem."

Jules opened her mouth to retort when the phone rang—"thank goodness it did," she would realize later. She grabbed the receiver, fully expecting to hear Mary Anne crying again, but she drew up short at the sound of Ronnie's voice.

"Ronnie, what's wrong?" She could hear Ronnie crying. "Where are you? What happened?"

"I'm out behind the diner." Ronnie sniffed. "I didn't know who else to talk to."

"What do you mean?" Jules asked. "What's going on?"

"Our pastor got me in his office yesterday," Ronnie said. "We stayed for a social after church, so I couldn't get away from him. He made me sit down, and he pulled another chair up close, and..." She started crying again.

Kelli was watching the expression on Jules's face and came closer. Jules tilted the phone so she could hear, her cheek next to Jules's.

"He put his hand on my knee and started sliding it up, under my damned dress," Ronnie mumbled almost unintelligibly.

Kelli's hand flew to her mouth, but Jules said, "What did you do?"

"I shoved him," Ronnie said. "I shoved him so hard, his chair fell backward. I ran from the office."

"What did he say or do?"

"I don't know," Ronnie said. "I walked home and changed into regular clothes. I threw the dress into the trash barrel and burned it. Steve was so mad when they got home. He wanted to know why I was disrespectful to the pastor." Ronnie laughed angrily. "He told me I had to go apologize. I told him I wouldn't go near that guy again and I'm never going back to that church. He said I had to go or get out from under his roof."

Jules closed her eyes. "What did your mother say?"

There was a long pause before Ronnie said bitterly, "Nothing. She stood there and didn't say anything."

"So what did you do?" Kelli asked.

"I packed an extra backpack with some clothes and took my school backpack and left," Ronnie said. "I slept in the diner last night. Sandy doesn't know. I have a key 'cause sometimes I open or close."

"Did you go to school today? Did anyone there act like they knew what happened?" Jules asked.

"I went, but no one said anything." Ronnie was quiet for a moment. "I don't know where I'll go. I can eat my meals here, but I can't keep sleeping here and I gotta shower—but not at school."

Jules bit her lip as she thought. "Whose phone are you using?"

"Trish's. She let me borrow it."

"Can I call you back at this number?"

"Yes," said Ronnie. "My break is almost over, but I'll ask Trish if I can hold on to it for a little while."

"Okay. I'll call you back in a minute."

Kelli looked at her as she hung the phone up and stood leaning against the counter. "What are you thinking? Are you going to bring her here?"

"God, no," said Jules with a shake of her head. She took a deep breath and picked the phone up again, punching numbers. "Mae?"

CHAPTER 22

As requested, Elaine kept Donna's birthday party small, just Jules and Kelli along with their veterinarian, Barbara, and her partner, Chris—"and Carrie," Kelli said under her breath as they entered the house. What Elaine apparently didn't tell Donna or Carrie was that she had also invited another woman, Yvonne, in what was a very transparent setup.

"I tried to talk her out of it when I realized," Donna muttered to Jules and Kelli as she poured them drinks, "but she thinks they might hit it off."

That seemed unlikely on the surface. Yvonne sported multiple tattoos and piercings and had shaved her head. The three of them watched from across the room as Elaine tried to engage Carrie and Yvonne in conversation.

"Not exactly conservative, is she?" Jules said in a low voice.

"Who knows?" Kelli said. "Appearances can be deceiving. Maybe Carrie has tattoos in places we can't see."

"She doesn't," Jules blurted. When Kelli and Donna both turned to her with questioning expressions, she burned scarlet and said, "She's afraid of needles. She told me."

Donna smirked. "Got out of that one, didn't you?"

Kelli, though, didn't smile. "I'm going to go over to say hello."

Jules took a big gulp of wine as Kelli left them.

Donna peered at her closely. "What's up?"

Jules didn't look at her. "Nothing. Why?"

"Why?" Donna looked over to where Kelli was shaking hands with Yvonne. "The tension just then was pretty obvious."

Jules shook her head. "It's nothing. I just—I was stupid. Carrie wanted to try bicycling, and I took her out on our bikes a couple of weeks ago without saying anything to Kelli ahead of time." Donna didn't respond, and Jules looked at her to see a shadow settling over Donna's features.

It's not what you did or didn't do with her, it's that you're bringing a third person into this relationship. That's the problem, and if you can't see that….

Those words suddenly rang in Jules's ears, only it had been years since Donna had said them to her—back when it was Stacy she was starting to spend time with.

Donna lowered her gaze. "I'd better check on…" She gestured toward the kitchen and disappeared.

"Shit," Jules muttered, turning back to the table to pour herself some more wine.

"What's the matter?"

She turned to find Carrie at her elbow. "Hi."

"Hi," said Carrie. "Are you okay?" She laid a hand on Jules's shoulder.

Jules gave a small shake of her head. "I'm fine." She turned, sliding out from under Carrie's grasp, and glanced meaningfully in Yvonne's direction, where she was engaged in a conversation with Kelli and the others. "So...?"

"Oh, well..." Carrie gave an embarrassed laugh. "She seems nice. She's an artist," she said as if that summed up all there was to say.

"That bad, huh?

"There's just not much in common, I think," Carrie said. "Not like—I mean, I could talk to you about anything. We've got so much in common." She seemed to be waiting for Jules to say something. "I'd just like to find someone I can really talk to, you know?"

Jules couldn't meet Carrie's earnest expression. "You will," she said as she swirled the wine in her glass.

"What if I already have?"

A prickly silence filled the space between them.

"Hey," Jules said, a little too enthusiastically, as Barbara came over to get some more wine. "How are things going at your practice?" she asked, breathing with relief when Barbara launched into a lengthy conversation about one of her animal patients.

A couple of hours later, Kelli and Jules were alone in their car, driving home.

"Are you going to talk to me sometime tonight?" Jules asked as she stopped at a light.

"I thought maybe you were talked out after Carrie had you cornered all evening," Kelli said in clipped tones.

"What are you talking about?" Jules said. "You talked to Yvonne all evening."

"She happens to be very interesting," Kelli said. "We were talking about her art and how difficult it is to get galleries and shops to carry your stuff."

"So, what's the problem?" Jules asked.

Kelli turned in her seat. "The problem is that Carrie was glued to your hip all evening. She was supposed to be Yvonne's date."

"It wasn't a date," Jules said. "It was an experiment by Elaine—one that didn't pan out. And she wasn't glued to my hip. We just have things to talk about—"

"Things that don't include me," Kelli cut in. "Carrie made that very clear when you were talking about the Latino boy."

Jules took a calming breath and reached for Kelli's hand. "It's not like that," she said, trying to defuse this tension that had come, it seemed to her, out of nowhere. Although, *is Kelli really that far off-base?* she asked herself, remembering the things Carrie had said, the way she'd been looking at her.

The light changed, and Kelli pulled her hand away.

They rode in silence for a few minutes.

"Don't you think some of this has to with Mary Anne and Brian's problems?" Jules asked. "You know as well as I do how often being around a couple having problems rubs off on others. I don't think this is really about Carrie, because there's nothing there to be concerned about." She took Kelli's hand again.

Kelli blinked rapidly and turned away to look out the window. "Really?"

"Really." Jules raised Kelli's hand to her lips. "I love you."

"I love you, too," Kelli whispered, leaning over to press her forehead against Jules's shoulder. "I'm sorry. Just being stupid."

Jules sat in algebra, in her usual last-row seat. She was supposed to be learning how to multiply binomials, but she kept glancing three seats to her left and one forward, to Tammy Dearing. She watched the graceful way Tammy held her pencil, the way she kept reaching up to tuck a stray strand of hair behind her ear as she bent over her paper. A sudden tapping on her desk startled her, and she realized Mr. Anderson was standing there next to her desk, tapping her paper with his finger. She quickly refocused on her own paper as he moved on, her face burning as she kept her head lowered. Hobie sniggered next to her, and she reached out to punch him in the arm while Mr. Anderson wasn't looking.

First, Outer, Inner, Last... what in the world did this have to do with anything? Math was stupid. Spanish and literature were much better—partly because Hobie had already introduced Jules to *Huckleberry Finn*, which they were now reading, and partly because Tammy Dearing asked for Jules's help in Spanish. Hobie and Jules had signed up for as many of the same classes as they could, but only got the same math and World History classes. Jules was secretly glad Hobie wasn't in her Spanish class.

"You're really good at Spanish," Tammy had said after the third week of their freshman year. "Could you help me, maybe?"

Jules had nodded dumbly, struck by Tammy's green eyes, which crinkled when she smiled. Somehow, she had a feeling Hobie would have known without her saying it that she thought Tammy Dearing was the prettiest girl she had ever met. She liked the tingle she felt in her stomach whenever she thought of Tammy, and she looked forward to study hall, when Tammy saved her a seat next to hers so Jules could help her with their Spanish homework. She tried not to think about the fact that Tammy was now asking her to just do her homework for her—"you're so much smarter than I am," Tammy would say with her prettiest smile, sliding her paper over in front of Jules.

On Thursday the week before Halloween, Jules was eating lunch alone in the Spanish classroom. Hobie had another headache and had stayed home from school, again. Jules hadn't said anything to him, but she'd noticed he had started having these headaches on gym days and was missing one or two days of school each week. Jules herself had gone home with supposed headaches a few times when her stupid period started. If she'd thought it was murder having to tell Mae she needed a bra, it was nothing to having to talk about menstruation. She knew from health class what was happening and had found a box of sanitary napkins in the back of the cupboard in the bathroom. She had no idea who they'd been purchased for—that was another thing they didn't talk about in their house. She supposed Mae must have noticed they were being used, because new boxes appeared in the bathroom when they were needed.

Rather than eating alone in the cafeteria, Jules had asked Mrs. Fulton, the Spanish teacher, if she would mind if Jules ate her lunch in her classroom, "so I can study while I eat," Jules had said. Mrs. Fulton had been most agreeable as she was at her desk grading papers almost every day at lunchtime anyway.

Jules pulled out a paper she had tucked into the back pocket of her notebook, a poem she'd been writing—a poem for Tammy. She rather liked it in English but thought it would sound even better if she translated it into Spanish. She munched on her bologna sandwich as she scoured her Spanish dictionary for the right words, occasionally asking Mrs. Fulton, "¿Señora, cómo se dice...?" if she couldn't find the right word.

The bell rang, and Jules packed up her notebook, throwing her lunch bag in the trash as she said "adios" to Mrs. Fulton and headed toward study hall. Tammy, as usual, was waiting for her.

"Hi," she said as Jules took the seat she'd saved. "I got you something." She placed a Snickers bar on Jules's desk. "I don't know if you like them."

"I do," Jules said, beaming. "Thanks." She bent over to put the Snickers bar in her book bag and bumped her elbow against her notebook, knocking it to the floor. Papers scattered everywhere.

Tammy reached from her seat to help pick them up. Jules held out her hand for the papers Tammy had retrieved, when she saw Tammy reading one of them, a strange look on her face. With a sensation like a rock dropping into her stomach, she saw that Tammy was reading the poem she'd written.

Jules snatched it from her. Her face burned.

"What are you—?" Tammy sputtered. The study hall teacher cleared her throat at them, and Tammy lowered her voice to a hissing whisper. "Are you queer or something?

Amy Curry told me you were weird and I should stay away from you. But I told her you were okay. You stay away from me, you hear?" She grabbed her books off her desk and moved to the other side of the room.

Jules pulled the hood of her sweatshirt up over her head and sat with her head low, her nose nearly touching her copy of *Huck Finn*, as tears dripped onto the pages, waiting for the bell to ring so she could escape. When it did ring at last, she didn't go to her literature class. She didn't even go to her locker to get her jacket. She made straight for the back door at the end of the hallway near the locker rooms and slipped out of the building. Once outside, she ran past the practice field and baseball diamond, empty now that the PE classes were being held indoors. She knew she would be in trouble with Mae when the school called to see where she'd gone, but she didn't care. She didn't care about anything except the look of repulsion on Tammy's face as she'd read Jules's poem.

She swiped her sleeve against her runny nose as she ran, trying to put as much distance between herself and the school as she could. Only now, she had to find somewhere to go for a couple of hours. A cold wind was already making her shiver in her sweatshirt. She made her way back to the dump road and crept up to Hobie's back door, hidden from view of her own house and Mae. Hobie's mom should still be at work, sewing down at the dry cleaner's, but she didn't know if Hobie might be in bed if he really was sick.

Tentatively, she knocked on the back screen door. A shadow moved inside, and a moment later, Hobie opened the back door.

"What happened?" He held the door open for her. "Why aren't you in school?"

"Why aren't you?" Jules asked.

Hobie turned to the kitchen table, where he had been pouring himself a glass of milk to go with a plate of cookies his mother had left him. He got a second glass down and poured for Jules. She sat with him at the table.

"I had a headache," he said lamely.

She looked at him closely. "You've had a lot of headaches lately."

Hobie stuffed a whole peanut butter cookie in his mouth and didn't say anything.

"Especially on gym days," Jules added.

Hobie's pale cheeks burned a telltale splotchy red, but he frowned and said, "I hate gym. We have to dress out, and the gym teacher is making us shower."

Jules looked at him. "Really? The girls have to dress out, too, but we don't have to shower."

"Well, I'm not going to." His face hardened. "Things are bad enough without that."

"But you have to go to gym sometime, don't you?" Jules asked.

Hobie swirled his milk in the glass. "I asked. If I have a doctor's excuse, they can't make me."

"But you don't have a doctor's excuse, do you?"

"I'll get one." He gave a wheezy cough that sounded very fake to Jules. "I think I have asthma," he gasped dramatically.

She laughed. "They'll never believe that."

"Then I'll think of something else." He ate another cookie. "So are you going to tell me why you left school?"

Jules blinked hard and shook her head. She didn't want to cry in front of Hobie.

"Hey," he said, leaning toward her. "It's okay. I've felt like this tons of times. Whatever it is, it doesn't matter to me."

———— ⊶⊰⊱⊷ ————

Jules lay on her side in the extra bedroom, Mistletoe curled up against her stomach, as she stared at the foxes on her night-light. Kelli would be home within the hour. They hadn't talked again about Carrie, but Jules's gut clenched every time she thought about it. Kelli was not a jealous person, and Jules knew she was crossing a line, just as she had with Stacy, only she had told herself—and Donna—back then that there wasn't much of a relationship left and that Stacy wasn't the real issue. *That was partly true,* Jules thought now, *but only partly.* Donna had wanted, early on, to work on whatever was causing the friction between them, but by the time Stacy came into the picture, Donna had distanced herself—"to protect herself," Jules realized as she thought back.

Kelli isn't like Donna, though, said a voice in Jules's head. *She isn't likely to walk away without more of a fight...*

"Why are you even thinking about walking away?" Jules whispered. "You should be hanging on to her as tightly as you can."

If she were truly honest with herself, she had to admit that she was flattered by Carrie's attention—*and her flirting,* prompted that obnoxious voice in Jules's head. Carrie had been more casually physical during their counseling sessions with Luís—mostly knees and thighs pressed together under the table as they sat side by side talking to him—and the way she looked at Jules sometimes, when they were alone in her classroom....

"Because you're not telling her to stop," Jules said. "Why aren't you?"

There was no answer to that.

With a frustrated sigh, Jules rolled over. Things felt as if they were somehow spiraling out of her control. Her phone call to Mae had resulted in Ronnie being taken in, not by Mae, but by Mrs. Fahnestock.

"What?" Jules had said when she heard this. "No!"

"Whyever not?" Mae had asked. "She's lonely over in that house all alone all these years. The girl needs a safe place to stay, and when I explained the situation, Bertha said she'd be more than welcome to stay with her. I think it'll be good for both of them."

That had been over a week ago, and Jules hadn't heard any updates yet on how that situation was working out. She wondered if Ronnie was staying in Hobie's room... Surely not. She couldn't imagine Mrs. Fahnestock letting anyone else stay in that room, though Jules hadn't been in there since—

"Stop!" she said loudly, making Mistletoe jump and hiss. The cat leapt from the bed as Jules flung herself into a sitting position, her elbows on her knees, forehead pressed into the heels of her hands. "God damn it," she muttered, reaching for the switch on the night-light and clicking it off.

She went down the hall to the office and, opening her laptop to fire off an e-mail to Ronnie asking for an update, she stopped abruptly when she saw there was a message from Ronnie in her in-box.

Dear Jules and Kelli,

Thank you so much for helping me find another place to live. Don't take this the wrong way, but Mrs. Calhoon was a little scary. Mrs. Fahnestock has been really nice. She seems really sad, though. She makes me dinner whenever I don't have to work, and she didn't want to charge me anything, but I told her I would only stay if she let me pay her something, so we agreed on $100 a month.

So far, I haven't heard a word from my mom. I knew I wouldn't—she's afraid of making Steve mad, but I thought maybe she'd try to get in touch with me at school or something. But this is better. I don't have to go back to that stupid church. All I have to worry about is getting through school. I'm just glad the summer vacation starts in a couple of weeks. Maybe they'll have a new target by next year.

The bell just rang. Gotta go.

Later,
Ronnie

Jules couldn't help smiling as she read the message. *Smart girl,* she thought. *Mae scares me, and I'm her granddaughter.* With a sense of relief, she closed her laptop. It sounded as if things were going well, better than she'd expected. Maybe Mae was right; maybe Mrs. Fahnestock was ready for company. *Mae's been right a lot lately.*

CHAPTER 23

KELLI BALANCED ON ONE foot as she used the other to prop open the door of Elaine's studio long enough for her to squeeze through, carrying a box loaded with new pottery. The bell tinkled, announcing her arrival, and she looked up to see Donna standing on a ladder, swishing a feather duster over an elaborate chandelier.

"What are you doing?" Kelli asked, laughing up at her. "Is this how you're going to spend your summer? Giving up teaching for custodial work?"

Donna looked down at her and grinned. "When you're married to the owner, you get tapped for all the things on the honey-do list."

Elaine popped up from behind an ornately carved teak armoire that she was polishing. "All hands on deck." She set her polishing rag down and came over to where Kelli was pulling her pots out of the box, placing them out on a table for Elaine's inspection.

"You don't have to take all of them," Kelli said. "I know things haven't been moving like they normally would—"

"But your pottery is one of my best sellers." Elaine inspected the glazing. "These are gorgeous. Do you have a list of everything you brought? And extra cards?"

"Yes," said Kelli. "And there's another box in the car."

"I'll get it." Donna climbed down from the ladder.

"Oh, thank you, sweetie," Elaine said distractedly, taking two of the pots and looking for places to put them.

A customer entered as Donna exited, and Elaine rushed over to greet the woman. Donna was back in a moment and brought the second box over to join the first.

"These really are nice," she said.

"Thanks," Kelli said. "How have you been? Feel any older now that you're forty?"

Donna nodded. "I do, a little. It's weird. I didn't think I would, but it feels different than thirty did."

"Forty didn't bother me," Kelli said, trying to recall. She frowned a little. "Jules will be forty this year."

Donna looked up at her. "Yeah. We're the same age."

"I wonder..."

"What?"

Kelli bit her lip. "I've been wondering... if maybe that's why, you know. Her moods and stuff. I mean," she added quickly, "there are times when she's completely normal, and everything is great between us, and then... for no reason I can tell, she kind of disappears again." She flushed at having revealed so much.

Donna didn't say anything for a moment. She glanced toward Elaine, who was happily showing the customer dining tables. She opened her mouth as if she were going to say something but then seemed to change her mind.

"What is it?" Kelli asked.

"Well," Donna said, looking hesitant. "I didn't like the way Carrie was behaving the night of the party."

Kelli lowered her gaze to the pot in her hand. "Jules didn't exactly discourage her."

"No, she didn't," Donna said coldly, and Kelli looked up in surprise. "I saw it," Donna said. "I was kind of pissed to tell you the truth—at both of them. It just—" She stopped abruptly.

"It brought up old memories?" Kelli asked.

Donna looked at her and nodded. "This is what she does. Or has done. I don't want it to happen again. Not to you," Donna said sincerely. Checking on Elaine's location and level of distraction again, she lowered her voice. "You've been really good for her. Not like Stacy. That situation was never good. And Jules and I were so young. But I'd hoped, with you, she was done with this... this thing she does."

Kelli swallowed the hard lump that had risen unexpectedly in her throat. "I wish we had some idea what triggers it. How do you fix something when you don't know what you did?"

Donna shook her head. "I didn't know it was happening until it was practically over, beyond fixing." Her eyes were glistening. "I've been thinking a lot about this. About what happened then and the things you've told me are happening now. I don't think it's us." She looked up at Kelli with eyes still wounded after all these years. "We get caught in the aftermath, but it's not us. It's her."

Kelli looked at her helplessly. "There's got to be something we can do."

"Maybe not," Donna said. "Maybe it's something she won't deal with until she hits some kind of bottom that makes her face it, like an alcoholic. We can't do it for her. And so far," she added darkly, "her pattern is to run from it anytime it gets too close."

Jules sat at her computer, trying to ignore the metallic clangs coming from the building maintenance staff attempting to fix the aging air conditioning system that could no longer cool the air in the central office. She punched numbers into the computer as she scored a test, cussing when she had to backtrack and re-enter an entire subtest because she hadn't been paying attention.

"Here you are."

Jules looked up to see Carrie's head peeking around the wall of her cubicle.

"Hi," she said, startled. "What are you doing here?"

Carrie dragged a chair from the empty cubicle next door and pulled it into Jules's space—way into her space, as Carrie's knees were almost pressed against hers as she sat.

"I never got to see you the last week of school," Carrie said. "We were supposed to have one more session with Luís."

"Oh, well, I had a last-minute child study meeting that week," Jules said, knowing full well she could have rescheduled with Carrie and Luís.

"I've been e-mailing you," Carrie said pointedly, glancing at Jules's computer screen where the e-mail program was open.

"I've got lots of testing I have to get scored and written up," Jules said.

Carrie leaned forward, resting an elbow on the desk and placing her other hand on Jules's knee. "If I didn't know better, I'd think you were trying to avoid me."

Jules looked around. She had no idea how many of the others were in their cubicles. Voices carried in this room. She stood abruptly. "I need to stretch my legs. Let's go get some air."

She pushed past Carrie and led the way out to a small employee break area with a picnic table under an awning that provided some shade.

"What are you doing?" Jules hissed when she had made sure no one else was within hearing.

"Why are you so upset?" Carrie asked.

"Why am I upset? Maybe because I'm not out at work, and you're being stupidly obvious," Jules said. "Why are you doing this?"

Carrie, far from looking upset, smiled at her. "You don't think people know, even if you've never said anything?"

"That's beside the point. I'm with someone."

"Someone you're not happy with," Carrie said, unabashed.

"What?" Jules choked. "Why would you say that?"

"Because it's true," Carrie said. "Anyone with eyes can see that you're not happy."

Jules stared at the ground. *This is all your fault. You let it get this far.* Bracing herself, she looked up at Carrie. "Whatever you think you've seen in me that's unhappy, that has nothing to do with Kelli. I'm sorry if I've given you the wrong impression—which I apparently have—but Kelli and I are fine—"

Jules broke off as she looked over Carrie's shoulder to where her eye had been caught by movement in the parking lot. Kelli was standing there with a large bag that Jules recognized as being from a local sandwich shop, stopped in mid-stride as she spied Jules and Carrie at the picnic table. She spun on her heel and headed back to the Tahoe.

"Kelli!" Jules called, but Kelli kept walking. Jules sprinted to the parking lot in time to see the Tahoe speed away.

Jules stood there, grinding her teeth, as Carrie came up beside her and laid a hand on her shoulder.

"You can call me if you need to talk about the relationship that's fine," Carrie said.

She walked on to where she had parked her car, turning for one more lingering glance in Jules's direction before getting in and starting the engine.

Jules went back to the building, cursing under her breath, nearly knocking over the assistant superintendent as she yanked the door open and charged through.

"Sorry," she mumbled, going back to her cubicle where she had to put Carrie's chair back into the neighboring space before throwing herself into her own chair.

"Damn, damn, damn," she muttered. She knew better than to think Kelli would answer the phone. She pulled out her cell phone and texted, *Kelli, that was not what it looked like. I can't talk now. I'll see you after work.*

Jules ran most of the way home from school. Hobie was off doing his paper route—"I'll get a real job when I turn sixteen," he kept saying, but for now, the paper route was easy money. Sometimes, Jules wished she'd thought of the paper route first, but she knew Hobie and his mom needed the money. She ran through the back door, letting the screen door bang shut behind her.

"How many times—" Mae started to scold her, but "sorry," Jules interrupted, tossing her book bag up the stairs to her room and heading out into the backyard with Friday who was dancing and jumping in her excitement that Jules was finally home. They played a little tug of war with a scrap of rope, Friday growling with feigned ferocity as she yanked on the rope. Jules let her win after a couple of minutes, and, together, they headed off to roam until dinnertime.

"Before high school, I used to like school," Jules said aloud to Friday as they walked down the sidewalk together, Jules's hand trailing along Friday's back. Friday glanced back at her as she listened. Jules didn't like to think about Tammy Dearing and that stupid poem—"why did I write it?" she'd asked herself over and over again. She wasn't sure Tammy had ever told anyone about that, but everyone seemed to know that she wasn't talking to Jules anymore, and, since Tammy was pretty and popular, that meant none of the other girls talked to Jules, either. She told herself they were stupid and it didn't matter anyway, but it always felt weird when everyone else in a class was talking about going to the football or basketball games and no one cared if she was coming or not.

Sometimes, she and Hobie went together to the home games, but Hobie didn't like sports and was soon bored, wishing he was home with a book. She never played ball with Joey Reynolds or his gang of boys anymore—not since she'd rescued Friday from their fireworks. Joey didn't mess with her, but he wouldn't talk to her, either. She'd thought about going out for track when spring came—she was a fast runner—but it would have meant having to travel with the team on the bus for away meets and she didn't want to have to face being left all by herself while the other team members were all chummy with each other.

"It's okay to be alone when it's your idea," Hobie had said knowingly more than once. "It feels different when it's not your idea."

"Who cares," Jules said now, reaching lower to dig her fingers into the fur at the scruff of Friday's neck, the place she liked to be scratched. "I have you and Hobie. I don't need anyone else."

She hadn't paid attention to where she was walking. She knew all the streets for blocks around and wasn't worried about getting lost. She glanced down a side street as she walked and stopped abruptly. Pappy's Dodge Dart was parked there.

"Come on," Jules said to Friday, and they turned down the street. She peered into the car. It was empty. She looked around, but there was no sign of him. "Let's find Pappy," she said, and the German shepherd, seeming to understand, lowered her nose to the ground and began following a scent trail. Together, they wandered back behind a house into a copse of trees that sat between the houses on this street and a neighboring farm. There, in the narrow stretch of woods, stood Pappy, looking around.

"Pappy," Jules called out, running over to him.

He looked down and seemed surprised to see her. "Jules," he said.

"What are you doing here?" she asked.

"Oh, nothing," he said.

She took his hand. "Well, let's go home."

He blinked down at her and nodded. "Yeah. We should get home to your grandmother. Lead the way."

Jules walked back to the car with him.

"You want to drive us home?" Pappy asked.

Jules's eyes got big as saucers. "You mean it?"

"You'll be driving soon enough," he said. "Might as well start giving you lessons."

Jules slid in behind the wheel, and Pappy adjusted the seat for her. He showed her how to use the turn signals and made sure she could reach the brake and gas pedals all right.

"You take the shortest way home, hear?" Pappy said. "We could get in trouble for this."

Jules turned the ignition and pulled down on the shift lever on the steering column. She let the car ease itself forward as she'd watched Pappy do a million times.

"You're a natural," Pappy said with a proud grin. "Which way you gonna go?"

Jules put the left turn signal on at the intersection and turned the corner. Within a couple of minutes, they were home.

"That was well-done," Pappy said as Jules jerked the Dart to a stop in the driveway and turned the ignition off. "Best we keep this our secret."

Jules nodded, her cheeks aglow. "Our secret."

The air conditioning unit on the side of the house was whirring when Jules got home from work, but she knew the chill waiting for her inside would not be from the AC. She found Kelli at work in her studio, bent over her wheel, her blonde hair hanging forward, curtaining her face from Jules's gaze.

She sat down on the deacon's bench, waiting. The cats, seeming to sense the tension in the room, meowed a couple of times and then left. When Kelli kept working with no sign that she even knew Jules was sitting there, Jules cleared her throat and said, "We need to talk. Since you're in the middle of a piece, I'll start and you can just listen."

Kelli gave no indication she had heard.

Jules braced herself and said, "Carrie came by unannounced today. I had no idea she was going to do that. I got busy the last week of school, and we never got to finish our counseling of the boy we were working with."

The pottery wheel kept spinning. Barely audible over the hum of the motor came Kelli's voice mumbling something.

"Sorry, what?" Jules said.

Kelli sat up at last, her expression stony. "And she missed you so much, she just had to come by and see you."

A hot flush crept up Jules's neck to her cheeks. "It's not like that—"

"Don't!" Kelli's head jerked up as she stopped the wheel. "Don't insult me. Don't pretend you don't see how she flirts with you and that you've been enjoying it. I've tried to ignore that. A little flirting can be good for anyone's ego. But don't try to pretend she doesn't want there to be something more."

She watched Jules's face, her eyes hard as she waited for a response.

Jules's shoulders slumped a little. "Okay, she does want more. She thinks—it doesn't matter what she thinks. I set her straight today."

"Did you?" Kelli asked, clearly not believing this.

"Yes," Jules said, though her conscience squirmed a little as she remembered Carrie's parting words. "I told her that I was sorry if I'd given her the wrong impression, but that you and I are fine."

Kelli looked down at her clay-caked fingers and picked up a wet rag to wipe some of the clay off of her fingernails.

"We are okay, aren't we?" Jules asked.

"I don't know, Jules. Are we?" Kelli asked in a dangerously quiet voice, and Jules suddenly wished she would yell or throw something. "I've told Donna that this isn't going to—"

"What do you mean, you've told Donna?" Jules cut in. "What are you doing talking to Donna?"

Kelli threw the rag down. "I needed to talk to someone who would actually talk back," she retorted. "And since you won't..." She paused and took a deep breath. "I don't want us to turn out like you and Donna or you and Stacy did," she said slowly, as if giving Jules time for the weight of her words to sink in. "But I'm not going to let myself be tossed aside while you fuck around with someone else."

Jules's temper flared at once. "Is this some kind of ultimatum? Bringing my failed relationships up to bring me to heel, teach me some kind of lesson?"

Kelli's expression became "pitying," Jules would realize with a shock when she thought about this conversation later, and she said, "I'm not giving you an ultimatum. I'm trying to tell you that I love you, and I want us to survive this... this whatever it is that's going on with you. But I can't do it alone. If we are going to get through this, you have to help."

Kelli got up and came to Jules. She stood before her for a moment and then leaned down and murmured, "Don't do this to us." She kissed Jules on the cheek and left her sitting there.

CHAPTER 24

"Why didn't you eat lunch with me today? Over."

Jules sat listening to the static on her walkie-talkie, waiting for Hobie to answer. They didn't use the walkie-talkies as much now, not as they used to when they were little. She didn't even know if Hobie had his turned on.

She went to her window, looking down at Hobie's house. "Are you there? Over."

Finally, "I'm here," Hobie said.

"What's wrong?" Jules asked. "Where've you been all day?"

They were in their first week of their sophomore year at school. So far, Jules's had been okay. To her immense relief, she wasn't in any classes with Tammy Dearing this year, and Tammy seemed to have decided that ignoring Jules when passing her in the hallway was the appropriate thing to do. But Jules couldn't help noticing that Tammy was even prettier this year.

She and Hobie only had British literature together this semester—"you have to take British lit," Hobie had said. "They do Macbeth and the classics. You can't miss this." So, Jules had grudgingly signed up for British lit. But with their separate schedules, the only other time they saw each other was at lunch, and today, Hobie hadn't shown up.

"I left school this morning," Hobie said in a hushed voice.

"Why?"

Nothing but static.

"Was it Joey and those guys again?"

"No."

Jules waited.

"It was the older guys," Hobie said.

Something in his tone scared Jules. "What did they do?"

"I... I can't tell you," he said.

"Hobie," Jules sank to her knees by her window, "you can tell me anything." Friday leaned against her, whining.

There was another long, static-filled silence before Hobie said, "They peed on me. Called me... called me stuff."

"But why?"

Hobie was crying now. "I don't know. I didn't do anything to them. I never do anything." He cried harder. "I had to come home and clean up while my mom was at work. I told her I was sick."

Jules pounded her fist on the windowsill. "You have to tell her. Let her go to the principal or—"

"No! I can't tell her," Hobie said frantically. "And you can't tell anyone, either. Promise me."

He sounded so desperate, so scared. "I promise," Jules said.

They sat in silence again for long minutes until Hobie seemed calmer.

"What are you doing now?" Jules asked.

"I'm writing," Hobie said, and he sounded angry.

"Writing what?"

"I'll make them sorry someday," he said. "When I'm a famous writer and they're still here, working at the mill like the losers they are."

Jules had never heard him talk like this. "Are you okay?" she asked, wrapping an arm around Friday and pulling her close.

"I gotta go," Hobie said.

"Okay. Over and out." Jules waited for an answer, but there was none.

<hr />

Jules paused the lawn mower, lifting the hem of her T-shirt to wipe the sweat out of her eyes. Gnats buzzed in her ears and tickled her as they tried to fly up her nose or into her eyes. Swatting them away futilely, she pulled the bill of her baseball cap lower and got the mower moving again. She was on the second day of a one-week vacation—"some vacation," she muttered as she pushed the mower through the overgrown yard. She immediately spit out a few gnats, mentally reminding herself to keep her mouth shut and not talk out loud to herself. Every July, she told herself she should have taken some time off in May before the heat and humidity picked up. And every May, she was too busy to take any time off.

She finished mowing and dumped the grass clippings onto the compost pile at the back of the yard, turning next to the shrubs, which were in desperate need of trimming. She had decided to push through one miserable day of yard chores while Kelli was at work and try to get all these overdue things done.

She felt as if she was walking on thin ice these past couple of weeks since the clash over Carrie's unwelcome visit. She had deliberately not replied to Carrie's continued e-mails and had deleted the voice mails Carrie had left on her cell phone. *She's got to get the hint at some point.*

Kelli hadn't been giving Jules the silent treatment and wasn't overtly punishing her, but she was cool, aloof. Physically, there had been nothing more between them than a peck upon leaving for work and no contact in bed at night. Jules knew she had some rebuilding and repairing to do.

"It is different this time," she kept insisting to herself. "I'm different. I wouldn't have done this before." She didn't want to remember too clearly what she had thought and felt before, what she had done—"or not done would be more like it"—with Donna and then Stacy. She tried to focus only on here and now.

Unfortunately, Ronnie's messages were making that difficult, as she'd started asking questions about Hobie.

You knew him, she says, Ronnie wrote. *What happened? What was he like? Why doesn't she talk about him?*

Jules replied in vague terms, never really answering her questions. "This was not what I had in mind when I asked Mae to help," she grumbled as she stuffed boxwood branches into a trash barrel. "Why the hell did I get involved in the first place?" She shook her head in disgust as she thought back—almost a year, she realized—to the day she'd found that stupid note slipped under the door of the bathroom stall.

She snipped angrily at the hedge. None of this was Ronnie's fault; she knew that, but still... She stopped with the hedge clippers and stood, staring off into space. It had all started with Pappy's funeral—no, *it started way before that.*

"You should come home and see him," Mae had said over the phone months earlier.

"What for?" Jules asked. "To watch him lie in bed like a vegetable? He was like that on my last visit to Aldie. I don't want to remember him like that."

"To talk to him," Mae said. "The doctors say he probably hears us, even if he can't show it. And they say he doesn't have long. You should come home. He loved you, you know."

But Jules had resisted, coming up with multiple excuses as to why she couldn't come back to Aldie to see Pappy in the nursing home, until, "he's gone," Mae had said one day last summer. "The funeral will be next week. You will be here for that, won't you?"

Jules had known her homecoming would be greeted by a disapproving chill. "I'll pay for this for a long time," Jules had said to Kelli as she packed. "But it's not like it'll feel any different from the way she usually is."

Jules hauled the barrel full of hedge clippings to the curb for pickup the next day, remembering how Kelli had cautioned her then, "You know she's hurting and vulnerable now." Jules had snorted, but Kelli insisted, "You are all the family she has left. Just be there for her."

"It's not her that's kept me out of Aldie," Jules had almost said that day. *Would it have made any difference if I'd told her then?* she wondered now as she hung the clippers back up and scraped all the clumped-up grass from the underside of the mower before wheeling it into the shed. She pulled some thick gardening gloves off one of the shelves and went to tackle the ivy that was creeping through the fence from the neighbor's yard again.

She yanked on the long strands that had woven themselves through the chain link. A few startled spiders scurried away from the unexpected commotion, some of them running up Jules's arms. Calmly, she blew them off and continued pulling.

"I almost told her the night her mom was diagnosed," Jules recalled. God, that seemed so long ago, but it wasn't. *Something always seems to happen whenever this starts to get close enough to the surface to talk about it,* she thought. *Maybe it's supposed to stay buried, where it belongs.* She paused, her eyes closed tightly for a moment, before she reached for another vine.

"Bad choice of words," she muttered.

———◆———

Kelli lay in the dark, listening to the soft sounds of Jules's breathing beside her. Gently, she reached out and laid her hand on Jules's back, feeling her warmth, her nearness. Tears stung her eyes as she lay there.

The first thing Kelli had noticed when she got home earlier that evening was that the grass had been mown and edged along the sidewalk and driveway. She took a moment to peer into the backyard before she went into the house. She smiled as she looked around.

"You got a lot done today," she'd said as she entered the kitchen through the garage.

Jules turned to her from the counter, where she was making a salad. "Hi," she said, her hands full of lettuce she was ripping apart.

"And you got sunburned," Kelli added, looking at Jules's neck and her arms. She came to her and ran her hands over Jules's arms. "Does it hurt?"

Jules shrugged. "Just stings a little. Forgot to put sunscreen on. And I'm still blowing gnats out of my nose."

Kelli's eyebrows rose. "That's a pleasant image. Thanks." She pulled Jules into an embrace and murmured, "Thank you. For everything you've been doing lately."

Jules buried her face into Kelli's neck and held her tightly, her fists still full of lettuce.

"Are you okay?" Kelli asked.

Jules nodded. "Just hold me."

Kelli wrapped her arms more tightly around Jules, and they stood like that as the cats came in and began twisting themselves sinuously around their ankles.

"Are you okay?" Kelli repeated.

Jules sniffed and pulled back. "I'm fine. I've just missed you."

Kelli laid a hand tenderly on Jules's cheek. "I've missed you, too."

Jules looked into her eyes for a long moment. "Go shower," she said at last. "I've almost got dinner ready. I'll feed the felines so we can eat in peace."

Kelli gave her a light kiss on the lips. "I'll be down in a few minutes."

She was back in a short while, fresh-smelling and hungry. "I'm starving," she said. "This looks wonderful."

They filled their plates and went to the table, where Kelli reached for Jules's hand. "Thanks again."

Jules raised Kelli's hand to her lips. "You're welcome."

They ate and talked about nothing important. Jules filled Kelli in on the yard work she'd tackled, and Kelli complained about the new chief of the nursing service, who was making life unpleasant for everyone. After dinner, they took glasses of iced tea outside to enjoy the evening cool-down in their backyard.

Sitting side by side in their Adirondack chairs, Kelli breathed in the scent of freshly mown grass and reached again for Jules's hand. "Have you heard from Carrie?"

She could feel Jules stiffen slightly. "No," Jules said. "Well, she's e-mailed and left voice messages, but I haven't responded."

"Why not?"

Jules hesitated. "I just haven't wanted to talk to her."

"You didn't have any trouble talking to her before," Kelli said in a carefully casual tone.

"That was before she started—" Jules paused for a moment. "She thinks we're not happy together or rather that I'm not happy with you."

Kelli turned to her. "Why would she think that?"

Jules forced herself to meet Kelli's gaze. "I honestly don't know. I haven't said one word about being unhappy in this relationship. She was asking a lot of questions about my past, and I told her a bit about growing up with Pappy and Mae and..." Jules turned back to the yard. "I don't know if she picked up on anything there and assumed it had to do with you. I'm not sure."

The silence between them was tense and thick with apprehension.

"Jules—" Kelli began, but at the same moment, Jules blurted out, "My best friend died."

"Wait, what?" Kelli said, not certain she'd heard correctly.

Jules pulled her hand free and sat forward on her chair, her elbows on her knees as she stared into her tea. "When I lived in Aldie, my best friend, Hobie Fahnestock, died."

Kelli took this in. "Fahnestock? Isn't that the name of the woman Ronnie is staying with, next door to your grandmother? The one you took some food over to?"

Jules nodded. "He and his mom moved in next to us when Hobie and I were in third grade. We were inseparable, until... we were in high school when he died."

"What happened?" Kelli asked gently.

The muscles in Jules's jaw clenched as she replied, "He drowned." Kelli was about to ask more questions when Jules sat back and said, "Anyway, I guess my visit to Aldie for Pappy's funeral got a lot of those old memories stirred up."

Kelli reached for Jules's hand again, and Jules grasped it briefly but then let go. "Why didn't you tell me this before?" Kelli asked, feeling an immense mix of sorrow and relief at finally knowing what was at the root of Jules's distance since last summer.

"I almost did," Jules said. "I planned to the night I came home and you told me about your mom's diagnosis. I couldn't tell you then, and after that, the next months were all crazy with you and Mary Anne helping your folks, and... something just always came up."

Kelli watched Jules's face closely as she stared fixedly out across the lawn. "You never told Donna or Stacy about this, did you?"

Jules shook her head jerkily. "I've never talked about it to anyone."

"Thank you for telling me," Kelli said.

Kelli lay in bed now, her hand still resting against Jules's back, feeling the rise and fall of her breathing. *I know what the monster is now. Together, we can deal with it.*

CHAPTER 25

I met someone! I noticed her hanging out in the library, and last week we were both looking for books in the fantasy section and reached for the same book at the same time. Her name is Ariel—like the Little Mermaid, only she says it's a Hebrew name. Isn't it beautiful? She is. She has blonde hair that's kind of curly, and her eyes laugh. She said she noticed me in the library. She noticed me!!! Can you believe anyone that beautiful would notice me? We got to talking about books and movies and school and everything. She and her family just moved to Aldie (not sure why anyone would move TO Aldie, but I'm glad she did!). She comes to the diner sometimes, but I hate for her to see me in my dorky hairnet, so I try to hide in the back when I know she's there. I know sooner or later, all the crap about my family and why I'm living with Mrs. Fahnestock will come up, but for now, we mostly meet at the library or get ice cream at the diner when I get off. Maybe I'll ask her to go to the movies with me this weekend. I'm so psyched. It's the first time

*I've ever felt like this about anyone. I'll keep you
posted. Hi to Kelli.*

Love,
Ronnie

Jules read this message over a few times, smiling a little
bitterly. She could remember the thrill of feeling the way
Ronnie was feeling right now, but she could also remember
how horrible it felt when it all came crashing down. *You
can't spare her from that,* she told herself. *It's something we all
have to go through.*

Upstairs, she heard Kelli emerge from the shower, and
a moment later, the hair dryer started up. She closed her
laptop and went to get her own shower. She gave Kelli's
naked rump a pat as she padded through the bathroom and
turned the hot water on.

"I'm excited about today," Kelli said, watching in the
mirror as Jules stepped into the shower.

"I'm so glad," Jules said wryly.

"Aren't you?" Kelli asked, running a brush through her
hair.

"I'm glad to be spending the day with you," Jules said.
"Spending part of my vacation going to a junk yard with
Elaine, not really."

"It isn't a junk yard," Kelli said. "It's a salvage warehouse.
Black Dog is huge. Wait and see. It's going to be so cool.
We're going to be sorry we didn't go with a bigger vehicle."

"And a bigger wallet," said Jules as the water ran over
her head. She started spitting and coughing. "No more
talking. Shampoo in mouth."

Kelli laughed as she went to get dressed.

Not long after, a horn beeped from out front.

"Ready?" Kelli called. "They're here."

Jules came running down the stairs, tugging a polo shirt over her head, her wet hair already pulled back into its ponytail. "All set."

They locked the door and went to join Elaine and Donna in the large cargo van Elaine had rented for their trip. The back was stacked with moving blankets, old towels, and rugs to pad whatever treasures Elaine managed to find to bring back for her shop.

"Everyone buckled in?" Donna asked as she put the van in gear.

Elaine pointed out the cooler sitting on the floor. "I packed us some cold drinks and snacks for the road. I really appreciate your help on this trip."

"We're looking forward to it," Kelli said. "I haven't been to Roanoke for ages." She reached for the cooler and pulled out a bottle of orange juice, handing it to Jules. She took a V8 for herself and settled back in her seat.

Jules glanced up and caught Donna watching her in the rearview mirror. She quickly looked away. They hadn't spoken since Kelli had let slip that she had been talking to Donna. Jules wasn't sure how to feel about that. Her initial instinct had been to be angry, but she kept reminding herself that Kelli had to talk to someone. And Donna knew her better than anyone, so it seemed natural that Kelli would have turned to her, but it was still weird, having her partner talking to her ex about their relationship.

She only half-listened to Elaine talking about some design project she was currently working on and what she hoped to find at the salvage yard. Jules's thoughts roamed as the others' voices droned on in the background. She smiled again—not so bitterly this time—as she thought about Ronnie's message and tried to remember what that blush of first love felt like, those early days when it was private and felt sacred, when it kept you up for hours at night, unable to sleep for the excitement of thinking and daydreaming about her, the ecstasy of reading her notes or hearing her voice... until one day, it wasn't any of those things.

"Hey."

Jules looked around to see Hobie standing next to her at her locker. "Hi," she said. She looked at him more closely. His face was flushed, his eyes bright. Her first thought was that something had happened again. She knew Hobie had basically stopped drinking anything all day long so he wouldn't have to use the bathroom while he was at school.

"I need to talk to you," he said in an urgent voice. "Tonight. After dinner. Meet me out back, okay?"

"Okay," said Jules, perplexed.

"See you." He hurried off for his next class.

Impatiently, Jules got through the rest of the day and wolfed down her dinner. She hurriedly did the dishes, almost pulling the plates out from under Mae and Pappy in her haste to finish her chores and get outside.

"What in the world is wrong with you?" Mae asked.

"Nothing," Jules said. "Just want to play with Friday some before bedtime."

She opened the screen door, and she and Friday went outside as she tugged a sweatshirt over her head to ward off the autumn chill. Friday promptly flushed a rabbit and chased it to the dump road before trotting proudly back to Jules, who had seated herself under the oak tree, where she and Hobie used to plan their futures together. She didn't have to wait long before Hobie emerged from the dusk and sat beside her.

"What's up?" Jules asked.

"I was talking to some people," he said, that urgent tone still in his voice. "And they were—"

"What people?"

"Just some people, guys I see sometimes in different parts of town on my paper route," Hobie said. "Anyway, they were telling me about this place."

He paused, looking scared to continue.

"What place?" she asked.

"A place where people like us go to hang out," he said breathlessly. "A place all our own. Where we don't have to worry about being beaten up or having people think we're... you know."

Jules stared at him in the gathering gloom. "What are you talking about? What do you mean, 'people like us'?"

Hobie looked at her, and there was just enough lingering daylight for her to make out the pitying expression on his face. "Just come with me," he said. "You'll see. Once we're there, you'll understand."

Jules's mouth hung open for a moment. "Go where? This is crazy!" she said, but Hobie wasn't listening.

"They're there every weekend, if the weather's good," he said. "I'm going this Saturday. Let's go together. But you probably shouldn't bring Friday. We'll tell my mom and your grandparents we're going to the movies so we can be out later." He seemed to have given this plan a great deal of thought, but Jules was still confused. "Just come," he repeated. "You'll see."

Saturday evening found them wandering to the cemetery.

"What are we doing here?" Jules asked. The cemetery hill was a good place to sled in winter, but why were they there in October?

Hobie didn't answer but led the way around the far side of the hill, the side above the river. There, worn into the hillside, was a footpath Jules had never noticed. The path was a little treacherous as it zigzagged down the bluff toward the river to a place where a group of people had congregated around a campfire. There were maybe seven or eight people, mostly guys, just two other girls. Two of the guys stood up to greet Hobie and made room for him and Jules on a log pulled up near the fire. The people gathered there exchanged first names, and the two girls introduced themselves as Vicki and Barb. Jules recognized them as seniors at school but had never spoken to them. Most of the guys' names she immediately forgot. Someone had brought beer, and they offered some to Jules and Hobie. They each accepted a can. Jules had never tasted beer, as Mae didn't allow any alcohol in the house, and she was sure Hobie had never had any. She took a taste and couldn't suppress the shudder as the bitter liquid slid down her throat. Hobie made a better show than she did of liking it, but she noticed he took only tiny sips as they sat and listened to the others talking. Hobie's face was flushed again, and Jules could tell he was hanging on to every word the others said. They all seemed to know one another well, but Jules couldn't tell how they knew each other. She stared at the fire, mesmerized by the flames dancing in the evening breeze as she listened to the sounds of the river swirling in the brush dams below them. There was movement on the other side of the fire, and she realized the two girls had gotten up and moved deeper into the shadows, away from the circle of light cast by the fire.

With a shock that nearly choked her as she took another sip of her beer, she realized the girls were kissing—each other. Looking around again, she realized other twosomes had similarly moved off into the darkness, where their shadows could be seen, no longer individual shadows, but undulating shapes melted together in the night. Jules sat there, her heart hammering in her chest as she tried not to stare, but... she knew. This was what she would have liked to have done with Tammy Dearing. She'd never been able to put words to those feelings before, not until this very moment.

Soon, only she, Hobie, and one other guy were left sitting by the fire. Far from looking uncomfortable, Hobie leaned toward the other boy—Lawrence, Jules remembered someone had called him—and said, "You guys are here every weekend?"

Lawrence nodded. "Yeah. You can come alone or bring someone." His eyes flickered curiously in Jules's direction. "We don't care, as long as you don't tell. You have to swear never to tell."

"We do," Hobie said quickly, speaking for both of them. Jules sat there, not saying anything and trying to ignore the writhing shadows around them. She didn't know where to look, so she stared at the fire.

"We should get home," she muttered to Hobie after what seemed like a long while.

"Yeah, okay," he said reluctantly. "But we'll be back."

"So, how's your summer?" Donna asked as they wandered through a forest of porch columns and stack upon stack of old wooden doors. Kelli and Elaine had detoured off toward the cast-iron fences and gates.

"Just peachy," said Jules.

Donna must have heard the chill in Jules's voice because she said, "Kelli told you we've talked."

Always direct, Jules thought. It had been something she hadn't appreciated about Donna until she was with Stacy, who was anything but.

"Yes," Jules said. "She told me." She paused, pretending to look at the detail in a carved fireplace mantel. "What exactly did you tell her?"

"It wasn't like that," Donna said. "She said you were becoming more distant after Pappy's funeral—something I asked you about a few times, if you recall. And then, when Carrie came into the picture..."

Jules flushed, still not looking at Donna.

"She asked to know more about how we ended," Donna continued, and Jules could hear the tightness in her voice.

"Why?" Jules asked, turning to look directly at Donna now.

Donna searched her eyes for a long moment. "She needed to know if the pattern was repeating itself."

Jules blinked and looked away again.

"Is it?" Donna asked.

"No," Jules said firmly. "It isn't."

She walked on, Donna following.

"I'm glad," Donna said when she caught up. "I told Kelli I thought she was good for you. Better than Stacy by far, and... better than I was, all those years ago."

Jules stopped short at this admission. "It wasn't you," she said in a low voice. "It was never you."

"What are you doing over there?" Elaine called out. "I need you to come and see what I found."

Elaine's find turned out to be a set of rusted finials off of some city's dismantled street lamps. "They'll make a wonderful border along a garden path," she said.

"They're filthy." Jules looked at the rust on her hands after testing the weight of one of them.

"They're weathered," Elaine said. "They have a beautiful patina."

"They're rusty hunks of metal," Jules muttered in an undertone to Kelli and Donna. Elaine, if she heard, chose to ignore Jules's comment.

Elaine negotiated a price, and soon, all four women— "no, not four, only three," Jules pointed out as Elaine managed to be busy elsewhere while the other three loaded the finials, some porch columns, and a disassembled railing with a full set of stairwell balusters into the cargo van.

"Look what else I found," Elaine said, hurrying to the van with a round side table. "The top was a wooden gear from an old mill."

She loaded the table into the back of the van, and they pulled out of Roanoke.

"Let's go back on Route 11," Elaine said. "We'll eat at some quaint eatery, my treat, and maybe check out some more antique shops on the way."

Jules suppressed a groan, feeling that she should have known this would end up turning into an all-day event. Kelli reached over and squeezed her hand. They stopped in Troutville at a small diner.

"This wasn't exactly what I had in mind." Elaine looked at the pickup trucks gathered around the place.

"I'm not sure what else you thought you'd run into along 11," Donna said. "But this is about as quaint as we're going to get. Come on. With this many trucks parked here, the food is probably good."

"At least we'll be able to pronounce everything on the menu," Jules whispered to Kelli, who elbowed her.

They were seated at a table in the middle of the restaurant. Like Sandy's, back in Aldie—*probably like every diner, everywhere*, Jules thought—there was a counter, filled with local men who all seemed to know each other. The four women were looking their menus over when an old man came in, looking around a little confusedly. Jules watched him.

"Hey there, Andy," said one of the men at the counter. "Come on over and take a load off." He beckoned to Andy, who shuffled over and took the seat next to the other man.

Jules's attention was pulled back to the menu in front of her when their waitress came back to take their order. "Um," she stalled, looking over the specials, "I'll have an open-face turkey sandwich, with mashed potatoes and gravy."

Kelli exhaled next to her, and Jules grinned as Kelli placed an order for a grilled-chicken salad.

"My turkey sandwich is going to taste a lot better than the white iceberg lettuce you're going to get in that salad," she said in a low voice so the waitress wouldn't hear.

When the waitress had taken all their orders and brought their drinks, Elaine raised her plastic cup. "To a successful trip. Thank you all so much."

As they sipped their drinks, waiting for their food, a harassed-looking woman came in, hair escaping from her ponytail, face glistening with sweat, a baggy T-shirt hanging nearly lower than her cut-off shorts.

"There you are, Grampa," she said, clearly exasperated. "We been lookin' everywhere for you."

She walked over to where Andy was seated at the counter. "Ernie, you know he don't know where he is half the time anymore. He wanders off an' then can't remember how to get home."

"We was just havin' a bite to eat, Sarah," said Ernie. "Then I woulda took him home."

"And how was you plannin' to get his truck home?" Sarah asked.

"You mean he drove here?" Ernie asked.

"Yes, he did," she said, while Andy sat there with a pleased smile on his face. "Come on, Grampa. Let's go home."

Elaine leaned across the table. "No secrets in a place like this," she said as Jules watched Sarah take her grandfather by the arm and lead him from the diner to a waiting car outside.

"Are you okay?"

Jules started and realized Donna had been watching her closely.

"Yup," she said, taking a sip of her drink.

"Did that remind you of Pappy?" Kelli asked.

Jules nodded. "He was like that for a long time. Years. I'd find him lost somewhere in our neighborhood or downtown. He'd pretend he meant to stop wherever he was, but I knew after a while that he couldn't remember how to get home." She swirled her Coke in her cup. "One day, when I was in college, the state police called. He'd driven all the way to Columbus from the mill and didn't know where he was. That was when he had to retire and stay home, where Mae could keep an eye on him."

"When did he go into a nursing home?" Donna asked.

Jules narrowed her eyes as she thought back. "A few years ago. He'd been fine, confused at times, but content to be home, puttering around in the garage or the garden. But then, all of a sudden, he just went blank. Almost catatonic. I didn't know Alzheimer's could do that. Mae tried to take care of him, but she couldn't handle him at home anymore. She had to put him in a nursing home then."

There was silence at the table for a long moment, and then Elaine said, "Well, this is a depressing conversation. Oh, look. Here's our food."

Jules half-listened to Elaine's chatter as they ate, but she kept glancing toward Ernie and the empty seat beside him, feeling as if it were Pappy who had shuffled in for a visit.

CHAPTER 26

MOONLIGHT STREAMED IN THROUGH the slats of the plantation shutters on the windows as Jules lay awake. Next to her, Kelli and the two cats were sleeping, small snuffles and snorts coming from all three of them. Carefully, she eased out of bed, trying not to disturb anyone. She padded across the room and went down the hall to the spare room, where she placed her night-light on the floor and sat with her back against the bed as she clicked it on.

Her mind had been filled with thoughts of Pappy for the past couple of days, ever since they got back from that damned trip to Roanoke. The one-year anniversary of his death was coming soon—*you knew this was going to hit at some point*—but, psychologically, she realized that the scene at the diner was the thing that had dredged up all these feelings and memories. *All it needed was a trigger.*

"There's my girl," Pappy had said during one of Jules's visits back to Aldie when she was in grad school. He was sitting in his chair by the garage, puffing on his pipe. "There's my Joanie."

"No, Pappy. It's Jules," she'd said. "Jules, not Joan."

He'd blinked at her, his blue eyes no longer twinkling with laughter, but watery and unfocused much of the time. His large hands, once so strong and deft, trembled now, and he dropped things. Mae had taken to giving him only plastic plates and cups as so much of their china had been broken.

"Jules?" He shook his head a little as if trying to clear it.

"Yes," she said, taking his hand. "Your granddaughter. Joan's daughter."

He smiled. "Oh, yes. Jules. Where are we going to fly off to today?"

Jules's eyes filled with tears now as she twirled her light to the geese scene. "There were so many places we were going to go," she whispered. "So many things we never got to do—"

—*because you took off and never looked back,* said a small voice.

Jules closed her eyes. "I had to. I couldn't stay, not after..."

She pulled a pillow off the bed and lay down on the carpeted floor, staring at the copper geese....

"Hey, wake up."

Jules started awake to find Kelli kneeling next to her, shaking her gently.

"Have you been in here all night?" Kelli asked.

Jules rubbed her eyes and sat up. "Oh," she groaned, stretching stiffly. "I am getting too old for sleeping on floors."

"You were right next to a bed," Kelli said drolly, extending a hand to pull her to her feet.

"I know." Jules wrapped her arms around her and let Kelli's warmth soak into her like a tonic.

"You okay?" Kelli asked.

Jules nodded into Kelli's neck.

"Well, speaking of getting old," Kelli said. "What do you want to do for your birthday next week? Want to go to Aldie?"

"No," Jules said emphatically. "Maybe go to Williamsburg for an overnight?"

"Sure," Kelli said. "We could do that. I'm going to go down and make coffee, and we can talk about it."

"Okay. I'll be down in a minute," Jules said, heading to the bathroom.

When she got downstairs, coffee was brewing and eggs were frying.

"Could you make toast?" Kelli pointed to the loaf of bread next to the toaster. "I told Mary Anne I'd go with her to take the kids to the pool today." She flipped the eggs. "You want to go?"

"This is my last day of vacation, and I don't want to spend it with kids," Jules said, waiting for the toaster to pop. "So, no thank you. How are they doing?"

Kelli slid the eggs onto plates. "Okay. Brian tries to do the weekend thing, but the kids are involved in so many sports now, he and Mary Anne still end up sitting together at their games and practices." Jules buttered the toast as Kelli continued, "They really should keep working on their marriage. I know they had problems, but it seems crazy for them to split."

Jules brought the toast to the table and sat. "Sometimes, one person is just over it. By the time they admit there's a problem, one is already emotionally gone."

Kelli glanced up at her sharply. "Are we still talking about my sister?"

"Yes," Jules said, meeting her gaze. "We are still talking about your sister."

Clearly not reassured, Kelli said, "But that's how you were; that's the point you got to with Donna and Stacy, isn't it?"

Jules set her fork down. "God, how many times do we have to go through this? Yes. That's where I was with them. It doesn't mean that's where I am now."

Kelli poked her egg yolk with her fork. "Then why were you in the spare room staring at that light?" she asked quietly.

Jules blinked rapidly, dunking her toast in her egg yolk. "It has nothing to do with us."

Kelli, watching her closely, said, "It was that old man in the diner, wasn't it?"

Jules dropped her head to her hand, rubbing her forehead as if trying to wipe away the memories. "I should have gone to see him more when I could," she said, her voice cracking.

Kelli reached for her hand. "Why didn't you?" she asked.

It was several seconds before Jules could say, "I couldn't. I just couldn't go back."

"I don't understand," Kelli said carefully. "Did he do something? Did you two have a fight?"

"No," said Jules. "It was nothing like that. It was—" but she couldn't say what it was.

"You could go see Mae," Kelli said. "While you still can."

Jules sat back and exhaled forcefully. "Maybe. I'll think about it." She reached for the television remote and clicked it onto the weather. "You'd better enjoy the pool while you can," she said. "It looks like that line of storms coming through the Midwest will be here tonight or tomorrow."

Kelli watched Jules for a moment. When Jules's silence signaled an end to the conversation, she finished her eggs and said, "All right. I'll be with Mary Anne and the kids through mid-afternoon. I'll be home in time for dinner."

———⊷⧓⊶———

Storm clouds blotted the daylight so completely that it seemed night had fallen hours early. Rain slashed at the windshield, and, even with the wipers on high, Jules could barely see twenty feet in front of her. She passed car after car that had pulled off to the side of the highway, waiting for the storm to pass, but she kept going, leaning forward, eyes straining as she tried to see ahead of her. Forty was as fast as she dared go as water sheeted over the asphalt on I-64, causing her Subaru to hydroplane briefly. Lightning forked through the sky, seemingly mere yards away, with such an explosion of thunder that the entire car vibrated with the sound.

"Shit!" Jules exclaimed as her heart leapt in her chest.

She passed a sign telling her that she was ten miles from Beckley. Not daring to take her eyes from the road, she picked her phone up and lifted it to the steering wheel, glancing again at the screen. Nothing. No bars and no calls. She dropped the phone back into the empty drink holder. Even if Kelli had received the messages she'd left, she couldn't get through now.

She quickly checked the clock on the dashboard. How could it be only two o'clock? It seemed hours and hours ago that Mae had called in a panic.

"Ronnie ran away," she said with no preamble when Jules answered.

"What do you mean, she ran away?" Jules asked. "What happened?"

She could hear crying in the background and knew Bertha Fahnestock must be there.

"Bertha says she came home upset a couple of nights ago. She went to the movies with a friend, but she came home early and ran upstairs crying," Mae explained. "She went to work at the diner yesterday, but when Bertha got up this morning, Ronnie wasn't in the house. She left a note in her room—"

Mae mumbled something, not into the phone.

"Mae? Mae!" Jules called. "What did the note say?"

She could hear more garbled voices, and then Mae was back. "The note said she was sorry, she couldn't take any more of this and she hadn't meant to be so much trouble."

Jules's face screwed up as she raised a clenched fist, wishing there was something to hit. Forcing herself to take a deep breath, she asked, "Have you tried calling the diner? Does anyone there know where she is?"

Mae hesitated for a second and then said, "She didn't show up for work yesterday or today. No one there has heard from her."

"Damn." Dimly, it registered that Mae hadn't scolded her for swearing and that she must be as worried as Jules was. "Did she take anything? A backpack, clothes, anything at all?"

Mae repeated the questions to Bertha and, after a moment, said, "She took one backpack that Bertha could tell."

"Okay," Jules said, thinking quickly. "I'm going to head your way as soon as I can get on the road. You keep Bertha there with you or wait with her at her house, but don't leave her alone."

"We're getting a bad line of storms," Mae said, and the line crackled as she spoke. "You shouldn't drive in this."

"I'll be fine," Jules said. "I'm coming."

She hung up and immediately called Kelli. She got her voice mail and left an urgent message asking her to call and come home as quickly as she could. Jules ran upstairs and threw a change of clothes and a toothbrush into a gym bag. She tried Kelli again, and again got her voice mail. She left another terse message and got in the car.

Now, her eyes stung and her head ached with the strain of concentrating to see through the storm-lashed windshield, but she kept up a steady speed, inching closer to Aldie.

Jules stared fixedly at her peanut butter and jelly sandwich, trying not to listen.

"Jules and I have found some cool places to go," Hobie was saying. "We'll show you around."

"That sounds great," said the new kid, Gilbert Bayliss.

He'd moved to Aldie over the summer before their junior year. Though his wavy blond hair and good looks had made him immediately popular with the girls, the guys for some reason didn't seem to like him much. But Hobie did. Hobie had noticed him right away, pointing him out to Jules as they sat in the cafeteria, watching Gilbert hunt for a place to eat. Catching his eye, Hobie had gestured to him, inviting him to sit with them. Jules had stared—Hobie, who never talked to any other boy in school, the kid the guys delighted in tormenting—he was inviting this strange boy over to eat with them.

"You're in my trig class," Gilbert said as he set his meal tray down at their table.

"Yeah," Hobie said, and Jules could tell he was pleased that Gilbert had noticed him. "This is my friend, Jules. This is Gilbert Bayliss."

If it seemed odd to Gilbert that Hobie already knew his name, he didn't say so. They struck up a conversation, and Gilbert told them his family had just moved to Aldie from Toledo when his dad got hired as an accountant at the mill.

Gilbert had joined them for lunch nearly every day since then, and, just like that, their group of two had become a group of three.

Gilbert was even coming to Hobie's house sometimes. Not that Jules wasn't invited. Hobie always included her, but she felt oddly like the one who didn't belong when they were together. There were still some things she and Hobie did just the two of them. They went to the cove—that's what they called the place behind the cemetery—nearly every weekend. At least Hobie did. Jules didn't always want to go. It made her feel weird to be there as a single when other people were paired off, but that never seemed to bother Hobie. He went even when Jules didn't—the only time he had ever insisted on doing something with or without her. He was different when he was there. She watched him sometimes in the firelight, laughing and talking like he never did at school, and she felt at times as if she were watching someone she didn't know.

He was kind of like that when Gilbert was around, *which is a lot lately*, she thought grumpily. When Gilbert was at Hobie's house, they usually played Monopoly, never seeming to tire of it. Jules soon hated Monopoly. Sometimes, they played chess, but then Jules had to sit and watch and there was no talking because they wanted to concentrate. It was funny, though, that Gilbert never invited Hobie to his house, Jules noticed. If it bothered Hobie, he never said so.

Then, one day, "I was thinking about taking Gilbert to the cove," Hobie said in an overly casual tone as they sat out back under the oak tree, Friday lying between them with her head resting on Jules's leg. Jules knew he was waiting to gauge her response.

Jules felt as if it was hard to breathe. She had known from that first night why she and Hobie were allowed to join the others at the cove, even if it was never said out loud. Sometimes, the people from the cove ran into one another in town, exchanging small nods and looks of greeting, but always discreetly so as not to be noticeable to other people. Jules knew she would have liked, in a scary kind of liking, to be doing what the others were doing when they moved away from the fire into the shadows, but she had never imagined actually bringing someone there, mostly because she didn't know any girl she could have taken to the cove. For Hobie to be thinking about taking Gilbert there was... it felt like....

"You can do whatever you want," Jules snapped, pushing to her feet.

Hobie looked up at her in consternation. "What? Why are you mad?"

"I'm not mad," she said over her shoulder as she stomped back into the house.

"Damn! Who turned the ringer off?"

Kelli stared at the screen of her phone showing five missed calls from Jules. Her niece, soaking wet from the pool, had been playing games on her phone early in the day.

"Give that to me," Mary Anne had said, drying the phone with a towel and tucking it safely into her beach bag.

Kelli listened now to the messages from Jules, growing more alarmed with each one.

"What is it?" Mary Anne asked as she tried to wrangle the kids and get them back out to the car.

"An emergency in Ohio," Kelli said. "She's already left. She's got a couple hours' head start by now. I've got to go."

It seemed to take forever for Mary Anne to get the kids loaded back in their minivan and get back to their house. With a hasty promise to call with an update, Kelli jumped into her Tahoe and drove home.

She ran into the house and skidded to a halt when she saw the answering machine blinking. There were two more messages from Jules, and then, "Jules, Kelli, this is Ronnie." Kelli could hear that she was crying. "I did something really, really stupid. I'm in Cleveland—" *What is she doing in Cleveland?* "—and I don't know what to do. The number at this phone booth is..." Kelli quickly jotted the number down. "Please call me," Ronnie finished with a sob.

Kelli tried dialing the number of the phone booth but had to start over three times as her hands were trembling so badly she kept punching the wrong buttons. Ronnie answered almost immediately.

"Hello?"

"Ronnie? This is Kelli."

Ronnie started crying again. Kelli could hear thunder and voices in the background.

"Ronnie, listen to me," Kelli said loudly. "Where are you? Are you safe?"

"I'm at a truck stop," Ronnie said. "I hitchhiked, and this guy dropped me off here."

"Are you okay?"

Ronnie sniffed. "Yes. I'm okay."

Kelli closed her eyes in relief. "All right. Listen to me. Jules is on her way to Aldie. I'm going to go there and get her, and we'll come up to get you, okay? Is the truck stop open? Is it a safe place to hang out and wait?"

"I think so," Ronnie said. "The sign says twenty-four hours, and I've got money."

"Then you stay put. We'll be up to get you as soon as we can, but it might be hours. Don't you dare leave with anyone, and don't hitch another ride. You understand?"

"Yes," Ronnie said in a meek voice.

Kelli hung up and ran upstairs as she tried Jules's cell phone. Nothing. Not even voice mail. She hung up and called Donna and Elaine while she threw a change of clothes into a bag.

"Hey," she said quickly when Donna answered. "We've got a situation. Jules is on her way to Aldie, and I'm getting ready to go. Can you guys look after the cats while we're gone?"

"Wait a minute," Donna said. "What's going on? Is it Mae? Are you and Jules okay?"

"It's not Mae," Kelli said. "It's Ronnie, the girl that Jules was e-mailing. Something has happened; I'm not sure what. Jules took off and I've got to get out there."

She could hear muffled voices as Donna covered the receiver with her hand. Kelli frowned as the voices grew louder even through the filter of the hand on the phone. Suddenly, Donna was back.

"I'm going with you," she said. "I'll be there in five minutes."

She hung up before Kelli could protest, but Kelli realized how relieved she was not to have to go alone. She fed the cats, overfilling their bowls with dry food and topping off the water bowl as she called Mary Anne to tell her she was leaving within a few minutes for Ohio.

"What's going on?" Mary Anne asked.

"I don't know yet," Kelli said. "I'll call when I know more. But I need you to check on the cats tomorrow."

The doorbell rang.

"Gotta go," she said. She hung up and hurried to let Donna in. "Thank you for doing this," she said sincerely. "Elaine wasn't happy, was she?"

Donna's eyes glinted. "She told me if I went, she wouldn't be there when I got back." She beckoned out toward the waiting Tahoe. "Let's go get her."

CHAPTER 27

W<small>HEN</small> J<small>ULES AT LAST</small> got to Aldie, her head was pounding in rhythm with the windshield wipers and her eyelids felt like sandpaper every time she blinked to clear her vision. She sent geysers of water out from beneath her tires as she drove through huge puddles of standing water. Nearly the entire town was pitch-black. *The power must be out.* She glanced at the clock and saw that it was only eight o'clock. She'd been driving in the dark for so many hours, it felt like the middle of the night to her.

The hardest rain had let up, and the thunder and lightning were more distant, with most of the lightning flashes now south of town. She pulled into Mae's driveway and ran to the front door. In answer to her frantic knock, a dim, bobbing light approached, and then Mae opened the door, holding a candle. She stepped back to let Jules in.

"You shouldn't have come in this weather," she said in a more gentle scold than would have been typical as she took Jules's wet jacket.

"I had to," Jules said. She slipped off her shoes and turned to Bertha Fahnestock, who was sitting on the couch, clutching a sofa pillow to her and looking very pale in the candlelight.

Jules knelt in front of her. "Tell me again what happened. When was the last time you saw her?"

Bertha said in a quavering voice, "Yesterday morning. She went out with a friend the night before and came home crying. She ran upstairs and stayed in her room. She got up yesterday morning and said she was going to work. I thought it was strange because she had a jacket and a backpack, but I thought maybe she was going out again after work. She still wasn't home when I went to bed last night, which was also strange. She's been very polite about not staying out late." Here, she had to stop as her eyes filled and her chin quivered. "And then today, she didn't come down for breakfast. I thought maybe she got up and left early for work or maybe she was sleeping in. But when I went up to knock, she didn't answer, and there was a note on her bed."

She reached into the pocket of her dress and pulled out a crumpled note. Jules took it from her, remembering the note that had brought Ronnie into her life in the first place.

I'm sorry to leave you like this, but I just can't take it anymore. I can't take this town and the people in it. I've had enough. Thank you for everything.

Good-bye,
Ronnie

Jules stared at the familiar handwriting. She handed the note back to Mrs. Fahnestock and got to her feet. "I'm going to look for her."

"Where?" Mae asked.

Jules looked at her grandmother. "I know a few places she might have gone. I'll be back as soon as I can." She slipped into her shoes, pulled her rain jacket back on, and hurried off into the rainy night.

Jules jogged through puddles on her way downtown. "Just focus on finding her," she told herself over and over. Most of Aldie seemed to have lost power. Isolated blocks were lit up, but most of the town was dark, and only a few cars were out, causing the standing water in the streets to wash up over curbs as they went creeping by. Jules got caught by an especially large wave that sloshed over her feet before she could jump out of the way. *Well, I can't get much wetter.* Her heart fell when she saw that the diner was dark and the closed sign hung on the door. Ronnie had already used the diner once as a hideout, and Jules had hoped against hope she had done so again. *She might still be in there.* Jules peered through the front windows, trying to detect any signs of movement inside. She went around to the back and banged on the employee door, but there was no answer.

...I can't take it anymore... I've had enough....

Jules jogged on to the library, but it, too, was in darkness and closed for the night. She wondered briefly if Ronnie could have found places to hide inside during the nights. It probably wouldn't be hard to stay out of sight of the staff as they closed... but her note had made it sound as if she were looking for a way out. *What happened to you?*

Jules wondered as she ran on, trying to figure out where she could look next. She ran to the elementary playground, though she knew it was a stupid idea. "She won't be here," she told herself, but she knew it was the first place they had talked, and she was half afraid Ronnie might have thought it would be a symbolic place to—"Don't be here," she pleaded. "Please don't be here." Warily, she scanned the high crossbar of the swing set, illuminated intermittently by flashes of lightning. Only the chains of the swings hung from it.

Jules stood there, rain running down her face as she stared into the darkness. After a long time, she turned and began walking toward the cemetery.

———— ◄►◄• ————

"Jules! Jules, stop!"

Hobie ran to catch her.

"Stop and talk to me," he pleaded when he caught up to her in the hallway. Other kids stared at them as they passed, but Hobie ignored them. "Why won't you talk to me?"

"Leave me alone," Jules said, turning back in the direction she'd been heading for her last class of the day.

"What is wrong with you?" he demanded.

She stopped and glared at him. "What's wrong with me? I'm not the one taking Gilbert Bayliss to the cove."

Hobie shushed her, looking around to see if anyone had overheard.

"Why should I be quiet?" Jules continued, knowing she should stop, but inside, she could feel all the jealousy and anger that had been eating at her the past couple of months as Hobie spent more and more time with Gilbert, leaving her feeling like an unwanted leftover of days that would never be recaptured.

"I'm not the one who took Gilbert Bayliss up to my room," she said, not bothering to lower her voice and savagely rejoicing at the look of panic in Hobie's eyes as she continued. "I was watching. I saw you two."

A few people had actually stopped and were listening now.

"You and your boyfriend," she hissed.

A crowd was quickly gathering. Hobie shook his head, his eyes shining with tears as he silently begged Jules to stop.

"I think you're disgusting," she flung at him. "You stay away from me, you homo fag."

All around them, there were mixed exclamations of surprise and jeers as Hobie turned and stalked away, his back ramrod straight. Jules turned and pushed through the throng, feeling as if she might throw up. She got to her science class and sat down, blinking hard to keep from crying.

"You're always sorry afterward," Mae had said to her so many times. "When are you ever going to learn to stop and think before you speak?"

Why did I do it? she asked herself over and over until the bell rang. She ran home through the rain, going straight to the Fahnestock house, but Mrs. Fahnestock said Hobie wasn't home yet. Jules went home and got into dry clothes.

"Whatever is the matter with you?" Mae asked when Jules hardly touched her dinner.

"You sick, Jules?" Pappy asked, laying a hand on her arm.

Jules shook her head and pushed away from the table. She went up to her room and pulled out her walkie-talkie. She went to the window. "Are you there?" she asked, but there was no response from Hobie's dark room.

Outside, the rain came down in buckets. "We're under a tornado watch," Mae announced from the living room as she watched the news on the television.

Jules crept to the back door, pulling on a rain jacket. Silently, she let herself out the door and pulled it shut. She went next door. "Can I talk to Hobie, please?" she asked when the door was yanked open.

Mrs. Fahnestock stood there, wringing her hands. "He's not home. He was here earlier, but he went out again. It's not like Hobie to stay away and worry me. He knows how I worry. I can't imagine where he's got to."

"I'll find him," Jules said. She turned from the house and stood on the sidewalk. She knew where she had to look.

"Thank God for GPS," Donna said when she and Kelli got to Aldie. Neither of them could remember precisely how to get to the Calhoon house, and everything looked unfamiliar in the dark and the rain.

When they finally got to the house, they saw Jules's Subaru in the drive. "I'm so glad she's here," Kelli said.

They ran through the rain to the front door and knocked. Mae answered, carrying a candle.

"Where in the world have you—?" She stopped short at the sight of Kelli and Donna on her stoop. "Come in out of the weather."

"Where's Jules?" Kelli asked, looking around.

"She's out looking for Ronnie," Mae said. "I thought you were her. She's been gone for a long time."

"I talked to Ronnie," Kelli said. "She's safe. She hitched a ride and got as far as Cleveland."

"Cleveland?" said a woman neither of them had noticed over on the couch. "Then she's all right?"

"Yes," Kelli said. "Why would you have thought she might not be okay?"

"She left a note," Mae said, patting the woman on the shoulder as she cried in relief.

"A note," Kelli said. "You thought she might have hurt herself?" She went to the couch and squatted down. "You're Hobie's mother, aren't you?"

Bertha nodded.

"This is Kelli and Donna," Mae said. Donna looked at her. "Don't be so surprised. I remember you."

Kelli tried Jules's phone again, but got nothing. "The storm has messed up cell coverage. I haven't been able to get hold of Jules all day. Do you know where she was going to search? Why has she been gone so long?"

Mae turned to look at Bertha.

Bertha's eyes were large as she raised a hand to her mouth. "You don't think—?"

"I don't know," Mae said.

"What?" Donna asked.

"There's one place she might have gone," Mae said grimly. "Especially if she thought the girl might have—"

Mae went to get a raincoat and flashlight.

"I'm going, too," Bertha said, standing up.

"No." Mae tied a plastic rain hat under her chin. "I don't think you should."

277

Bertha, despite her mousy appearance, said firmly, "I have to go."

Kellie and Donna exchanged puzzled looks.

"Where are we going?" Kelli asked as Mae went to get another raincoat for Bertha.

"To the cemetery," Mae said.

Together, the four women headed out into the rain.

"Why are we going to the cemetery?" Donna asked. "Pappy?"

"No, not Carl," said Mae. "Hobie."

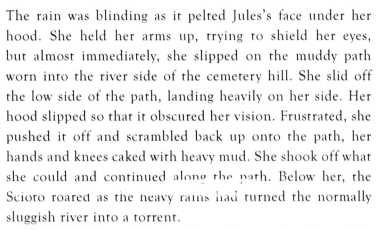

The rain was blinding as it pelted Jules's face under her hood. She held her arms up, trying to shield her eyes, but almost immediately, she slipped on the muddy path worn into the river side of the cemetery hill. She slid off the low side of the path, landing heavily on her side. Her hood slipped so that it obscured her vision. Frustrated, she pushed it off and scrambled back up onto the path, her hands and knees caked with heavy mud. She shook off what she could and continued along the path. Below her, the Scioto roared as the heavy rains had turned the normally sluggish river into a torrent.

"Hobie!" she yelled, but her voice was barely audible over the sounds of the storm. "Hobie!"

She kept calling as she slid down a switchback in the path. Her throat felt as if it was tearing as she screamed the name over and over, trying to make herself heard. Turning sideways, she let her feet slide in the mud, reaching for the rocks that littered the trail, using them to stop her downward motion through the mud and rain. Her foot hit one rock crookedly, twisting her ankle and causing her to fall again. She grabbed her ankle and sat for a moment, waiting for the throbbing pain to subside. When it didn't, she got back on her feet, using words she knew Mae would have punished her for saying as she limped onward, making her way down to the cove.

No one. Through the flashes of lightning that lit the night, she could see that the fire pit and logs around it were empty. Of course they were empty. What kind of idiot would be down here on a night like this? Jules stood there, her hair plastered to her head, rain running down her neck inside her shirt, her rain jacket useless in this downpour. Below her, the river churned and swirled. Lightning flashed again, and she thought she saw something down there.

Barely able to put weight on her injured ankle, Jules sat and slid on her butt down the grassy bank to the river's edge, but the water level was several feet higher than normal. Her feet were in the water before she could stop her momentum. The current tore at her, pulling her in. She turned and scrabbled, her hands grasping at bushes, grass, whatever she could reach to pull herself inch by inch back up onto the bank and out of the greedy tug of the water. Panting, she sat there and looked back down at the angry brown river below her.

Another flash of lightning made her gasp.

"Hobie!" Jules screamed. She could have sworn she'd seen a pair of blue-jeaned legs down in the brush dam tangled up near the water's edge.

Holding her breath, she waited for the next flash of lightning. There it was. Someone was down there. She slid back down the bank, looking for something she could brace her feet on as she gingerly lowered herself back into the raging water. She felt a log under her and placed her feet on it, reaching forward, trying to grab what looked like a jacket billowing in the current, but her injured ankle buckled and she slid under the surface.

She held her breath too late and inhaled a mouthful of water. The undertow pushed her into a submerged log whose branches tore at her jacket like hands that were trying to pull her under. Panicking, she grabbed at the log, trying to hold on and use it to get her head above water. Breaking through the surface, she gasped for air, coughing and choking. The swirling water around her kept pulling at her. She held on as tightly as she could, her nose and mouth only sometimes above water, afraid to let go even to get back up onto the bank. Shifting her grip a little, she looked over. She saw a hand reaching for her.

"Hobie," she gurgled through a mouthful of water, straining to grab his hand. He was just out of reach. Hooking one arm around a branch, she stretched her other hand out, reaching, trying to get to him. She managed to grasp a handful of jacket and pulled, but the current was too strong. She couldn't dislodge him from the branches that had him pinned. She tried again and again until she was exhausted.

"Hobie," she sobbed, clinging to her log. "I can't get you out. I'll be back."

She inched her way along the log toward the bank and managed to climb up without getting sucked back into the river.

"Help," she gasped. "Got to get help."

CHAPTER 28

"I DON'T UNDERSTAND," KELLI said. "Why would she blame herself?"

The town was deserted as they drove to the cemetery.

"Because she couldn't save him," said Mae. "She tried to pull him out of the river, but she couldn't." She glanced over at Bertha, who sat beside her in the backseat, wearing one of Mae's plastic rain hats and Carl's old raincoat over her dress, staring straight ahead. "It was a night almost exactly like this. The rain was coming down, and the river was up. She had to come back and get help, and by the time they got there... it was too late."

Donna twisted around in her seat. She hesitated, taking in Bertha's stark, white face. "Was he still alive when Jules found him? Could she have saved him when she got there?"

Mae shook her head. "They said not. They said he'd been in the water for a while, but I don't think that mattered to Jules." She pointed. "Just here. Follow that drive around to the right side of the hill. Then we'll have to walk."

Kelli drove carefully, leaning forward to see, as the rain seemed to swallow the headlights.

"Stop. This is as far as we can drive," Mae said.

The four women got out of the car and made their way on foot, guided by the meager beam from Mae's flashlight.

"I don't know what it's like back here now," Mae said in a loud voice over a renewed surge in the rain. "Not sure anyone's been here since that night."

Kelli offered her an arm, and Donna did likewise for Bertha. They found an old path, muddy now, zigzagged against the hillside. They changed to single-file, Kelli leading with Donna bringing up the rear. Slipping and sliding, they made their way down the hillside toward the river roaring below. They reached a point where it looked as if part of the trail had been washed away.

Kelli turned to Mae and Bertha. "I think you should stay here," she yelled over the noise of the water. "We'll go down and see if we can find her."

Mae nodded, handing them the flashlight. "We'll wait here for you." She linked an arm through Bertha's as the younger women half-sat, sliding downhill through the mud and grass that covered the hillside.

Playing the flashlight back and forth through the night, mostly what Kelli saw was the reflection of the raindrops. It was hard to make out anything more than a few feet in front of her.

"What's that?" Donna called out from behind her. She reached over Kelli's shoulder, pointing to the left.

Kelli swung the flashlight in that direction and saw a shadowy silhouette. They scrambled along the trail and found Jules sitting, hunched and bedraggled, on a log next to an old stone-lined fire pit.

They sat down on either side of her.

"Jules?" Kelli placed an arm around her shoulders.

"Are you okay?" Donna asked.

Jules murmured something. They could barely hear her over the churning, gurgling sounds of the water.

"Jules, let's go," Kelli said. "We need to get you out of here."

But Jules sat, staring down toward the swirling river below. With the power out, there wasn't even any reflected light, only the intermittent flashes of lightning, which forked down on the far side of the river.

"Jules," Donna hollered. "It wasn't your fault. Mae said he was already drowned by the time you found him. You couldn't have saved him."

Jules shook her head. "No. It's my fault he was here in the first place."

Kelli took Jules's arm. "You can explain it when we get you back to the house. Come on. We have to go. Mae and Bertha are standing up there in the rain, waiting for us. And we have to get Ronnie. Come on."

Jules looked around at that. "Ronnie?"

"Yes," Kelli yelled. "She's safe. She's in Cleveland, waiting for us to come and get her. We have to go."

Jules allowed herself to be helped to her feet, and the three of them began making their way back up the muddy path to where Mae and Bertha were standing. When they saw the bobbing light of the flashlight, Mae stepped forward and pulled Jules into a hug. Jules wrapped her arms around her grandmother, and they stood like that for a long time.

"We need to get out of the rain," Kelli said.

Hand in hand, they made their way back up the trail to where the Tahoe was waiting. Within a few minutes, they were all seated around Mae's kitchen table as she put a kettle on to boil.

She retrieved blankets for each of them to wrap up in, pursing her lips at the mud and water all over her kitchen floor. "A cup of piping hot tea is what we all need," said Mae as she got five mugs down from the cupboard. She glanced worriedly at Jules, who just sat at the table, staring at the speckles of the gray Formica tabletop.

"Mae, is your telephone working?" Kelli asked.

"I believe so," Mae said. "Big lot of help your fancy cell phones are when the weather gets nasty. Good thing I've got a real telephone."

Kelli pulled a scrap of paper out of her pocket and dialed the number written there. "Ronnie? It's Kelli. We're here in Aldie. We found Jules... I'll explain that later. Anyway, we're coming up to get you now. Tell me exactly what truck stop you're at."

She wrote as Mae handed out mugs of tea.

"I should go with you," Jules said, cradling her mug in her hands as Kelli came back to the table.

"You've been through enough for tonight." Mae glanced at Bertha, who hadn't said a word but was watching Jules with an almost haunted look in her eyes. "I'll go with Donna and Kelli, and we'll get the girl and bring her home."

Kelli opened her mouth to protest but followed Mae's gaze to Bertha's face and then to Jules, who was now staring into Bertha's eyes. "Okay," she said.

They finished their tea and went to put their wet shoes back on. Kelli wrapped an arm around Jules's shoulders. "We'll get Ronnie and be back as soon as we can."

Jules nodded, squeezing Kelli's hand and giving Donna a small smile.

The kitchen door closed behind them, and then it was just Jules and Bertha.

"I don't understand. Why would any of it have been your fault?"

"For twenty-three years, I've dreaded having to answer that question," Jules would say to Kelli later when she told her about that night.

She looked at Bertha Fahnestock now and knew that it was time—time to confess, time to give Hobie's mother the answers she'd never had, time to face up to herself and what she'd done.

"That last day," Jules began haltingly. "The day he died, we had a fight at school. I said awful, horrible things to him." Her throat tightened painfully, but she forced herself to continue. "I wanted to hurt him, and I did."

Bertha looked at her questioningly. "But what could you have said that—"

Clenching the folds of her blanket tightly, Jules said, "Hobie was gay. Me, too. We knew when we were in school. We're both gay."

Bertha shook her head. "Did Hobie think that would matter to me? I knew he was sensitive, different." Her pale blue eyes searched Jules's—*funny, how I never noticed Hobie had her eyes,* Jules realized. "I knew other boys thought he was a sissy and they beat him up," Bertha continued. "But he always had you to stand up for him. He was so proud to have you as a friend."

Tears spilled from Jules's eyes as she tried to hold back the enormity of her remorse and guilt. "I wasn't his friend then, towards the end. He... he met someone..."

"Gilbert?"

Jules nodded. "I was jealous and hurt because Hobie wanted to be with Gilbert, and I said... I said horrible things." She covered her face with her blanket and cried. "That night," she choked, "when he didn't come home, I knew where he'd gone. I found him down at the place we all used to go... I couldn't pull him out. I tried, but I wasn't strong enough." She couldn't go on, and she sat rocking as she sobbed.

Bertha came to sit in the chair beside her and held her.

"Hobie knew you didn't mean those things you said," Bertha crooned as she held Jules tightly. "He loved you."

It was several minutes before Jules could talk again. "I never got to tell him I was sorry," she whispered. "I never got to tell him I didn't mean it, and then he... because of me, he..."

Bertha sat up and took Jules's hand in her own. "You think Hobie took his own life?" she asked. "You think he went into the river on purpose?" She shook her head emphatically. "No. My Hobie would never do that to me. The firefighters who got him out—" Her chin quivered. "The ones who pulled him free of the river, they said the bank was a mud slick. They said he slid into the water and got caught in the current and couldn't pull himself out." She looked into Jules's eyes. "It was an accident. An accident."

Jules searched Bertha's eyes—so sure, so full of her conviction. *God, I want to believe that.*

"There are things," she whispered to Bertha, "things Hobie wrote, that you should have."

Bertha shook her head sadly. "I thought there would be. He was always writing. But when I searched his room... there was nothing."

Jules unwrapped herself from her blanket and stood. Holding a hand out, she said, "Come with me."

———•⊗•———

When Kelli and the others got back to Aldie, it was nearly three a.m. They found Mae's house empty. Jules was asleep on Bertha's living room sofa, while Bertha sat in her chair with the old oil lamp burning on the table next to her, holding a collection of papers and books in her lap.

"Hobie's journals and stories," Bertha said, her face lit up with a happiness Mae hadn't seen there since that horrible night. "They were hidden under a floorboard in his room. Jules got them for me." She clasped one of the journals to her chest. "I feel like I have a bit of my boy back."

Kelli knelt next to the sofa, where Jules was sleeping, her face more peaceful than it had been in ages. "She's okay?" she asked, turning to Bertha.

Bertha watched Jules for long seconds. "No. Not yet. But I think she will be."

Ronnie came to Bertha's chair and said, "I'm so sorry, Mrs. Fahnestock. Running away was stupid. I didn't mean to worry you, and I didn't know about—" She gestured toward Hobie's photos on the mantel.

"It's late, and we're all tired," Mae said. She glanced over at Jules, who was still dead to the world. "Why don't you come to my house?" she said, looking at Kelli and Donna. "There are two beds upstairs. I think we can leave Jules here, and you, young lady," she said, looking at Ronnie, "you'd best get up to your room."

Ronnie smiled. "Yes, ma'am."

"We can all talk tomorrow," Mae said, looking at her watch. "Or later this morning."

CHAPTER 29

JULES WOKE TO BRIGHT sunshine pouring in through the front window. Blinking, she sat up and looked around, trying to get her bearings.

"The storm has passed," said Bertha as she pulled back the curtains.

Has it? Jules looked around. "You haven't had the curtains open in a long time."

"Twenty-three years," said Bertha, turning to look at the photos of Hobie sitting on the mantel. She picked one up and held it lovingly. "I've kept him in the dark for too, too long."

There was a knock on the front door, and Mae entered, followed by Kelli, Donna, and Ronnie, who were all carrying to-go cartons and bags.

"Downtown has power back," Mae said, "but they say it'll be mid-afternoon sometime before we get it back. We got breakfast at the diner."

Jules followed them into the kitchen, where Kelli pressed a carryout cup of fresh coffee into her hands. Jules closed her eyes and sniffed deeply. "Thank you."

Ronnie reached into one of the bags and pulled out a Styrofoam container, passing it to Jules.

Jules smiled when she opened it. "Chocolate pie."

"Trish said you always order chocolate pie when you come in," Ronnie said.

"Let's eat, and then we'll talk," said Mae with a stern glance at Ronnie.

They all sat down, looking a little the worse for the previous night's adventure, as no one had been able to shower. Jules realized she still had dried mud on her hands and got up to wash.

"All right, young lady," Mae began as soon as they had finished eating. Jules couldn't help feeling a little sorry for Ronnie, as she herself had been on the receiving end of so many of those "young lady" talks. "Suppose you tell us what happened that was so bad you felt you had to run away."

Ronnie's face burned scarlet, and Jules felt a renewed sense of sympathy for her. She opened her mouth to protest that maybe this conversation should be between Ronnie and her, but Mae silenced her with a glance.

"You had all of us worried to death yesterday and last night," Mae said. "What was so terrible?"

Ronnie sat, pulling at a hangnail as she struggled to know what to say.

Could you have done this in front of all these people? Jules asked herself. "Was it Ariel?" she prompted.

Ronnie blanched, looking fearfully at Mae and Bertha.

"Ronnie," Kelli said gently, leaning forward. "Jules, Donna, and I are all lesbians. It's okay."

Kelli turned to Mae, who blustered, "Well, for heaven's sake, I'd have to be an idiot not to have known that all these years."

"And my Hobie was gay," Bertha said bravely.

Ronnie looked around at all of them as they waited patiently. "We—Ariel and I—have been spending a lot of time together. I thought she liked me... the same way I like her. We went to a movie, and she was leaning against me, you know, like our shoulders and knees were touching..." She paused, looking totally humiliated as she continued. "And then I tried to hold her hand, and she yanked it away and whispered what was wrong with me, and... she left."

Her eyes filled with tears. "I was so stupid for thinking she could like me that way. Look at me! She's beautiful, and I'm big and klutzy and—"

"—and brave and strong," said Jules. "You stood up to that pastor instead of letting him do what you knew was wrong, even when it cost you your home."

"But you have a new home now," Bertha said. "For as long as you want to be here. I don't care if you're gay."

"You're too young to be thinking of such foolishness anyhow," said Mae—*most unhelpfully,* Jules thought—but Ronnie's tearful face broke into a smile as Mae added, "You've got scholarships and college to be thinking about. Time enough to be thinking of those other things later."

Jules reached for Ronnie's arm. "Your senior year might be tough. Seeing Ariel in school, especially if she tells anyone about... you know. Are you going to be able to deal with that? Without feeling like you have to run away again?"

Ronnie looked at Bertha. "I won't do that to you again. I'm sorry."

"I was worried about you," Bertha said.

"We all were," Kelli said.

Ronnie looked around at all of them. "Thank you. I'll be okay. I'll get through it, somehow."

"We're all here to help if you need it," Jules said. "All you have to do is ask."

"The same goes for you," Mae said, looking at Jules.

Jules's eyes filled with sudden tears, and Kelli reached for her hand. "I know," Jules managed to say. "I've just been carrying it around for so long. I don't know how to let it go."

"You won't," said Mae, and there was an odd tone to her voice. "Not completely. Some hurts go too deep to heal."

Jules looked at her grandmother and "for the first time, I knew, I really saw how much my mother's running away had hurt her," she would say to Kelli later.

"But," Mae continued, "now that it's out in the open, it can start to get better. Bad things fester in the darkness of being kept secret."

"I remember you said something like that once before," Jules recalled.

Mae had a funny look on her face, and opened her mouth as if to add something but took a sip of her coffee instead.

Jules looked at Ronnie. "You said Trish was working this morning?"

Ronnie nodded as Jules pushed back from the table. "There's something I need to do," Jules said.

—✦✧✦—

"That's his house," Hobie had pointed out on more than one occasion when he dragged Jules down that street, hoping to see Gilbert somewhere outside.

Jules found it again now, walking down streets littered with the debris from the storm—downed branches from trees, piles of gravel and silt deposited wherever the water flow had slowed as it ran along sidewalks and curbs, flower beds ruined with pitiful-looking plants flattened by the downpour. Near the end of Grady Street was the white bungalow she sought, fixed up more neatly than she remembered with shutters painted a cheerful red and flowerboxes under the main floor windows. Gilbert was outside, raking up leaves and branches and placing them in trash barrels to be hauled to the dump.

He stopped raking as Jules approached.

"We need to talk," she said.

He pressed his sweaty chin against his T-shirt sleeve as he leaned on his rake. "I figured I'd be seeing you." He set the rake down and gestured toward the house. "Come on in."

Though she and Hobie had spied on the house a few times, Jules had never been inside. The interior was as neat and nicely decorated as the exterior. Gilbert led her back to the kitchen.

"Something to drink?"

"Uh, sure," she said. "Water? Orange juice? Whatever."

He poured two glasses of orange juice and invited her to sit at the table. He took the chair opposite.

Jules took a small sip of her juice and asked, "Why did you think you'd be seeing me?"

Gilbert shrugged. "Ever since that day at the diner, I just figured it was inevitable." He looked at her, and she was startled to see tears shining in his eyes.

"I've never been able to talk about him," he said, his voice cracking. "Not to anyone."

"Me, neither," said Jules. "But not for the same reason." Just as she had with Bertha, Jules took a deep breath and forced herself to say, "We had a fight, Hobie and I, the day he died. At school. About you. I'd seen the two of you in his room, and I—" She had to pause and wait a moment before she could trust her voice. "He loved you. And I just couldn't deal with that."

Gilbert's handsome face contorted as he tried to control his emotions. "You know," he said in a strangled voice, "I love Trish, and I know it's stupid to think that two seventeen-year-olds could have lasted a lifetime, but... when a love is allowed to die a natural death, you can let it go. If we'd grown apart when we went off to college, if we'd met someone else and broken up—it would have been so different. But when a love is cut off like that, with no end to it, it becomes a ghost. It haunts you." He closed his eyes and pressed his fist against his mouth, almost as if he were trying to stifle the sobs threatening to escape. It was a long time before he could talk again.

"Did he do it on purpose?" he whispered.

Jules shook her head. "I don't know. His mom swears it was an accident, but... I don't know."

"The funny thing is," he said, blinking hard, "I don't think I, or anyone else, could ever have come between you. He talked about you all the time." Gilbert managed a weak smile. "He admired you more than anyone he knew. And as much as he may have loved me, he loved you more."

———◆◄━━►◆———

Kelli and Donna rode silently, each lost in her thoughts, until they were nearly in Charleston.

"Have you talked to Elaine?" Kelli asked.

Donna shook her head as she drove. "Left messages, but she hasn't called me back."

Kelli turned to look at her. All the way to Aldie in the storm and all during the last three days, her attention had been focused solely on Jules and Ronnie. Only now did she stop to consider that Donna might be going back to a breakup.

"Oh, Donna. Are you all right?" Kelli asked.

Donna didn't answer immediately. "I knew what I was doing. Elaine has never been okay with Jules and me still being friends. I don't know why she feels so threatened by that, but I wasn't going to sit back when Jules was in such trouble."

"I feel like I dragged you into this," Kelli said.

Donna glanced over. "You don't have anything to feel guilty about. I couldn't let you do that drive by yourself, not knowing what you might find when you got there..."

"Did you know?" Kelli asked. "About Hobie?"

Donna shook her head again. "Not in detail. I guessed something horrible had happened, but I had no idea how bad it was or how much Jules felt like she had caused it."

"But you thought there was a chance she could hurt herself?" Kelli pressed, expressing her own fears for the first time.

"I did," Donna said. "She's always had times when she went to some dark place, but it had seemed really bad this past year, ever since she was in Aldie for Pappy's funeral. I've been afraid for her. For both of you."

Kelli's throat caught. "I'm still afraid—for all of us."

Donna reached over and squeezed Kelli's arm. "Did she say when she would be coming home?"

Kelli shook her head. "No." She had to try a couple of times before she could say, "She actually didn't say if she was coming home."

Jules stood at her window, looking down at the Fahnestock house. The bushes and trees had all been trimmed; the grass was recently mowed with fresh edging cut in along the sidewalk. The place looked more cheerful and lived-in than it had in over two decades.

"You don't have to do this," Bertha had said over and over the past few days as Kelli, Donna, Jules, and Ronnie all chipped in to help. When they insisted on continuing, she cooked for them—*just like she used to for Hobie*, Jules thought with a small smile.

They were still in Aldie for Jules's fortieth birthday. The celebration was bittersweet, as she and Bertha looked at each other across the chocolate cake she had made, and Jules knew they were both thinking the same thing. She looked at the women gathered around the table—women who had loved her and stuck by her no matter how hard she tried to push them away, and, scrunching her eyes tightly shut, she wished Hobie could have been there as she blew out her lone candle.

Turning from the window now, she went back and sat on one of the beds. *Kelli.* Jules closed her eyes. *And Donna.* It felt in some ways as if someone had pushed a reset button on her life, and she couldn't help wondering "what if?" Her insides twisted with guilt every time she thought of what she had put them both through.

But they both came, said Jules to Jules. *For you.*

She couldn't help wondering how different life with Donna might have been if it hadn't been for that damned class reunion setting her off again. *Would we have still been together if I hadn't screwed things up? And what about Kelli now?*

Her introspection was interrupted by footsteps coming up the stairs, and Mae appeared in the doorway.

"Can I come in?" she asked.

Jules couldn't ever remember Mae asking to come into her room. "Yes."

Mae sat down beside her. "Sometimes," she began, "when I come up here to clean, I sit down and remember." She glanced around the room, and, suddenly, Jules realized how old and sad her grandmother looked.

"Joan was such a dear girl when she was little," Mae said, talking about her daughter for the first time that Jules could remember. "Not a little hellion, like you." She shrugged. "She became a hellion later." Mae pursed her lips, and Jules thought maybe she was close to tears.

"The other morning, after the storm," Mae went on, "I said that things fester when they're kept secret. There's something I never told you." It seemed she needed a moment before she could continue. "Six years ago... Joan, your mother, she came home."

"What?" Jules asked, turning to face Mae.

Mae's jaw worked back and forth for a minute, and she was blinking rapidly. "She was a mess. All scrawny and sickly. I didn't ask, but she looked like those people you saw on the television who had that AIDS. Carl thought maybe she came home to be with us, but—" Mae paused, her jaw jutting forward as it did when she was angry. "All she wanted was money. Her inheritance, she said. She asked about you, where you were, but I didn't tell her anything. And I stopped Carl from telling her. I was afraid she'd come after you for money and you might not be able to tell her no." Jules looked down and noted Mae's hands, red-knuckled and worn from a lifetime of hard work, tightly clenched in her lap on top of her flowered apron. "I sent her away. And I told Carl we could never tell you. He was getting bad by then, but it wasn't long after that he stopped talking. I think it broke his heart to see his girl like that."

Mae shifted on the bed to face Jules.

"I did what I believed was best," she said, raising her gaze to meet Jules's. "Maybe I did wrong. I don't rightly know anymore. It felt right at the time, but now... I realize how hurtful it can be to never have a chance to say good-bye to someone. And I didn't give you that chance with your mother. I'm sorry."

Jules sat there, trying to take this in. "Did she say where she'd been all this time?"

"All kinds of fancy cities like New York and Los Angeles, to listen to her," Mae said. "But—and it pains me to say this—I think she'd have said anything to us if it got her what she wanted." She stood up. "I just thought you had a right to know," she said and left Jules alone again.

Jules lay back on the bed, staring up at the old posters still papering the ceiling. If her mother had had AIDS, or even if she didn't yet but was doing drugs, it wasn't likely she was still alive. Jules found herself feeling angry—not with Mae, but with her mother, for not caring enough to come back earlier. *Funny,* she realized. *I never really wanted her to come back, but I always, always pictured her still alive somewhere. It never occurred to me that she might have died alone, addicted and sick.* Slowly, her anger turned into sadness. Sadness for the pathetic life her mother had had, and sadness for the way it broke Pappy to see her like that.

Tilting her head to look up at the Brady Bunch, Jules was half-tempted to rip all the posters down, but "no," she told herself. "Better to keep thinking of her as Pappy's other girl."

CHAPTER 30

"Is THIS EVERYTHING?" KELLI asked as she carried a large cardboard box inside and upstairs to the spare room.

"For now," Donna said, following her with another box in her arms. "I told her the rest of my stuff could stay there until I find a place. I don't think she'll do anything to it." She set her box down and turned to Kelli. "Are you sure about this?"

"Absolutely," Kelli said. "We have plenty of room here, and this is no imposition at all. Plus—"

"I told you," Donna interrupted. "This is not your fault. Elaine and I were headed in this direction anyway. It just took the right thing to push us over the edge." She looked around with a vacant expression on her face. "I'm not sure I can even remember what brought us together in the first place. Funny, how being with someone can become a matter of habit, not want or desire or love..." She looked at Kelli. "Have you told Jules I'm staying here?"

"Not yet," Kelli said. "She'll be fine with it. But she's going to be in Aldie another week. I figure whatever she's dealing with there is enough for her to be thinking about right now. She said her supervisor gave her a little grief about taking more time off, but Jules reminded her they complain if the psychologists take time off during the school year, and they complain if they take it in the summer, so her supervisor approved the time."

They went downstairs and got cold drinks.

"Does she seem okay?" Donna asked as she followed Kelli into the family room.

"I think so," Kelli said. "She and Mae are talking more than they ever have. Mae told her her mother did come back to Aldie a few years ago, just before we got together."

Donna choked on her drink. "What?" She coughed.

Kelli nodded. "Apparently, she was all wasted away, probably on drugs, maybe had HIV, and only wanted money. Didn't want to stay. Mae and Carl wouldn't tell her where Jules was, and they kept it from her."

"How is Jules taking that?" Donna asked.

"She seems like she's taking it well," Kelli said. "She says she understands Mae was trying to protect her and did what she thought was best."

"Wow." Donna sat back. "That's got to take some getting used to, to think all these years that she never came back and then to hear this."

They sat in silence for a few minutes—until two meowing felines came in, demanding attention. The cats jumped up into laps and settled, purring loudly.

"I keep thinking about Hobie," Kelli asked. "How horrible it was for him to have died that way, with so many questions about how and why it happened."

"I know," Donna said. "She never named him to me. Sometimes, she would say things that let me know high school was hell for her, but I never knew what. Any time I tried to ask, she would just shut down."

"All these years, thinking she'd driven him to take his own life," Kelli said. "No wonder she ran from it any time it reared its head."

"It does help everything else make sense." Donna looked at Kelli curiously. "Do you believe Bertha… that his death was accidental? That he didn't commit suicide?"

"I want to believe it," Kelli said. "For Jules's sake, I'm going to believe it." She glanced at her watch. "I'd better get to bed. I'm working tomorrow."

They took their glasses to the kitchen, and Donna followed Kelli upstairs. "Good night," Donna said. "And thanks again."

"No problem," Kelli said. "Make yourself at home tomorrow."

Donna went into the guest room and changed into pajamas. She went down the hall to the guest bathroom and brushed her teeth. Back in her room, she turned the bedside lamp off and pulled down the covers on the bed. That's when she noticed Jules's night-light sitting there. She clicked the switch and lay down, turning the light slowly from geese to fish to foxes. Her eyes filled with tears, and she cried quietly in the low light of the cowboy sitting at his campfire.

"Found them!"

Jules emerged from the garage with two stiff baseball mitts and an old baseball. She tossed a mitt to Ronnie, and they headed out behind the garage to the backyard. They both squeezed and flapped the mitts, trying to work the stiffness out of the leather. Jules tossed the ball to Ronnie, who caught it easily and threw it back.

"You know how to throw," Jules said with a grin.

"Of course I know how to throw," Ronnie shot back. "What kind of lesbian would I be if I didn't know how to throw a ball?"

Jules laughed at Ronnie's easy use of the word *lesbian* now. "Hobie didn't know. His dad died young, and no one ever taught him." She threw the ball back. "That's how we met."

"Mrs. Fahnestock seems really different now," Ronnie said, throwing a grounder. "Not as sad as she was."

Jules nodded as she squatted and scooped it up. "I think most of her died with him." She fired a fast one that Ronnie caught. "He would have been a great man. He would have changed the world. I think we're all a little poorer because we didn't have him here to challenge things."

"I wish I could have known him," Ronnie said. "Mrs. Fahnestock said I could read some of his stories."

"You should," Jules said. "He always wanted to be a writer. Like you. You two would have gotten along great. I think sometimes he just shook his head with me."

Ronnie paused with the ball in her glove. "Is he... you know, everything that happened, is that why you became a psychologist?"

Jules thought. "Maybe. I never really made the connection. I felt so lost when I finally got out of Aldie and got to college. Wasn't sure what I wanted to major in, but I know Hobie's death influenced every decision I made—probably every decision I've ever made since then."

Ronnie tossed her the ball.

"Have you called your mother?" Jules asked, throwing the ball back.

Ronnie made a face. "I called her at work. I won't talk to her at his house." She refused to call Steve by name. "I told her I was staying with a friend's mother, but she didn't ask who." Ronnie made a wild throw in her anger, forcing Jules to jump to catch it. "Sorry. I think she's just relieved not to have to deal with the tension between me and her stupid husband anymore."

"Don't judge her too harshly," Jules said, speaking with a newfound humility in realizing now how much Mae had kept locked up inside all these years. "I know it must feel like she chose them over you, but you're probably in a better situation now that you're away from them, and your mother might not have your strength. It was probably tough, raising you on her own, and now she doesn't want to jeopardize the security she has with what's-his-name."

Ronnie grinned. "That's how I'll address my Christmas card—" She stopped mid-throw, her face falling as the prospect of the future hit her hard. "Is this it? Am I never going to have my mother back? What about graduation?" She turned away, not wanting Jules to see her crying.

Jules came to her and wrapped an arm around her shoulders. "I don't know," she said. "Just don't cut off ties with her. Keep calling. Send her letters or cards. She may find a way to stand up to Steve." She gave Ronnie a gentle shake. "Take it from me; it's never too late to make things better."

Ronnie sniffed and wiped her sleeve across her eyes. "You're still leaving tomorrow?"

"Yes," said Jules. "I have to get back to work. But we've already discussed having you and Mae and Bertha come out to us for Thanksgiving. And we might be able to get back out later this summer. We'll see."

Ronnie turned and looked at Jules. "You've changed my life. I can't tell you how many times I've thought about that day at the diner, how I almost chickened out and didn't slide that note under the bathroom door. But if I hadn't..."

"I know," Jules said. "I never told you this, but I can't tell you how many times I tried to get rid of it. I didn't want another connection to Aldie. I didn't want some snot-nosed loser of a teenager screwing up my life." She grinned. "Shows how wrong I can be, doesn't it? That turned out to be one of the best days of my life."

Ronnie's face sobered. "I hope I never let you down."

"You just work to not let yourself down, and that'll always be enough for me."

Later that night, Jules sat in the dark of her room. She pulled out the old walkie-talkie and turned it on. Like before, there was a soft hiss of static. She depressed the talk button and whispered, "Are you there?" She listened for a long moment and then pushed the button and murmured, "I just want you to know I'm okay, and I miss you. Over and out."

CHAPTER 31

THE DRIVE BACK TO Virginia felt a little surreal to Jules, as she couldn't recall much of the drive to Aldie nearly two weeks ago. "Two weeks! I haven't spent that much time in Aldie since I left home," she'd said to Kelli. The night of the storm was a blur, mostly because, for Jules, those two stormy nights had blended together. *I was so sure I was going to find her down there,* Jules mused as she drove. *Just like I found him.*

Jules had had to go all the way down to the river with them. No one could have found him in the dark and the rain if they didn't know where to look. "Hurry," she shouted, ignoring the throbbing in her ankle. "He was reaching for me, but I couldn't get him." The riverbank quickly became a churned-up mess of slick mud that caused more than one rescue worker to slide into the turgid water just as Jules had done. The night was filled with yells and spotlights and bursts of radio static. "You should leave now," a concerned firefighter had said to Jules when they were finally able to reach Hobie with a grappling hook and dislodge his body from the tangled branches that had trapped him, but Jules had stayed put, wrapped in a blanket someone had placed around her shoulders. Numbly, she watched as they pulled him to where they could grasp him and drag him up to a level spot. She stared, transfixed, at his ghostly white face, strangely peaceful in the midst of all the chaos, as they briefly examined him and then zipped him into a plastic body bag.

Jules realized she was strangling the steering wheel. She hadn't let herself relive that scene for years. Only in her worst dreams had she been back there—the only time she couldn't stop her brain from revisiting that awful night. *Will the dreams go away now?*

She savored the mountain views along I-64 as she got closer to home. The blossoms on the trees were long gone at this time of the summer, but everything was lush and green. The closer she got to home, however, the more anxious she became. Kelli had finally told her that Donna was living with them temporarily while she looked for a place of her own.

"You're kidding. She and Elaine have really split up?" Jules had asked, aching for the pain Donna must be feeling, but kind of relieved to see that relationship come to an end. "They're not going to try and patch things up?"

"It doesn't seem that way," Kelli said. "Her coming to Ohio with me was the last straw for Elaine."

"Oh." Jules understood immediately. Elaine had given Donna an ultimatum—"Jules or me"—and Donna had chosen.

After reliving so much of her past over the last couple of weeks, the present felt unsettled. "It's almost like I've had amnesia. Everything feels like I'm starting over," she said aloud, as she rehearsed how to explain what she was feeling to Kelli. The past, including her relationships, felt almost as if it belonged to a different person. "Well, I guess I am different now."

The psychologist in her recognized that she was going through a normal adjustment period after facing a traumatic event from her past. "You need to analyze this rationally," she had reminded herself over and over, but the emotional side felt as if she were being ripped apart. Kelli and Donna—her current love and her first real love, both living in her house....

When she got home, Donna's Toyota was in the driveway. Jules pulled her bag from the car and went in. "Hello?" she called. "Anyone here?"

Holly and Mistletoe came trotting out right away, scolding her for staying away so long. She bent down to pet them, and when she straightened, Donna was standing in the doorway.

"Hi," Jules said.

"How was your drive?" Donna asked.

"Long, but traffic was light." Jules noticed how Donna's hair gleamed in the late afternoon sunlight. *So different from Kelli. One so fair and the other so dark.* "Anyway," she said, giving herself a mental shake. "Is Kelli still at work?"

"Yes," Donna said. "I made some dinner. Hungry?"

"Yeah, I am. Let me take this up. I'll be back in a minute."

Upstairs, she deposited her bag in the master bedroom and then quietly went down the hall, past the office to the spare room that Donna was using. She inhaled, smelling Donna's perfume. Stepping farther into the room, she saw that her night-light was in a different place on the nightstand, closer to the bed. She stood, staring at it for a long moment, until Donna called her from downstairs.

Jules hurried down to the kitchen, where Donna was dishing out freshly made potato salad—"your mom's recipe," Jules remembered—and cold fried chicken and another salad of mixed beans, dried cranberries, and walnuts.

"I've been trying to make things that don't have to be kept hot on the nights Kelli is working late," Donna said, handing Jules a plate. "You still like dark meat, right?"

Jules nodded, smiling as she accepted the plate. They sat at the kitchen table, where glasses of iced tea waited. "Mmmm, this is good," Jules said with her first bite of potato salad. "As good as your mom's."

Donna laughed. "Don't let her hear you say that."

Jules picked up a drumstick and tore a bite off. "I'm sorry about you and Elaine."

"Don't be," Donna said. She kept her eyes on her plate. "It's not easy, but it's been coming for a long time."

"It can't have helped that I was the reason," Jules said.

Donna raised her gaze to Jules's. "When Kelli called me, I had to go. I couldn't have stayed here when..." She stopped, her face eloquent with so much that lay unspoken between them.

Jules looked away first. "I put you through a lot," she said quietly.

"You've been through a lot," Donna said. "I wish you'd been able to talk about it before. I wish I could have helped."

"I never wanted to have to deal with that again." Jules sighed. "I fought it every time something happened that would have dragged me back there, back to that night. I couldn't stand the thought of what I'd done." She closed her eyes.

Donna reached out and laid a hand on Jules's arm. "What you thought you'd done."

Jules's eyes fluttered open, and she and Donna sat for a long while, staring into each other's eyes. As if by mutual consent, they broke eye contact and turned back to their plates.

They were washing up the dishes when Kelli got home.

"Hey," she said, hurrying over to give Jules a tight embrace. "I'm so glad you're home. I'll go shower and be right down."

Donna fixed a plate for her, and she and Jules joined Kelli as she sat to eat.

"So, tell us how you left things with Mae and Bertha and Ronnie," Kelli said as she ate. "I know, you've probably already told Donna, but tell me anyhow."

Jules reached down and picked up Holly, who settled contentedly in her lap. "Ronnie's having a hard time accepting that her mom has chosen between her husband and her daughter, but she's strong. I'll think she'll be okay. Bertha still retreats into her shell sometimes, but she is much better. And Mae is just Mae."

Holly crawled forward on Jules's lap and sniffed the aroma of chicken coming from Kelli's plate.

Kelli reached for Jules's hand. "And how are you?"

"Um," Jules said, squeezing Kelli's hand and then withdrawing. "I'm okay. It's good to be home. I'll be going back to work tomorrow."

Kelli's gaze moved from Jules to Donna and back. "You sure you're rested enough to go right back? Don't you want to take another day off?"

"No," Jules said. "This way, I'll only have a three-day week. What's your schedule for the rest of this week?"

"I'm off tomorrow and Thursday. Mary Anne and I were going to take the kids up to see Dad tomorrow," Kelli said, pinching off a piece of chicken and giving it to Holly. She turned to Donna. "Would you like to go?"

Donna smiled. "Thanks, but no. Summer is my vacation away from kids."

Jules grinned. "See? Told you. We get all our kid time during the school year."

"I'm going to go see a couple of houses for rent," Donna said. "I'll try to get out of your hair soon."

"I don't know." Kelli scooped up another forkful of potato salad. "The way you cook, we might just have to keep you here."

Kelli lay in the dark of the bedroom and swept an arm over the empty mattress beside her, the place Jules should be and wasn't—the place she hadn't been since she got home.

"What is it?" she had asked that first night when she emerged from the bathroom to find Jules standing in the middle of the bedroom.

Jules had stood frozen as Kelli tried to enfold her in an embrace. "I can't do this right now," she'd whispered.

"Can't do what?" Kelli asked, holding Jules by the shoulders and looking at her worriedly. "What's wrong?"

"I can't be here with you," Jules said.

"Why not?"

But Jules could only shake her head and say, "I need to be by myself."

"I don't understand." Kelli felt her heart sink. She remembered how Jules had recoiled from any physical contact while they were in Aldie. Even upstairs, when the two of them had been alone while Donna slept on Mae's couch, Jules had been standoffish, gently pulling away from Kelli's tentative attempts to hold her and staying in her old bed with no invitation to Kelli to join her. Kelli had told herself Jules was still dealing with the trauma of having to relive the night of Hobie's death and the scare Ronnie had given them, and it would all get better once she was back home.

Only it hasn't, Kelli thought now as she lay alone in their room while Donna was alone in the guest room and Jules slept on the futon in the office. She had refused to give way to her fears by getting up in the night to check that the sleeping arrangements hadn't changed. "Jules wouldn't do that," she whispered out loud in the dark. "Donna wouldn't do that."

"I wouldn't be so sure," Mary Anne had said just that afternoon, when Kelli had confided these latest developments to her sister as they took a delivery of new pottery to Elaine's studio.

Donna was out looking at a couple of townhouses for sale in Huntwood and Jules was at work, so they had the afternoon to themselves.

"Why would you say that?" Kelli had asked. She regretted telling Mary Anne anything. She was still so bitter over her split with Brian that she had developed the nasty habit of assuming that no one was faithful and no one could be trusted.

Mary Anne looked at her as if she were having to explain something very simple to someone very obtuse. "You have her old lover living here with you—something I think would be a little weird under any circumstances. Not sure why you ever agreed to that. And you have Jules acting like a shell-shocked veteran coming back from a war zone."

"Don't say that."

"Well, think about it!" Mary Anne said sharply. "You say she had this horrible trauma that's all fresh in her mind; she hasn't let you touch her in weeks; she insists on sleeping alone—though I don't believe for one minute that's happening," she added in a sarcastic tone.

"Neither of them would do that," Kelli insisted.

"I wouldn't be so sure," Mary Anne said as they pulled into the parking lot. They each retrieved a box of pots from the back of the Tahoe and carried them inside, where Kelli stopped so abruptly that Mary Anne ran into her and nearly dropped her box.

"What the hell—?" Mary Anne swore as she caught the box before it hit the floor.

"Carrie," Kelli said. "What are you doing here?"

Elaine came hurrying over. "Hi, Kelli."

"Hey, Elaine," Kelli said. "This is my sister, Mary Anne."

Elaine said hello as she took the box from Mary Anne. "Carrie is helping me out here at the studio while she's got some time off this summer."

Kelli noticed Carrie had turned very red. She mumbled a hello and busied herself elsewhere in the studio where she was hidden from sight by tall pieces of furniture while Elaine looked over the contents of the boxes.

"These look wonderful," she gushed. "And I've got a check for you from the last batch. They nearly all sold."

"Thanks," said Kelli, still looking around for a sign of Carrie as Elaine went back to the office, but Carrie was staying out of sight. Elaine came back a moment later with a check. "See you soon," Kelli said.

"What was that all about?" Mary Anne asked as soon as they were back in the Tahoe. "Who was that other woman?"

"A teacher who was making a play for Jules," Kelli said darkly. "Looks like she's changed her target."

Mary Anne shook her head. "You do realize how incestuous this is. All this switching of partners? It's weird, Kelli."

"It's not like we have a monopoly on this," Kelli said. "You said the people at your country club do the same thing."

"Maybe," Mary Anne admitted with a scowl. Brian's taking his new fling to the club and flaunting her in front of their friends was still a very raw topic for Mary Anne and usually elicited at least a half hour's rant on what an asshole he was. "But at least we're not stupid enough to all pretend we're staying friends."

Kelli rolled over in bed now, restless and agitated. She got up and crossed to the bedroom door, her hand on the knob. "No," she whispered. "You are not going to do this. They're each in their rooms, and you're going to trust them." She forced herself to go back to bed, cursing herself for listening to her sister.

She'd thought the worst was over. Jules had faced the monster she'd been running from for over twenty years. She'd conquered it—*or so I thought*. But it felt now as if they'd simply entered a new phase of torment, one Kelli didn't completely understand, one that was pulling Jules away from her again—or at least dividing her.

In some vague way, Kelli could feel that Jules stood torn—torn between her and Donna. And Kelli strongly suspected that a third choice might be to simply walk away from both of them and begin again with someone new, someone who hadn't been tainted by Jules's past. A completely fresh start.

Kelli knew—had known from the beginning—that Donna had never completely recovered from loving Jules. She could see it and had often wondered why Jules couldn't. It was a feeling Kelli had understood, empathized with, but now she wondered if there was a part of Jules that had never stopped loving Donna as well.

She lay there, forcing herself to consider whether she could live as part of a threesome. Donna was already here in the house. The two of them got along well, but Kelli wondered if they could really share Jules. She could just imagine Mary Anne's reaction to that arrangement.

She flung her arms over her face. *You've held on this long,* she reminded herself. *Just hang on a little longer. Jules will come around. She will.*

CHAPTER 32

KELLI WAS IN THE kitchen when she heard the front door slam. She hurried into the living room to find Donna standing there with an armful of clothes.

"What's the matter?" Jules asked from the couch, where she'd been reading.

"Carrie was there!"

"Really?" Kelli stepped farther into the living room.

Donna dropped the clothes onto an empty chair. "I know you said you saw her at the studio," she said to Kelli. "But now, she's at the house! My stuff was all lying on a bed in a spare room, so I've been moved out of the master, presumably to make room for her." She flung herself into another chair and sat staring at the floor. "That didn't take long."

Kelli came to sit beside Jules. "Are you okay?" she asked, watching Donna worriedly.

Kelli and Jules looked at each other when Donna burst out laughing. "I knew I was well rid of her. But Carrie—" She gave Jules a reproachful look. "What you were thinking with that one, I will never know. They're perfect for each other."

Kelli smiled in relief. "How about some wine?"

Donna scowled. "I may never drink wine again in my life. I want a goddamned beer!"

Jules laughed and went to the kitchen, emerging a moment later with three bottles of Corona, fresh slices of lime squeezed into each one. They stood, holding the bottles aloft as Donna said, "Here's to fresh starts!"

"To fresh starts," Jules and Kelli echoed. Kelli looked askance at Jules to see if the words of the toast had triggered anything for her. In an instant, the atmosphere prickled with tension as the three of them glanced warily from one to the other.

Kelli hesitated, wondering if this was the right moment, but—*this has gone on long enough*—heard herself saying, "We need to talk."

Donna immediately turned to the chair where she had left her clothes and scooped them up in her beer-free arm. "I'll take—"

"No," Kelli cut in. "No. You're part of this, whatever this is. We all need to talk."

Donna put her clothes back down and took her chair again as Jules and Kelli resumed their positions on the couch, Kelli now sitting a cushion away so that they were sitting in a triangle. *How appropriate,* Kelli thought wryly, and she almost laughed out loud at the absurdity of this situation. She took a calming breath and tried to slow her heart.

"You've been home for almost two weeks now," Kelli said to Jules. "Clearly, something is still bothering you." She glanced at Donna. "I have the feeling it involves both Donna and myself."

Donna stood again. "I've interfered with the two of you for too long," she said. "I'll find somewhere else—"

"No," said Jules and Kelli at the same time.

"It's not you," Jules said.

Kelli leaned toward her as Donna took her seat once again. "Can't you tell us what's going on?"

Jules lowered her gaze to her bottle, swirling the lime inside. "It's not you," she repeated. "Either of you. But it's to do with you." She took a deep breath and let it out slowly. "I've not been on my own since I was twenty. There were a couple of girlfriends before you," she said, gesturing to Donna, "and then... from you to Stacy to you," she said, looking to Kelli. "I've never spent any time as an adult, dealing with my past, alone. Just me and my mistakes. I don't want to hurt either of you. I just have to figure some things out."

Donna looked startled, and Kelli's cheeks burned as if she'd been slapped. "I guess that's what I get for asking," Kelli said shakily.

<hr>

Can't you tell us what's going on?

Jules sat at her desk, staring unseeingly at the report on her computer screen. She closed her eyes, trying to shut out the pained expression on Kelli's face. "You may not have meant to hurt me, but you did," she seemed to say.

Jules knew she had put Donna in an awkward position, too, leaving her feeling as if she'd come between them. But even Kelli seemed to know that wasn't the case. A strange bond had developed between Donna and Kelli, almost as if they were looking to one another for comfort as they waited—*waiting for me to choose.*

Restlessly, she muttered to no one in particular that she needed a file. She walked the halls of the building and nodded absently to the few people she passed.

What if you don't choose? Jules asked Jules.

It might not be up to you, came the unexpected answer. *What if they decide they've had enough of you? What if they don't just sit around and wait for you to make up your mind?*

Jules stopped in her tracks. Alone. She'd said she needed to work through this alone, but she wasn't alone. Not really. She still had Kelli and Donna there. What if they both told her to go to hell and left her well and truly alone? *I'd deserve it.* For some reason, it hadn't even occurred to her that the choice might not be hers to make.

"What are you thinking about?"

Jules sat in a chair pulled up to Pappy's bed. He'd lost another five pounds, Mae had told her. He hadn't looked at her when she entered and called his name. He stared at the ceiling, a slight smile playing across his gaunt face, legs bent at the knee as he curled into a position the nursing staff was forever trying to get him out of, but as soon as they straightened his limbs, he curled up again.

He lay there now, hands folded across his chest as if in prayer, lost in his world, wherever that was. Jules sat there, talking to him and getting no response. *Why did I come back for this?*

"I've got a busy schedule next week," she'd protested to Mae.

"We've all got something to set aside," Mae said over the phone. "He's fading fast, and you're going to be sorry if you don't get back down here and spend some time with him while he knows you."

So, Jules had reluctantly made plans to go to Aldie for the weekend. She hadn't invited Stacy to come, and to her relief, Stacy hadn't wanted to come. *Good. I didn't want another argument.* They'd been arguing a lot lately. It was getting tiresome.

Once in Aldie, she had avoided seeing Mrs. Fahnestock— "don't worry," Mae said when she noticed. "You won't see her. She hardly ever comes out of that house anymore."

Jules had seen her only two or three times in the years since Hobie's funeral. "Of course, you have to go," Mae had insisted when Hobie's funeral arrangements were announced. "I know it's hard, but sometimes the right things are hard."

"We'll be there with you," Pappy had said.

It was Jules's first funeral, and she was afraid of what she might see—"but how could it be any worse than what you've already seen?" she would ask herself afterward. She could tell from across the viewing room that the casket was open. "We get in line and give Bertha our condolences," Mae prompted. Jules was herded along, shuffling reluctantly up toward the casket, where Mrs. Fahnestock stood, a crumpled handkerchief clutched in her hands, as her sister stood beside her. Jules mumbled something incoherent while Mae wrung Bertha's hand and Pappy said something kind about what a good boy Hobie was, and then Jules was led over to the casket.

"He looks peaceful," Mae said.

He looks drowned, Jules thought. Hobie looked almost as he had when they pulled him out of the river. His face was still white but now with fake-looking patches of blush on his cheeks, his hair slicked back in a way that he would have hated. She stared down at him and felt the warm weight of Pappy's hand on her shoulder.

She reached now for his hand as he lay in the nursing home bed. His hand lay limp in hers. She remembered how these hands had been able to fix anything, how they had rubbed her back to calm her when she was upset, how they had held her when she was finally brought home that night after the rescue workers had pulled Hobie from the river.

"I'm sorry I haven't been home more often," she whispered. "I just couldn't... I had to get away. I hope you understand."

I'm typing on my own computer! Mrs. Fahnestock said I need one for when school starts next month. She said she'd buy the computer if I can split the Internet bill and teach her how to use the Internet. She said I had to get my mom to give her permission for the school to use this as my new address, and Mom did it. She met me at school, but she didn't ask me how I'm doing or anything.

You wouldn't recognize this place. We got rid of the old curtains and put up blinds that let light in. We've been painting the downstairs rooms. It doesn't feel depressing here anymore.

I've been reading more of Hobie's stories and journals. You said you never read them. You should. You were in a lot of them. I feel like I'm getting to know you in a whole different way, seeing you through Hobie's eyes. It makes me gladder than ever that I slipped you that note.

Give my love to Kelli and Donna,
Ronnie

Jules smiled as she re-read Ronnie's latest message. What a godsend she'd become. "Jeez, I sound like Mae," she muttered as she realized what she'd just thought. Still, Ronnie had made a huge difference in all their lives. She shook her head again as she pulled the carefully folded note out of her wallet—"the note that wouldn't be destroyed," Kelli had christened it. "Some things," she declared, "are meant to be."

Or not to be.

Jules's expression sobered. Kelli was downstairs in her studio, and Donna was down the hall in her room, reading. She'd found a nearby townhouse for rent, but the current tenant wasn't scheduled to vacate until the end of August.

"I understand if you guys want your space back," she said. "I forgot how hard it is to find rentals in this town that aren't surrounded by students."

"You are not in our way at all," Kelli had assured her. "I think it's pretty poor form of Elaine not to go ahead with refinancing if she wants to keep the house. You need your half of its value."

Donna shrugged. "She's worried that she won't be approved on her own as someone who's self-employed."

"That's her problem," Jules said. "If she can't get the loan, the house goes on the market. It's pretty simple."

"I know," Donna said, shaking her head glumly. "I'll have to push her to do that soon. I just hope it doesn't come to that. She could make things ugly."

"No shit," but Jules bit the words back just in time. She felt lately as if she didn't have much room to criticize Elaine or anyone else.

Kelli and Donna were honoring her wish to be left mostly alone to deal with her issues. Kelli, in particular, had withdrawn—"well, I did my withdrawing years ago," Donna would have said pragmatically if they had talked about it. *Maybe they are talking about it,* Jules realized. The three of them ate most of their meals together, watched television together, or sometimes sat quietly together to read, but Kelli and Donna had hours together on Kelli's days off while Jules was at work. She was beginning to feel as if she was becoming the intruder on their relationship, and she couldn't help wondering how long the other two, Kelli especially, would be content to do this. She, herself, felt kind of numb. Flat. She felt no desire to be physically intimate—with anyone. There had been no more tears, but no real happiness either. Not much of anything lately. Just work and sleep and brief moments with Kelli and Donna that broke through the sameness of the days.

Sometimes, Jules felt she owed it to Kelli to offer her a breakup, without forcing Kelli to be the one to initiate it. But she couldn't seem to make herself do that, either. She found herself watching Kelli, the way her hair changed to varying shades of gold when she moved her head and the light hit it differently; the way her eyes lit up when she laughed—which was more often at something Donna did or said lately; the occasional glance from her in Jules's direction, her eyes still so full of love and tenderness that Jules had to look away.

What is wrong with me?

Jules had asked herself that question a million times over the past weeks. The worst should be over. She didn't understand why she couldn't just move on. She lay in the dark on the futon, staring at the ceiling as she tried to figure out what was stopping her from just going down the hall to Kelli and crawling into bed with her. She sat up and swung her feet to the floor. *Just go. She'll welcome you back.* She opened the door of the office and padded down the hall to Kelli's door. She reached for the doorknob and froze. She pressed her forehead against the door and stood there for a long time. She turned to go back to the office and stopped when she saw Donna standing outside her bedroom door, watching her. Soundlessly, Donna went back into the bedroom and closed the door.

———— ❧ ————

"Just tell her to get the hell out."

Mary Anne was breathing hard from the mat next to Kelli's as they were supposed to be doing their yoga routine—"in a meditative silence," Kelli had reminded her sister three times already, to no avail.

Kelli had tried to keep to her routine, forcing herself to do all the usual things. It was how she'd coped during the months after her mother's death. This felt almost like that, as if she were in mourning for something that was gone forever—*but it's not gone,* she kept telling herself. *You just have to believe she'll come back.*

Mary Anne had wheedled the latest update from Kelli, becoming increasingly more indignant as Kelli reluctantly explained that the current living arrangement had continued. She'd been avoiding this topic with Mary Anne, not wanting to hear any more of her thoughts on the matter, but even Kelli's patience was starting to wear thin as she wondered when, or if, things would ever get back to normal.

"Which her?"

Mary Anne panted as she tried to hold a plank. She finally collapsed onto her mat and gasped. "Both."

"I can't," Kelli said. "I don't want to. Donna will be moving in a couple of weeks anyhow, and I'm not ready to give Jules an ultimatum."

Mary Anne reached for the remote and turned off the DVD. "Enough of that." She rolled over and looked at Kelli, who continued working through a series of warrior poses. "What do you think is going on with Jules? Do you think she still loves you?"

Kelli didn't answer immediately, lowering herself into runner's pose and then into a plank and downward dog before saying, "I do. I catch her watching me sometimes, and I can see she still loves me. That's why I'm not ready to give up on this relationship yet. But..." She dropped to her mat. "I also see her watching Donna sometimes. I think..." She reached for a towel and mopped her sweaty face. "I think she honestly loves both of us. At least a part of her still loves Donna."

Mary Anne snorted. "That's just creepy."

"No," Kelli said slowly. "It's almost like Jules is getting in touch with feelings she hasn't let herself acknowledge for years and she has to work through them."

"Why doesn't she go see someone? I can give her the name of my therapist," Mary Anne said. "She's really expensive. It's costing Brian a fortune."

Kelli pressed her towel to her face and said in a muffled voice, "That's one area where Jules is more like her grandmother than she would ever admit. She would never talk to a stranger about her problems."

"If she keeps this up, strangers may be her only option," Mary Anne said. She eyed Kelli shrewdly. "And what if she decides to go back to Donna? What if you're the one left out? Someone is going to be hurt here."

Kelli flopped over on her back, trying not to think about the fact that Mary Anne had just given voice to her own deepest fear. "I don't think any of us will come out of this unscathed."

CHAPTER 33

JULES PULLED INTO AN empty driveway, exhausted from a day spent sitting through a webinar on executive functioning. She needed the credits for her license, but it was frustrating to spend hours listening to someone who wasn't imparting much new information.

"Hello?" she called as she came into the house, depositing her briefcase on the bench in the foyer. No answer. She checked the garage. No Tahoe. She couldn't remember the last time she'd had the house to herself. She went to get the mail and sorted through about ten catalogs as she brought the bundle back inside. Tucked amidst the catalogs was a large manila envelope. It was from Ronnie. Intrigued, Jules slit the envelope open and pulled out a sheaf of papers, along with a handwritten note from Ronnie.

Dear Jules,

I was reading some of the last parts of Hobie's journal and found some things I thought you should read. I showed them to

Mrs. Fahnestock, and she said we should copy them and mail them to you.

Love,
Ronnie

Scrawled underneath Ronnie's signature was a short postscript.

I hope this helps.
Bertha

More apprehensive than curious now, Jules carried the bundle upstairs and closed the office door behind her. She repositioned her pillow so she could sit back against the wall as she read in Hobie's tiny block writing:

I feel bad that I made such a big fuss about Mother's Day. I finally have some real money to spend, and I was going on to Jules about how I was going to buy Mom a new outfit and take her out to dinner. I only wanted to show Mom how much I appreciate everything she's done without all these years to make things as good for me as she could. I didn't think it would bother Jules. She's never acted like she missed her mother at all, but I think now

that we're sixteen and things like graduation
and college are getting closer, she's starting
to think about it more. I can't imagine having
a mother who never bothered to see me or
even call to see if I'm okay. I feel sorry for
her.

Jules remembered that Mother's Day. Hobie was right—it had hit her out of the blue as she watched him excitedly making plans to do something special for his mom. She supposed she could have done something for Mae, who had been more of a mother to her than her own, but Mae would have said something like, "That's a fool waste of money. I can cook as good as we'd get out for a whole lot less. You save your money." For the first time in her life, she had spent that Mother's Day wondering what her mother was doing and where she was.

Jules was glad, as she sat there staring at the page, that she hadn't known at that age what her mother was really up to. She wasn't sure how she would have reacted had she known. She slid that journal entry aside and began reading the next.

Jules had to have Friday put to sleep today.
The vet said the cancer had spread from
her liver to her spine and there wasn't
anything he could do. Mae and Pappy told her
it was best to put her out of her misery.

She told me when they got back from the vet. She just said it, all matter-of-fact, and then walked away. But tonight, I heard her crying out by the oak. I stood in the dark and listened to the sound, like a wounded animal, and it made the hair stand up on my arms as I listened. She never cries, not that I've ever seen or heard. As I stood there, I was torn. Part of me wanted to go and comfort her. I think maybe I'm the only one she would let near her right now. Like she was the only one Friday would let near in the beginning. But the other part of me felt like maybe she needs to cry, needs to let out all the bad things she's feeling. I've never had trouble doing that, but Jules keeps things bottled up inside. I worry about her sometimes.

Jules's eyes filled with tears now as she recalled that horrible day. Friday's back legs had become so weakened in the weeks prior that Jules had had to fashion a sling out of an old sheet to help support her to go out and relieve herself. But no matter how weak she was or how painful it had become to walk, Friday still tried to follow Jules everywhere. At last, Pappy had had to sit Jules down and say, "It's not right to let her go on like this, Jules. Sometimes, when we really love someone, we have to let them go when it's the right thing to do." Jules had managed not to cry on the way to the vet, sitting in the backseat of the Dart with Friday's head resting on her lap, or sitting on the floor of the vet's exam room, still holding Friday's head and whispering in her ear as the vet started the IV and pushed the plunger, or as she watched Friday's breathing slow and eventually still completely. She hadn't cried on the way home or when she told Hobie or for the remainder of the afternoon, but as darkness fell and she felt the empty space at her feet where Friday should have been lying, she couldn't hold it in any longer. She had retreated to the oak tree out back, far enough away from the house that she wouldn't be heard, and there, she'd given way to her grief. She'd never had any idea that Hobie had heard her. Until now. "What else did you know?" Jules whispered as she turned to the next page in the sheaf.

I think I'm starting to fall in love. I can't believe I'm writing that for the first time in my life! I always imagined what it would be like, but it feels more wonderful than anything I could have dreamt of. I want to shout it out, but I know I can't. Not in Aldie and not when it's another guy I'm falling for. I'd like to tell Jules. I know she's felt like this about some of the girls at school, but she's so private, so protective of her feelings. She never says anything. Her heart has been

> broken too many times. She's the bravest
> person I know. She'd stand up to anyone and
> has, but falling in love scares her. I think
> for her, it will have to wait until we're away
> from here and in college. Then, she'll be able
> to be herself. If the right time comes, I'm
> going to tell her.

Jules closed her eyes and leaned her head back against the wall. Tammy Dearing had been the first, but there had been others—infatuations, crushes on other girls in school. But never had Jules worked up the courage to tell any of them how she felt. Tammy's reaction to that stupid poem had killed any belief in Jules that another girl could feel the same way for her. Hobie had been so much braver about things like that than she'd ever been. She reached for a tissue and blew her nose, not really sure she wanted to keep reading, but unable to stop—*like watching the proverbial train wreck.* She flipped the page.

> I tried to talk to Jules today, but she's
> furious. She saw Gilbert and me kissing,
> and she said—I'm not sure how to handle the
> things she said. Everyone heard. I know she's
> really just afraid—afraid I'll leave her, afraid
> someone like Gilbert could come between
> her and me, but mostly afraid it will make

> her face herself if I have a boyfriend. I
> don't know what to do. I can't talk to her
> yet. I need to think. It's storming, but I'm going
> to go for a walk in the rain. I'll write more
> later.

"He was going to write more later," Jules whispered, clutching the paper in her hands as she stared at the words written there.

<hr />

Jules wasn't sure what time it was when she woke in the dark, lying on her side with the copies of Hobie's journal pages tucked next to her. She had a vague recollection of having heard noises from downstairs, and she thought maybe someone might have opened the office door and spoken to her, but she wasn't sure. She lay there, listening to the nighttime sounds of the house, and she could hear crickets chirping from outside—*funny how that sound carries even with the AC on,* she mused groggily.

She'd been dreaming about Hobie. They'd been down to the dump and had found all kinds of good stuff to bring home, and when Jules opened an army rucksack she'd hauled back, Friday climbed out of it. She smiled in the dark. It was the first good dream she could remember for ages.

She rolled over and looked at the clock. Nearly three a.m. She sat up on the side of the futon. Her stomach growled noisily, and she realized she hadn't had any dinner. She went down the hall to use the bathroom and brushed her teeth while she was in there. As she came back out into the hall, she paused at the door to the office. Her stomach growled insistently, and she went downstairs to get a bowl of cereal. She sat at the kitchen table, illuminated only by moonlight as she ate, her first couple of bites flavored with toothpaste.

She's the bravest person I know... but falling in love scares her. Hobie had seen right through her bravado and her defenses. He was right. She'd been scared most of her life. Even when she used to stand up to Joey Reynolds and the other kids, it was because she didn't want them to see her scared. It was all bluster, and it worked. "Up to a point," she whispered to the moon. But there had come a time, a time when it was her heart that was at risk, and then she wasn't brave anymore. Then, it had become easier to shut herself off whenever things got too close. With every relationship she'd had since high school, there had been an emotional boundary no one was allowed to cross. She looked up at the ceiling. Sleeping up there were the two women who had stuck with her, despite being stopped firmly at that border. They'd felt it, tried to get her to let them cross it, but she had rebuffed their efforts and kept them on their side of that divide.

Her breathing quickened as she weighed what to do. She carried her bowl to the sink and crept back upstairs, pausing a moment at Kelli's door but then going to the end of the hall to the guest room. She opened the door silently and closed it behind her. As she sat down, her weight on the mattress awakened Donna, who sat up, looking at her in the faint light coming into the bedroom through the curtains. Jules could hear the pounding of her own heart and thought, surely, Donna must hear it, too.

They sat for long minutes, looking at each other. Donna waited—"waiting for me to make the first move," Jules would realize later. Jules reached for Donna's hand and felt it trembling.

"I've been so unfair to you," Jules murmured. "You were my first real love, and I shut you out. I never told you about... everything that happened, and it put a wall between us." She paused, but Donna remained silent. Jules could hear her shallow breathing. "The wall has been torn down now, and you've seen everything, every ugly thing, every cowardly thing I've done. I never stopped loving you. I just couldn't stand letting you see the truth about me."

Donna moved at last, apprehensively drawing near to Jules.

Jules met her with a kiss, a long, tender kiss filled with yearning and sadness and hope. She leaned toward Donna, pressing her back to the bed, remembering how familiar and wondrous Donna's mouth and body had been as Donna pulled her close.

Abruptly, Donna turned away, breaking the kiss and pushing against Jules's shoulders. "No," she gasped.

Jules sat up, still leaning over Donna, whose hands gripped Jules's arms, pushing her away and holding her near at the same time.

"This is wrong." Donna sounded as if it was costing her every ounce of strength she had to say it. "God, I've wanted this for so long." Her voice cracked. "I've hoped and waited, but... we can't go back. And we can't do this to Kelli."

She cried softly as Jules pressed her lips to Donna's palm and left the room.

The kitchen crackled with tension the next morning as the three of them ate breakfast. Kelli looked from Jules to Donna and back as they avoided looking at one another.

"I'm going to go stay with Barbara and Chris for a week or two until the townhouse is ready for me to move in," Donna announced as she sat down with a couple of scrambled eggs and a piece of toast.

Kelli looked up. "But why? You don't need to move out of here. It's only a couple more weeks." She glanced quickly at Jules, who kept her eyes on her oatmeal. "Jules?"

Jules shrugged. "You are more than welcome to stay here," she said, "but I'll be okay with whatever you decide."

She looked up, and she and Donna locked eyes in a glance that went through Kelli like a lance. Shaken, Kelli turned back to her coffee as Donna said, "I've imposed on you two long enough. I think this would be the best thing to do. I'll move out today, and you'll have your place back to yourselves by this evening."

Jules glanced at her watch. "I'm running late. Gotta go." She rose and carried her bowl, still half-full of oatmeal, to the sink. "We'll see you soon, Donna."

Donna nodded. "See you." Her tone was casual, but Kelli saw that she was blinking back tears as Jules walked out of the room.

Kelli never remembered much of the remainder of that morning. When she got off work that evening, she took her time driving home, even taking a few detours along less-traveled roads. Donna had said she expected to be moved out by this time, but Kelli didn't know—didn't want to know—if she and Jules had spent any time together during the day. Work had been a blessing, keeping her so busy she had only had odd moments to think, and thinking was not a good thing today... As much as she had seen over these past few weeks that Jules was torn between the two of them and had tried to prepare herself for the possibility of the three of them somehow making a home together, the scene this morning—

She braked to a full stop in the middle of the street, one block from their house. She squeezed the steering wheel, trying to calm the panic rising within her. She'd tried so hard to be open, to wait until Jules was ready to come back to her, but now it seemed like the stupidest thing to have done. "I should have fought for her," she said aloud, thinking bitterly how Mary Anne would react to hearing that Jules was getting back together with Donna.

Startled by a car horn behind her, she turned the corner onto their street. Jules's car was in the driveway. Kelli pulled into the garage, wondering what would be awaiting her once she got inside.

She came into the kitchen from the garage and found it empty. She opened her mouth to call out but couldn't. *What if this is what it's like from now on?* The cats looked up sleepily from the family room when she peeked in. She went upstairs and saw that the office door was shut. She stood there for a moment, considering barging in to demand to know what was up, but turned, instead, to the master bedroom. She peeled off her clothing, stepped naked into the bathroom, and turned the shower on. While she waited for the water to get hot, she turned to the mirror, reaching down to grab the small love handle at her waist. She turned around to look at her butt. At forty-five, it was getting harder to keep the extra weight off, no matter how many miles she biked or how much yoga she did or how many weight workouts she did. Jules was five years younger, Donna's age....

She turned away from the mirror. "If that's the choice she's made, this isn't helping," she told herself harshly as she stepped into the shower.

A few minutes later, toweled off and changed into clean clothes, she went downstairs to find Jules in the kitchen, holding out a glass of wine. Kelli couldn't read anything in her expression.

"Are you hungry?" Jules asked.

Kelli's stomach had felt upset all day after the anxiety of the scene at the breakfast table. She'd barely touched her lunch. She knew drinking wine on such an empty stomach was probably not a good idea, but "I'll drink my dinner," she heard herself say, accepting the glass.

Jules gestured toward the backyard. "Want to watch the fireflies? We need to talk."

Kelli's face turned to stone at those words, but she led the way out to the backyard and the lawn chairs. Jules angled hers so that she was partially facing Kelli as the sun settled beyond the treetops, throwing long shadows across the grass.

"Kelli, I—" Jules began, but before she could go any further, Kelli cut in, saying, "So help me, Jules, if you give me one of those 'it's not you, it's me' speeches, I am going to throw this wine in your face."

To Kelli's surprise, Jules laughed. "And I would deserve it," she said. She tilted her head, looking at Kelli. A single ray of sun broke through the branches of the trees, and, with the clarity of a photograph, Kelli could see the edge of Jules's face, her eyelashes, her hair—all gilded in golden light. "But, in this case, it's true," Jules said. "It has been all me—me who pulled away, me who put walls up, me who has kept you at arm's length for so long now. You know most of why—all the stuff to do with the night Hobie died." She paused. "Do you have any idea what it feels like to be able to say those words out loud? To be able to talk about him and think about him and dream about him—in a good way—after all this time?"

Kelli refrained from reaching out to take Jules's hand. Instead, she took another sip of her wine, having a hard time swallowing as she waited to hear what was coming next.

"But ever since the night Ronnie ran away," Jules continued, "I have felt like I've been given a chance to make old wrongs right or at least take a second look at why they went wrong in the first place."

"Is this the part where you tell me you're getting back together with Donna?" Kelli asked, and the light tone of her voice sounded horribly forced, even to her own ears. As much as she didn't want to hear whatever Jules was going to say, it was better to get it over with.

Jules's eyes locked on Kelli's, and she leaned forward, elbows on knees. "It's true, I felt like I was standing on a fault line between you. Go back and try to fix what I ruined all those years ago, or stay and fix what I was ruining now. But... trying to figure out how to make that choice, who to go to..." She dropped her head, staring at the wine glass in her hands. "I went to Donna last night," she said quietly.

Kelli looked away to where fireflies were beginning to light up the deepening shadows of the backyard as the sun sank completely below the trees. She watched the little lights dotting the yard in a random pattern while she waited for the other shoe to drop.

"I had to apologize to her for everything I put her through," Jules said. "I had to tell her that I still loved her and wished things had been different. If I'd been able to deal with all of this a long time ago, things between Donna and me probably would have been different, and I never would have met you."

There was only the distant sound of a neighbor's lawn mower and, closer, a dog barking.

"So, why is Donna gone?" Kelli forced herself to ask.

"She told me we couldn't go back, and we couldn't hurt you," Jules said.

A long moment passed as Jules's words sunk in. Kelli turned to look at her. "So, now that Donna has turned you down, you can come to me?" she asked coldly. "I'm better than nothing, but I wasn't the one you came to first." She stood up. "Normally, I would tell you I have to think about it, but I'm pretty sure there's not much to think about."

She went inside, slamming the screen door as Jules sat back in her chair and looked up at the deepening purple of the summer sky.

———◦❯◦❮◦———

Mary Anne stood outside the door of the room Kelli had been using for the past three nights. "Kelli? I brought some dinner up. You hungry?"

When Kelli had arrived on Mary Anne's doorstep, stating, "I don't want to talk," Mary Anne had known it was serious. "Just let her have some space," she'd told the kids, who didn't understand why Aunt Kelli wasn't downstairs with them.

Kelli had worked twelve-hour shifts each of the next three days, taking an extra shift for another nurse. She left before the rest of the house was awake, coming back to Mary Anne's house in the evenings, where she showered and stayed up in the guest room.

Now, with the kids fed and settled in front of the television, Mary Anne figured enough was enough. She knocked again and opened the door to find Kelli sitting up on the bed.

"You need to eat something," she said, handing her sister the plate.

She went around to the other side of the bed and propped the second pillow against the headboard while Kelli picked at the food, eating a few forkfuls.

"You look awful." Mary Anne observed the dark circles under Kelli's eyes that made them look bruised.

Kelli didn't say anything.

"I've left you alone long enough. What the hell happened?"

Kelli's eyes filled with tears. "She made her choice," she managed to gasp as she shook with her sobs.

Mary Anne stared at her. "She's going back to Donna? That goddamned bitch."

Kelli shook her head, but Mary Anne had to wait a few minutes before Kelli could say, "She's not going back to Donna, but only because Donna said no."

"What?" Mary Anne shifted on the bed, sitting cross-legged to face her sister. "Tell me everything."

Kelli set the plate on the nightstand and pulled a tissue out of the box there. She dabbed at her eyes and blew her nose. "Jules went to Donna the night before I left. I could tell that morning there was something weird between them. Jules told me she went to her to tell her she was sorry for screwing up their life all those years ago and that she still loved her."

Mary Anne's mouth opened and closed a couple of times. "So, why aren't they together?"

Kelli shrugged. "I guess Donna told Jules that they couldn't go back to the way they were before and they couldn't hurt me."

"So then she comes to you? After Donna turned her down?"

"That's what I said," Kelli said with a bark of bitter laughter. "The hell with that."

"Damn straight. I would've told her to go fuck herself."

They sat silently for long minutes.

"I don't get it, though," Mary Anne said with a shake of her head. "I thought this was what Donna wanted. Jules couldn't have screwed this up more if she tried. It's like she did it on purpose."

Something shifted in Kelli's expression. She stared at her sister. "What did you say?"

The house was dark, but Jules wasn't sleeping when she heard the door open downstairs. She listened to the familiar footsteps coming up the stairs, and then the office door opened unexpectedly and Kelli stood there, breathing hard.

Jules sat up. Moonlight illuminated the room enough for them to make out each other's features.

"You did it deliberately," Kelli said. "You went to Donna first to give her the chance to end it this time, on her terms. And now, you're doing the same to me."

Jules sat silently. Kelli came over and sat on the side of the futon. "You're giving me the chance to put an end to us, instead of you walking away like you always have."

Jules just looked at her.

"Do you want us to end?" Kelli asked.

"No," Jules managed to croak, letting Kelli pull her into a bone-crushing embrace as tears ran down her face. "I don't want to lose you," Jules gasped.

"You're not going to lose me," Kelli whispered in Jules's ear as she rocked her. "You're not going to lose me."

They sat like that for a long time until Kelli slid her cheek along Jules's and pressed her lips to Jules's eagerly waiting mouth. They kissed deeply, clinging tightly to each another. Kelli pulled away long enough to pull her shirt over her head and then she lay down on top of Jules, kissing her hungrily as her hands slid under Jules's T-shirt to her breasts, where the nipples were hard, begging for Kelli's mouth. She ripped the T-shirt up and took first one, then the other nipple in her mouth, eliciting a moan from Jules, who lifted her hips as Kelli slid Jules's underwear down over her hips.

A long while later, both of them physically exhausted from their frantic lovemaking, Jules lay with her head resting on Kelli's shoulder. Kelli's hand rested against Jules's neck, where she could feel her pulse, strong and steady.

"Were you so sure Donna would turn you down?" Kelli murmured.

"Not really," Jules said.

"What would you have done if she hadn't said no?"

"I would have gone back to her," Jules said quietly. "I'm not sure we could have ever been as happy as we were before, but I would have honored that commitment."

"A do-over?"

Jules nodded against Kelli's shoulder.

"Do you still love her?"

"I never stopped loving her," Jules said carefully as she struggled to explain. "I stopped loving me. Part of me does still love her. I don't know if it could ever be enough, though." She lifted her head and looked at Kelli. "Because now, I'll always love you. I think she knew that. She deserves better than that, but at least this time, it was her choice." She laid her head back down. "You deserve better, too," she added softly.

"I don't deserve anything," Kelli said, wrapping her arm more tightly around Jules. "That's not how love works, Jules. You can't deserve it or earn it. I should be kicking your butt to the curb for what you tried to do, but I can't. I love you."

Jules squeezed Kelli tightly. "I'm sorry I've put you through so much."

"I'm just glad you're here, in my arms, all of you," Kelli murmured. She placed her fingers under Jules's chin and raised her face so she could look into her eyes. "Do I have all of you? Nothing went with Donna? Nothing left down at the river?"

In response, Jules sat up and turned on the lamp on the side table. Kelli shielded her eyes at the unexpected glare as Jules reached into a drawer and pulled out a small bundle of papers. Wordlessly, she handed them to Kelli, who sat up against a pillow and read. When she got to the last entry, she gasped and placed a hand over her mouth. She looked up at Jules.

"Then, he didn't—?" she said.

Jules shook her head. "No. He didn't. I don't think I truly believed it until I read that. But now, I'm sure." She took the papers back, holding them reverently. "It's almost as if he's given me absolution."

Kelli kissed Jules's hand. "Let's go back to bed. Our bed."

Jules started reaching for her clothes, but Kelli stopped her. "No need to bother with those. They're just coming off again."

Jules smiled and turned toward the master bedroom, but Kelli went the other way. "What—?"

Kelli went into the guest room and emerged again a moment later, carrying something. She went into their bedroom, set Jules's night-light on the bedside table, and plugged it in. She lay down beside Jules and reached over her to click the light on. The amber glow washed over them as they looked at the copper geese flying away to places unknown.

"I think," Kelli said softly, "this belongs in here, with us."

###

About Caren J. Werlinger

Caren was raised in Ohio, the oldest of four children. Much of her childhood was spent reading every book she could get her hands on and crafting her own stories. She completed a degree in foreign languages and later another degree in physical therapy. For many years, her only writing was research-based, including a therapeutic exercise textbook. She has lived in Virginia for over twenty years, where she practices physical therapy, teaches anatomy, and lives with her partner and their canine fur-children. She began writing creatively again several years ago. Her first novel, *Looking Through Windows*, won a Debut Author award from the Golden Crown Literary Society in 2009. In 2013, *Miserere*, *In This Small Spot*, and *Neither Present Time* all won or placed in the 2013 Rainbow Awards. *In This Small Spot* won Best Dramatic Fiction in the 2014 Golden Crown Literary Awards.

Connect with Caren online
E-mail her at: cjwerlingerbooks@yahoo.com
Visit her website: http://www.cjwerlinger.wordpress.com

Other Books from
Ylva Publishing

www.ylva-publishing.com

Coming Home

Lois Cloarec Hart

ISBN: 978-3-95533-064-4
Length: 371 pages

A triangle with a twist, *Coming Home* is the story of three good people caught up in an impossible situation.

Rob, a charismatic ex-fighter pilot severely disabled with MS, has been steadfastly cared for by his wife, Jan, for many years. Quite by accident one day, Terry, a young writer/ postal carrier, enters their lives and turns it upside down.

Injecting joy and turbulence into their quiet existence, Terry draws Rob and Jan into her lively circle of family and friends until the growing attachment between the two women begins to strain the bonds of love and loyalty, to Rob and each other.

Barring Complications

Blythe Rippon

ISBN: 978-3-95533-191-7

Length: 374 pages

It's an open secret that the newest justice on the Supreme Court is a lesbian. So when the Court decides to hear a case about gay marriage, Justice Victoria Willoughby must navigate the press, sway at least one of her conservative colleagues, and confront her own fraught feelings about coming out.

Just when she decides she's up to the challenge, she learns that the very brilliant, very out Genevieve Fornier will be lead counsel on the case.

Genevieve isn't sure which is causing her more sleepless nights: the prospect of losing the case, or the thought of who will be sitting on the bench when she argues it.

The Return

Ana Matics

ISBN: 978-3-95533-234-1
Length: 300 pages

Near Haven is like any other small, dying fishing village dotting the Maine coastline—a crusty remnant of an industry long gone, a place that is mired in sadness and longing for what was and can never be again. People move away, yet they always seem to come back. It's a vicious cycle of small-town America.

Liza Hawke thought that she'd gotten out, escaped across the country on a basketball scholarship. A series of bad decisions, however, has her returning home after nearly a decade. She struggles to accept her place in the fabric of this small coastal town, making amends to the people she's wronged and trying to rebuild her life in the process.

Her return marks the beginning of a shift within the town as the residents that she's hurt so badly start to heal once more.

Conflict of Interest

Jae

ISBN: 978-3-95533-109-2

Length: 466 pages

Workaholic Detective Aiden Carlisle isn't looking for love—and certainly not at the law enforcement seminar she reluctantly agreed to attend. But the first lecturer is not at all what she expected.

Psychologist Dawn Kinsley has just found her place in life. After a failed relationship with a police officer, she has sworn never to get involved with another cop again, but she feels a connection to Aiden from the very first moment.

Can Aiden keep from crossing the line when a brutal crime threatens to keep them apart before they've even gotten together?

Coming from Ylva Publishing in 2015

www.ylva-publishing.com

Getting Back

Cindy Rizzo

Elizabeth Morrison has ascended the ranks of her industry and now runs one of the most successful publishing companies in the US. But even after three decades, she has never been able to get past the devastating end of her relationship with Ruth Abramson. As she approaches her 30th college reunion, she must face the woman who long ago acceded to the demands of her famous father, regarded universally as a national hero, to marry a young man and start a family. It doesn't make it any easier that Ruth, now a US District Court judge and divorced, is the class luncheon speaker.

As Elizabeth and Ruth face one another and attempt to reconcile their past, Elizabeth must carefully decide whether she is more distrustful of Ruth or of herself. Is she headed for another fall with this woman? Or does she just want to get close again, so she can be the one to walk away?

When it comes to reuniting with the love of your life, it's not always easy to know the difference between getting back together or just getting back.

Cast Me Gently

Caren J. Werlinger

Teresa Benedetto and Ellie Ryan couldn't be more different, at least on the surface.

Teresa still lives at home. As much as she loves her boisterous Italian family, she feels trapped by them and their plans for her life. Their love is suffocating her.

Ellie has been on her own for years, working hard to save up enough to live her dream of escaping from Pittsburgh to travel the world. Except leaving isn't that simple when she knows her brother is out on the streets of the city somewhere, back from Vietnam, but not home.

When Teresa and Ellie meet and fall in love, their worlds clash. Ellie would love to be part of Teresa's family, but they both know that will never happen. Sooner or later, Teresa will have to choose between the two halves of her heart—Ellie or her family.

Set in 1980, the beginning of the Reagan era and the decline of Pittsburgh's steel empire, Cast Me Gently is a classic lesbian romance.

Turning for Home
© by Caren J. Werlinger

ISBN: 978-3-95533-323-2

Also available as e-book.

Published by Ylva Publishing, legal entity of Ylva Verlag, e.Kfr.

Ylva Verlag, e.Kfr.
Owner: Astrid Ohletz
Am Kirschgarten 2
65830 Kriftel
Germany

www.ylva-publishing.com

First edition: March 2015

Credits
Edited by Sandra Gerth
Cover Design by Streetlight Graphics